DOWNPOUR

A NICK VENTNER ADVENTURE

ASHTON MACAULAY

CONTENTS

PREFACE

"Of course, you want to hear about South America. Land of the Dead, nothing but bones, angry corpses, and a lack of proper booze…" Nick gulped the lager in front of him and sighed in relief. The Haven may have been grungy, but it had decent beer and strong cocktails. He took a long look at the woman sitting opposite him. *Why would she want to know about the Land of the Dead?*

A lanky man leaned on the bar for support and turned to Nick. "This time you've gone too far…" He let out a belch that could have shattered glass and slumped away to the dimmest corner he could find. Most tables at least had flickering lights above them, unlike the booth farthest from the jukebox. People used it for sleeping off whatever Jimmy served them and preferred to do so in semi-darkness. Slumping onto the worn vinyl bench, the lanky man soon snored softly, clutching a half-drunk glass of questionable brown liquid to his chest.

"Well, it doesn't really matter if *you* believe me, Marcus," Nick called out. "Wasn't talking to you anyway." Marcus didn't even twitch. Nick turned his attention back to his date, remembering that he was not at The Haven to debate Marcus and the other drunks hiding in the shadows. "Sorry about that." He made a dismissive gesture in Marcus's direction.

She sipped a gin and tonic while staring at him intently. "Happen often?" A sly grin spread across her face as she set the drink down.

"More often than I'd like." There was something familiar in her eyes, but Nick couldn't quite place it. *God, I hope I haven't been on this date before.* It wouldn't have been the first time. *Why, oh, why did I take her to Jimmy's?* The answer was simple. He had never intended to spend the entire night there. Nick had put on his best clothes: a faded suit jacket, slacks that barely fit, and a pair of shoes he had stolen off a corpse. After, he wracked his brain for the names of the fanciest bars he knew, realized he could afford none of them for long, and opted to do the bulk of the night's drinking at The Haven.

"Now, where was I?" asked Nick, trying to assuage the urge to tell Marcus off again.

"You were about to spout some lies about how you've been to the Land of the Dead," said his date, her eyes shining with the tiniest hint of menace in the dim bar light. "It's not the worst opening line I've heard, but it's close."

Nick looked to Marcus, who was snoring louder than ever and groaned as he noticed a barrel of a man pushing through the western-style double doors that concealed the bathrooms. Albert sported a long, unkempt beard, overalls, and a larger-than-necessary crossbow that remained strapped to his back. It said something about one's mental state when they needed to take medieval weaponry to the toilet. Then again, monster hunters were a paranoid bunch.

The man pulled at his overalls. "Why don't you save us all a few hours and skip to whatever ending you've concocted this time."

Nick flushed. He had told many lies at The Haven, that was for sure, but lately, real-life had been too compelling to embellish. "They're not lies," he said with a sigh. "When have I ever lied to you, Albert?"

Albert's eyes glazed over, the wheels of his mind spinning. "I think it was…" he paused, scooping up an empty glass from a table and trying to drink it. Dismayed that it was indeed empty, he set it back down and scratched his chin. For a good minute, he sat there, staring at the ceiling, muttering to himself in mental calculation. Eventually, he returned from his sumptuous reverie and declared: "Yesterday. Yesterday you were trying to fill us with some cock and bull story about a man who fancied himself Bigfoot and murdered some folks in Clearwater."

"That one was on the news, Albert!" Nick was growing exasperated. He looked to his companion for confirmation.

A flicker of recognition crossed her face like she was about to say something, but she picked up her phone instead. Nick couldn't be sure, but he suspected she was googling the incident.

"Oh sure, Local Eye. Hell of a paper that is. Good thing too, I was worried Elvis actually was dead for a while there." Albert let out a hearty laugh and zigzagged through the mess of tables toward the bar. "But that's none of my business. She'll see through you soon enough anyway."

Nick cursed the day that Albert had wandered out of his mudhole and into the city. "Usually," started Nick, trying to regain the flow of conversation. "Usually, it's not this bad."

"So, the great Dr. Ventner is a tale spinner, eh?" The woman finished her drink.

Never said I was a doctor. Nick didn't bother to correct her and finished his own glass, motioning to the bar for another. "Mostly, yes," he admitted. "But sometimes, just sometimes, I've got a tale or two that are true, and this is one of them. If you're not satisfied by the end, the door is there." This was a desperate play, and Nick knew it. Tonight was the first date he had been on in years, and indeed, he had given her the excuse she needed to leave.

A sleepy bartender shuffled over and plopped a glass down. It fizzled and popped with acidity. He placed another gin and tonic next to Nick's companion. "Compliments of Mr. Albert over there," said Jimmy, and he walked back to the bar to polish dirty glasses and watch his TV.

"You have this much time to impress me," said the woman,

motioning to the height of the glass. There was a joking manner to it, but Nick knew there was also a little bit of truth.

"Right, well, no time like the present." He took a drink of the fizzy mixture, and confidence rushed through him in an instant. "Well, it all started when I took what some would consider to be a rather ill-advised trip into the Amazon…"

PART I

THE JUNGLE

1

———

PARADISE LOST

Rain slapped the windshield of the cockpit, and my stomach turned as the plane lurched toward the jungle below. The old Cessna had come cheap, but in the middle of that storm, I wished we had sprung for something a little sturdier. It's funny how being thousands of feet in the air can cure a miser of his shallow pockets. I thought about the money we had saved and remembered that it had funded a noble cause—the nearly empty bottle I was clutching between my hands.

The plane shuddered again, making a terrible groaning noise. I looked out the rain-spattered window and, to my relief, saw that the wings were still attached. "Are you sure this thing can handle the storm?"

Lopsang sat confidently in the pilot's chair. He wore a classic fur-lined aviator's jacket and a leather cap to match. They had been the first things he spent his money on after the Nepal incident; flying lessons came second. If we hadn't been in a rickety old leisure plane, it would have been easy to mistake him for a fighter pilot. He waved a calm hand at me. "This is nothing. We had worse on the mountain, don't you remember?"

"At least then, we had our feet on the ground." I had never liked flying. Something about sandwiching myself in a tin can at the mercy of a pilot unnerved me.

Lopsang patted a cartoon image of a yeti that had been plastered above the center console. "Migoi can make it through anything."

The name made me wince. I had forbidden him from saying 'yeti,' so he had taken to using the word from his native tongue. "I'm still not sure why you'd name a gift after something that nearly killed us."

Lopsang only smiled. "It's the reason we had to buy the plane, isn't it?"

He wasn't wrong. I was about to argue the point further when the plane dropped several feet. My legs went out from under me, and I fell facedown in the center aisle surrounded by our spilled gear. "You do know it's only you that's immortal, right?" I groaned and pushed myself back up to a low stoop, the only height the plane's cabin allowed for. A bright flash illuminated the trees far below and was followed by a deafening thunderclap that shook the plane's metal frame.

For the first time, Lopsang's face showed a flicker of unease. "That was close," he said, eyeing the thunderous skies. Taking a deep breath, he returned to his calm demeanor and flexed his fingers around the flight controls.

I tried to take a drink from the bottle I had held on to so tightly but found it had emptied in the tumble. Luckily, I spotted my flask wedged in the co-pilot's chair and grabbed it, thankful that it made a sloshing sound. "Be careful." I knew there wasn't much good in caution now that we were already in the storm, but saying it made me feel better.

As I made my way back through the cramped cabin, I spotted a parachute pack attached to the back of the pilot's chair. I didn't want to offend Lopsang, but I also didn't want to take any chances. With what I assumed was ninjalike stealth, I unhooked the parachute and slung it around my back. *Better safe than sorry.* Skydiving was one of the many activities I had never wanted to try, but it was a better alternative to a fiery death.

"You really have no faith in me, do you?" Lopsang said, eyeing me. He chuckled and returned his eyes to the tormented sky.

"Don't take it personally. You know I don't have faith in anything." The plane lurched again and sent me sprawling into the passenger seat. I clutched the straps of the parachute, taking what little comfort I could from them.

"Woah there," Lopsang said, patting the plane's center console. "Easy now."

"Pretty sure that isn't helping." I took another drink from the flask and tried to savor the fire that poured out of it. Either I was too drunk, too scared, or both because I felt nothing. I could barely hear the beating of my own heart over the gale outside and the constant whine of engines struggling to keep us aloft.

The plane's cabin was an absolute mess. Our supplies had been upended by the turbulence, some of which were less than safe to be around. Leather-bound tomes were scattered across the aisles among knives, stray bullets, and various trinkets that were meant to ward off evil.

The plane lurched again, sending one of the knives into the air. It landed with a soft thunk in the chair's armrest, the blade buried about a half-inch into the fabric. "Nothing is worth this," I moaned. If Lopsang hadn't said the forecast was 'clear skies,' I never would have gotten on the plane.

"Don't worry, my friend. Now is not our time." Lopsang's tone was easy, and his calm demeanor was infuriating.

"Don't say that! That's what people say right before the plane crashes and they're never heard from again." I didn't put much into superstition, but jinxes were not worth meddling with. As a distraction, I tried to look out the window and get my bearings. There was nothing but uniform dark-grey clouds streaking by, mixed with the constant pelting of rain. Another flash of lightning illuminated the hellscape of the storm, churning around our plane like a sky-bound maelstrom.

In the cockpit, a red warning light flashed, and a siren blared.

"Lopsang?" The sound made me wince. Alarms and flashing

lights were never a good thing, adding fuel to a wicked hangover. "I'm guessing that isn't good."

Lopsang was frantically flipping toggles and switches, trying to turn the alarm off. "Nothing to worry about, Nick." He reached beneath his seat and pulled out a large book labeled 'Owner's Manual.' Other lights turned on and flashed until the plane's controls looked like a god-damned Christmas tree.

The plane shook violently, knocking the flask from my hand and sending what little booze remained inside pouring onto the floor. I looked down in utter dismay. "I think we should turn back." A cold dread had spread through my extremities. It was impossible to tell if it was the drink or the fear that was responsible.

I watched Lopsang turn from the owner's manual to the console repeatedly, trying more buttons with the detached interest of a documentary cameraman. All at once, the noise outside lessened. Already knowing what it meant, I turned to look out the window. One of the engine's props had ceased to spin. Most planes are designed to survive a single engine failure, but like I said, we had bought it on the cheap. Almost immediately, the plane's nose dipped toward the horizon.

The last of the warning lights turned on, and Lopsang finally admitted what was obvious. "Alright, we're in trouble." The altimeter spun backward, fueling the horror of the situation. Lopsang, however, remained completely calm and did his best to control the descent.

"Any ideas, Lopsang?" I yelled, struggling to be heard as the wind picked up around the falling plane.

Lopsang turned back with a half-hearted chuckle. "You're not going to like it." He yanked heavily on the flight stick, trying desperately to point us in a direction that wasn't straight down.

The parachute was never meant to be more than a safety blanket. I knew how to use it but jumping into the middle of uncharted territory by choice was another matter entirely. "Oh, hell, no."

"You're the one who put it on." Lopsang looked out of the cockpit window. We were passing through clouds, but I had a feeling that if we could see the canopy, it would be too late.

"I know nothing about the Amazon!" I had planned on reading more about it but ended up drinking instead.

"Well, I know a thing or two about plane crashes. Namely, you won't survive it.

I cocked an eyebrow. "Wait, why aren't you jumping?"

"And leave Migoi? Not a chance." Lopsang patted the console again.

"It's a hunk of metal, Lopsang. I'll buy you a new one!"

"You're as broke as I am." Lopsang set his jaw and stared firmly ahead. "If you're going to jump, you'll need to do it soon. We're going to be too low in a minute." His voice was ever calm as the altimeter continued to spin backward, bringing us closer and closer to doom.

"There's no fucking way." Lightning struck the other engine, and it erupted into a ball of flame. "Oh, come on!" One of the windows blew open, and cold rain sprayed through, slapping my face.

"Time to go, Nick. You can't find him if you're dead."

It was the one thing Lopsang knew I couldn't ignore. "You really are a bastard." I stumbled out of my seat, grabbed my gear bag, and staggered toward the plane's door.

Lopsang looked back. "I'll see you soon, Nick." He laughed and pulled a pair of flight goggles over his eyes.

The bright red emergency handle was like a lighthouse in a chaotic storm. I reached for it, and a lump formed in my throat. *Come on, you can do this.* I grabbed the handle, wrenched the door open, and before I could jump, the wind sucked me into the fury of the storm. The plane quickly disappeared, nothing but a red fireball hurtling toward the distant horizon.

My stomach fell out from under me as I spun violently into the storm. For the first few seconds, all I could do was scream, but even that was soon swallowed up by the raging wind around me. Rain blurred my vision and stung my eyes, making it impossible to see. Eventually, survival instinct kicked in, and I slapped a numb hand to my parachute, fumbling with the ripcord. It took a few clumsy attempts before I was able to get a grip and pull it free.

The parachute shot out of the pack and opened with violent force, snapping my head back. Stars blotted my vision, and I was acutely aware of the fact that my descent wasn't slowing. Above, the cords of the parachute tangled together, preventing the canvas from opening fully. "Last time I let you save my life!" I screamed into the wind, hoping that somehow, Lopsang would hear my ire.

A bolt of lightning flashed across the sky, illuminating the forest. I was never good at math, but one look below told me there wasn't much time left before I would smack into it. My heart leaped into my throat. Desperately, I fought with the lines, trying to get them straightened but succeeding only in making matters worse. The parachute flapped and fluttered in the wind but ultimately did nothing to forestall my doom.

Despite my better instincts, I looked down. The last thing I remember thinking was: *Oh shit, this is actually happening.* Then I hit the canopy and blacked out.

"How'd you survive?"

Nick jumped. Somehow over the course of the story, Marcus had risen from the corner booth and moved directly behind him. *Sneaky little bastard when he wants to be.* "I nearly didn't. Believe me, after a fall from that height, I wasn't feeling too well when I woke up." Nick did his best to recover his composure after the embarrassing scare.

"You expect us to believe that you fell out of a plane, in a storm, at low altitude, without a functioning parachute, and lived to tell the tale?" Marcus shook his head in disbelief. "I've flown with better men who were killed by less." He parted his coat to reveal the royal cross dangling around his neck that might as well have been permanently affixed. "You would have splattered on the ground like a bag of rotten fruit." He slammed a palm on the table and blew a raspberry, illustrating the point.

Nick's companion remained silent throughout the inquisition. If anything, her wry smile encouraged Marcus's aggressive questioning.

Well, at least she's listening. Nick wished that Marcus would flee back to some hole and sleep it off. Most nights, he could have handled the drunk bastard's critiques, but most nights, there wasn't a date involved.

"I got caught in the canopy, Marcus."

Marcus looked at him, eyes squinted, weighing the explanation. "Which jungle was this, eh?" The berating tone was still there, and he slumped down in his chair a little.

"The Amazon. Were you even listening?"

"I was until you started spinning bullshit again!" roared Marcus. Then, as if startled by his own voice, he quieted down. "Sorry 'bout that. Continue then, Nick."

Nick shot an apologetic look to his companion.

She laughed. "It's quite alright, Marcus. It's nice to know someone here is keeping him honest." The mischievous look had returned to her eyes.

Something about those eyes. Nick had always possessed a weak spot for mischief.

Marcus took a massive gulp of his beer. "Tha's me, always keepin' 'im honest." It seemed that the more Marcus drank, the more syllables he dropped. "Amazon, big trees thar. Canopy. Go'it. Continue on then." His head drooped low toward the table.

"Right, well, now that I have Marcus's permission…"

2

SOFT LANDINGS

When I awoke, it was to the patter of warm rain through the jungle canopy. Light filtered through the thinning clouds, but the rain showed no sign of letting up. I blearily tried to get my bearings and had the sensation of falling. I threw my arms and legs out instinctively, trying to grab for anything that would slow my descent. My fists closed over nothing but air, and my body swung gently in the breeze. A soreness crept through my shoulders where the parachute straps were digging in. I was getting angry about it when I caught a glimpse of the ground about thirty feet below me. My stomach turned.

There was no time to revel in the fact that I was alive as my longevity was still up for debate. I looked around for a way to get to the forest floor that didn't involve dropping like a stone. Above me, I saw the tangled straps of my parachute intertwined with the branches of the canopy. It was a mess, and the fact that I hadn't broken bones falling through it was nothing short of a miracle.

As my senses returned, the sounds of wildlife slowly grew. Birds sang, insects chirped, and somewhere in the distance, I could hear the howl of monkeys. It was enough to make me realize how deep the shit I was in went. Instantly, I regretted not reading up on the expanse of the jungle between us and our destination. *This wouldn't have been an issue if we had made it to Dedos Ligeros like we planned.*

The original idea was to fly to a small smuggling town known for its jungle guides and thievery. Most of the time, their business was guiding tourists out into the wild, robbing them blind, and then leaving them to rot, but I had a few friends that owed favors. I hadn't called ahead per se, but I was confident that they would help us with a little persuasion. Not that any of that mattered from my precarious perch high above the forest floor.

Looking down at the sprawling green expanse below, I knew immediately that I was out of my depth. To my surprise, my gear appeared to have landed safely. While it was a blessing, there was still the issue of being thirty feet above it. Ordinarily, I would have been excited to get a vantage point and survey my surroundings, but the forest was so thick, I could hardly make anything out a hundred feet to each side.

To my untrained eye, it seemed like a bit of bad luck that I had landed in a clearing. There was nothing to grasp or to help me find my way down. The easiest solution was to unclip from the harness and hope for the best, but I wasn't quite that desperate yet. As I began to formulate a plan, the branches above me rustled.

I looked up and, to my horror, saw a gargantuan, green snake inching slowly toward me.

"Oh, come on…" The irony was not lost on me that I had fallen into one of film's most fantastic adventure tropes by developing a fear of snakes, but something about the way they slithered was unnatural—that and, of course, the venom they carried. As a child, I was bitten by a cottonmouth and barely survived. After spending a day in the hospital, limbs swollen, chills wracking my body, I developed what I thought to be a healthy respect for the creatures. As it turns out, healthy respect can rapidly turn into a phobia.

Being stuck beneath one of these creatures was as close to my worst-case scenario as I could get. To my right, twenty feet away, was another large tree with thick, gnarled branches. They looked strong, and in the presence of the snake, I thought up a plan that was more than a little foolhardy. Like a child on a swing set or

Tarzan with a vine, I would kick my legs, build my momentum into a consistent arc, unbuckle at the top, and fly safely to the adjacent tree. It wasn't perfect, but it ended without me being turned into snake food.

Action films from my childhood were always the primary source of my half-baked plans. There were times when they landed me in trouble, but surprisingly, they worked more often than not. Kicking my legs out in front of me, I rocked back and forth. The branches above me groaned, and the snake moved quicker, perhaps sensing the urgency in its prey.

I cursed aloud and tried to focus, moving my feet rhythmically with the small swing I had generated. Somewhere above me, a branch cracked, and I winced, half expecting to plummet to my death for the second time. Miraculously, it held.

I kicked again, my swing growing wider with each passing moment. Above, the snake continued to slither closer, murder in its cold, dark eyes. Reaching out with my fingers, I could almost touch the opposite tree. "This is going to work, this is going to work." Repeating the mantra made it feel like I had a better chance. Sparing one last glance at the snake above, I put my hand on the clip that would release me from the harness and kicked. At the top of my swing, I unbuckled. The straps slid from beneath my arms, and my forward momentum stopped abruptly.

I tried to grasp the opposing tree, but my hands found nothing but air. Falling in slow motion, I looked up at the snake staring down at me with disappointment. Through the paralyzing fear, I managed to give it the finger. A second later, I smacked into the ground, violently expelling all the air from my lungs.

For a while, I lay there, eyes closed, not wanting to move for fear of finding out I couldn't. A profound soreness radiated in a painful spiral from my back. Raindrops fell on my forehead, tracing cold lines down the contours of my face. *I am so well and profoundly screwed.* As the seconds passed and turned into minutes, I wondered if I would ever be able to walk again. The pain in my back did not dissipate and instead kept up a low throb, reminding me of my idiocy.

Eventually, I opened my eyes and looked up at the canopy. Sure enough, the snake was winding its way lazily through the treetops, no doubt reveling in my misery. "You're a bastard," I croaked. Through throbbing pain, I pushed myself to a sitting position. Surprisingly, my back held the weight. The damp forest floor sunk down, enveloping my palms. It was the first stroke of luck I'd had in days. Hell knew I needed it.

After a few minutes of sitting, trying to come to terms with the fact that I was stranded in the jungle, I struggled to my feet. The jeans and jacket I wore were caked in muck and soaked throughout. I cursed myself for not picking more functional clothing, but then again, trekking through miles of uncharted terrain hadn't been in the brochure. "I was supposed to be drinking with a bandit king by now!" I yelled to no one in particular. The sound of my own voice echoing through the trees was enough to spark throbbing in my temples. *Ah shit,* I thought, realizing my flask was empty, and I was about to endure the mother of all withdrawals.

I thought wistfully to the bottles that had shattered in the plane crash. Then my mind drifted for the first time that morning to Lopsang. I wasn't so much concerned for his well-being, given that he was a demi-god, but I was angry that he hadn't jumped with me. *All this for a stupid airplane.* I did my best to brush the mud off my clothes and surveyed the clearing.

Thick vines and creeping moss ran from the forest floor up trunks of trees and into the canopy. Beneath me, I could almost feel the scuttling of a thousand unpleasant critters that no doubt lay in hiding. Lopsang had prepared an entire dossier on the area, but I hadn't exactly been in the studying mood. All it took was a blurb about the Amazon playing host to fifteen different species of venomous snake for me to toss it aside and never pick it up again. I shivered at the idea of the hundreds of unknown species that hid in the jungle's depths.

Of all the places in the world to land, why did it have to be here? I trudged across the clearing, looking for my bag. Every snapping twig beneath my feet and every distant bird call brought fresh waves of fear. Anything could be hiding in the dense foliage. Without any of my weapons, I didn't like my odds. *Come on, if Paul Mansen can hack it out here, then so can I.*

Paul had been the host of a television show on National Geographic, back in its heyday. He had gone all over the world, hunting for oddities, examining ancient ruins, and making passes at local archaeologists. In my opinion, he was one of the worst kind of idiots with the best kind of luck. In his travels, he had uncovered more precious artifacts in the name of ratings than most respectable scientists found in a lifetime.

Over the years, we had developed a sort of enmity. Partly due to repeated attempts to discredit and impugn his honor, but mostly because he was kind of a dick. For my money, I thought the man had sold his soul for fame in a literal sense. Unfortunately for my curiosity, none of my contacts in the dark arts trade had heard tell of such a deal. I counted myself lucky that the man was gone. A few years earlier, I had the misfortune of witnessing his brother's death, and knowing Paul, he would have found some way to blame it on me. As I walked through the forest, it did not escape me that it was the same part of the world he had disappeared in.

I found my bag in a bush, covered entirely with red ants. I grabbed it and shook off the irksome creatures. Several had already started to scuttle up my arm. To my dismay, they were biters. I shook the bag, attempting to rid myself of the fiery, little bastards, and heard the jingle of broken glass. Unzipping the canvas, I found a broken bottle of vodka, the remnants of which quickly evaporated into the air.

I swore loudly, the sound echoing off the forest. Birds flew from their perches in attempts to flee my vulgarity. Despite the heat, a cold chill ran down my spine. I was reminded distinctly of prey in the moments before being disemboweled by some shapeless predator. *Do they have panthers here?* One more reason I should have read the pamphlet. I later found out they did not, but there were jaguars, which were oh so much worse. Where a panther would stalk and kill you, Jaguars liked to play with their food, leaving it alive.

Trying to occupy my mind, I rummaged through my bag. It contained a map of the region, totally useless when I had no idea where I landed. A tarp was bound into a cube by bungee cords, a water purifier, dried military rations, a large machete, and waterproof matches. I had never forgotten the lesson I learned almost freezing to death on a mountain, and from then on, I always brought matches. While the contents were varied, they were only meant for a few days' survival, which meant I had to move quickly. Without the promise of more drink, my confidence was waning.

By Lopsang's estimate, we were only twenty minutes or so from landing when the plane crashed, but it could take days on foot. There was also the fact that the storm might have taken us off course. Even if I paid attention to the direction the plane was crashing, the fall had spun me around so much that I completely lost my bearings.

I opened the map and said a silent thank you to Lopsang for encasing it in plastic. Everything in the jungle was damp and terrible. Dedos Ligeros had been marked with a large red X. A dotted line left from the small airport where we had taken off and followed the Amazon river straight towards its source in Iquita. A sense of renewed hope filled me. If I could find the river, I could follow it to our destination.

I looked up from the map, hoping to get a sense of direction, but the dense green foliage spread out in a circle around me made it impossible. Other than my parachute pack hanging from the trees, there were no distinguishing features. Looking up at the sun, I guessed it was still on the rise and decided heading west was my best option. At least that would give me some barometer to ensure I wasn't walking in circles.

Soggy and hungover, I stuffed the map back into the bag and pulled the machete out. The broken bottle inside slashed along my hand, and blood trickled down my wrist to the forest floor. I wondered whether predators would be able to smell it as a shark would. Wiping my hand on my pants and trying not to think about it, I turned away from the rising sun and set off.

I held the machete in front of me, doing my best to imitate the caricatured explorers of old. They had lived long enough for people to tell stories about them, so clearly, they were doing something right. The machete provided the illusion of safety, even if it wasn't great for much more than clearing brush. My spirits lifted. Despite leaving my adversary behind, I kept my eyes on the canopy, watching for more snakes. I only wish I had directed my attention to the path before me and watched my surroundings a little more carefully…

3

THE MIGHTY JUNGLE

The sun rose, burning off low rainclouds and replacing them with oppressive, muggy heat. While the towering canopy provided shade from direct sunlight, it also trapped the jungle's damp warmth. Initially, I thought the heat might be a reprieve from my soggy hell, but somehow, it was far worse. I was out of water and unable to find another source to drink from. The irony was not lost on me that I would die of dehydration next to the world's largest river in a so-called rainforest.

The insects were incessant, swarming around me in a thick cloud. I would fling a hand out and they would disperse, only to return a few seconds later. Every inch of my exposed skin was covered in bumps and rashes. I stopped to scratch and wallow in my own misery, but even my self-pity didn't last. My dismay truly began with an intense itching sensation on my lower thigh—not that abnormal, given the thousands of bugs trying to suck my blood with every breath. Then, it was like something had set fire to my skin. Desperately, I rolled up my pant leg, the pain growing with every passing second until a wave of nausea and disgust washed over me.

A centipede more than a foot in length had wrapped its body around my leg. Now, I've stayed the night in a cabin surrounded by vampires with nothing but a dollar-store portrait of the Virgin Mary for company, but that was nothing compared to the sight of a blue-grey shell with far too many yellow appendages scuttling across my skin. Centipedes, when you think about it, are like snakes with the addition of a hundred poisonous legs. So, naturally, my rationality fled like a bog monster from soap. My heart beat frantically, reminding me of the immense pain the creature was causing me with every slight movement it made.

I looked deep into the centipede's eyes, or at least what I thought were its eyes, trying to project calm. What I wanted to do was hack it into a hundred equal segments with my machete and burn the carcass, but it didn't need to know that. The centipede, having millions of years of evolution on me, saw through this charade. In an almost cordial gesture, it wiggled it's curled red antennae and sank its pincers into my already ravaged skin. The pain was immediate and overwhelming. If I hadn't seen the insect, I would have been sure someone had taken two red hot pokers straight from the forge and plunged them into my soft flesh. I was frozen in agony, right up until the moment the creature started a purposeful march toward my groin.

With each step, the centipede's feet blistered my skin. Rising through the pain and revulsion, I grabbed my machete and swung at the creature with the flat end, careful not to sever my own leg in the process. The blade struck and sent it writhing to the ground, but before I could complete my mission of hacking the little shit into bite-sized morsels, it scuttled into the underbrush.

Still reeling in pain, I checked my surroundings to make sure there were no more crawling nightmares lying in wait. My leg throbbed, swelling and growing hotter with each passing second. I looked down and gasped in pain. Parallel lines of blisters ran in a serpentine pattern from my ankle to below my thigh. Where the pincers had gone in, two purple bumps had raised, oozing what I hoped was only blood.

"That's not good." My words came out slow and heavy. *Better keep a move on.* Shouldering my pack, I continued a struggling march toward civilization, hoping to hell that centipede venom wasn't something I needed to treat immediately. Something told me the cure would have been some straight whiskey coupled with a moratorium on jungle exploration, but that wasn't in the cards.

The day wore on, and the temperature managed to rise even higher. The farther I walked, the more aware I was of how carelessly sweat wasted every precious drop of water I had. The centipede bites continued to swell, and my head ached with a throbbing tempo usually reserved for the aftermath of vicious weekend benders. I had been wandering in the jungle for half a day and already had dreams of gleefully bulldozing the lot of it and reclining back in my apartment with a brand-new set of custom souvenir rainforest coasters.

The thought of home and a cold drink caused the trees to shimmer. It might have been the centipede venom, dehydration, or wishful thinking, but I could see a tumbler floating in the forest beyond. I found myself wishing for a frigid blast of mountain air, even if it meant confronting a yeti again.

The disturbances in my vision steadily worsened, and I wished to hell I had our medical bag. I couldn't remember reading about anyone dying from a centipede bite, but then again, I hadn't done much reading. Either way, a numbing lotion, or any way to assuage the pain from each chafing step, would have been a godsend. The jungle around me blurred, and several times green eyes shone out at me from the trees. I shook my head—trying to clear the hallucination—and focused on the action of putting one sodden foot in front of the other.

The sun sunk toward the horizon, bathing everything in its red glow. I needed another rest, only without any venomous interruptions this time. While not precisely clearing, there was a mossy rock that protruded a few feet above the ground. Through pain and exhaustion, I hoisted myself up and sat.

Wanting something to distract from my unfortunate reality, I unshouldered the gear bag and looked for the leather-bound tome I always carried. It contained the half-coherent ramblings of a man who treated drinking like a professional sport but somehow still managed to be occasionally useful. Henry had been a miserable companion, but at least his apprentices managed to live through his 'work-study.'

The pages of the tome had been perfectly preserved in their original, filthy state. The enchantments that had bound the book kept everything pristine, protecting Henry's writings from harm. Of course, given that the magic hadn't involved drinking, the bastard had never written the steps down.

The encounters inside were loosely organized by geography. I flipped through the pages, searching for anything that might relate to South America or the jungle. After passing plenty of accounts of goblins, ghosts, and goblin-ghosts, I came upon a page depicting a mythic snake devouring a fishing boat. "No, thanks." A few pages later, I found an entry describing the spiritual entity known as La Madremonte.

I first encountered this creature after a long evening of drinking in a river village.

Shocker there. He had been a testy old man, but a fair bit of fun when the mood struck him.

Most of the locals would have you believe that La Madremonte is region-specific, only appearing within Columbia's borders. I am not surprised to say that once again, this localization is incorrect.

I had found the same to be true in most of my travels. Every region is convinced they have their own unique brand of scary, but I've encountered vampires in Barbados and crocodile men in Tokyo. Variety, it seems, is the spice of life. Things that go bump in the night don't give a damn about the artificial borders set by society.

As I stepped out to relieve myself, I could feel something watching me from the jungle.

I thought back to the eeriness of the clearing, and my spine prickled. *Only the venom slowly killing you.* I returned to reading.

A pair of green eyes blinked at me from the forest, quiet and watchful. The next thing I knew, I was walking in after them, where I became hopelessly lost.

The similarities between his story and mine were beginning to make me uncomfortable.

I wasn't able to get a good look at her. She stuck to the trees, blending with the foliage as she moved at the edge of my vision. What little glimpses I caught showed a walking pile of vines with no distinguishing features aside from bright green eyes. A woman whispered to me in Spanish. I didn't speak it and couldn't remember enough to translate, but the voice came from the forest around me.

I stopped reading, struck by how quiet the jungle had become. There was no bird song, the trees had ceased to sway, and even the hum of insects had fallen off. I looked at the trees and saw nothing but tangled greenery. The hollowness crept back into my stomach, and I knew for sure that I was being watched. Every bead of sweat was electric, and my heart slammed into my ribcage with each thundering beat.

"Estas perdido?" a raspy voice whispered in my ear.

An involuntary chill wracked my body with violent shivers. The warmth that had been omnipresent went cold and clammy. I longed for Old Faithful—a harpoon gun that had gotten me through much worse than a vengeful bush spirit. Slowly, I lowered my shaking hand to my side and tentatively grasped the handle of my machete. My vision wavered in great lines, partly due to the centipede venom and partly due to whatever supernatural fuckery was happening behind me.

I took a deep, shuddering breath, and turned around in a swift motion, swinging the machete in a wide arc. There was a loud thunk as the blade caught in a tree; the sudden stop sent me sprawling onto my back. "Who's there?" I yelled, scrambling to my feet while trying my best to ignore the pain shooting through my back. As a rule, I don't usually call out to potentially aggressive spiritual entities, but I didn't have the holy water or chalk needed for my traditional paranormal welcome mat.

The vegetation swallowed up my voice without so much as a timid echo. I tried to keep myself still, listening for even the slightest rustling of leaves but hearing nothing other than the pumping of blood desperately trying to make its way through my veins, telling me to take off running. The forest had become a still life without even the slightest hint of movement.

What remained of the red sunlight was blotted out by dark rainclouds. The soft pattering of water broke the silence. When the first raindrop hit my lip, all memory of my aggressor left me for a guttural calling too strong to be ignored. I scrambled to grab my canteen, fashioned a small funnel from a leaf, and collected freshwater, completely forgetting the threat of the disembodied voice. Much of the rain spilled due to my shaking hands, but lucky for me, there was plenty.

What started as a light drizzle quickly turned into massive sheets. The rain fell over my tired body, washing away the day's grime and stinging my wounds. I rolled up my pant leg and rinsed the bites as best I could, wincing and cursing anything with more than two legs. While I was thankful for the brief respite, I knew the sodden gear was only going to make traveling that much worse. The tome, which I had dropped on the forest floor in my confusion, made for an odd sight as it repelled the falling water. Henry might have been a drunk, but he had thought of everything when it came to protective spells. *If only he had saved a little of that magic for himself.*

Not wanting to waste time, I repacked my bag and set off. I had to keep reminding myself that there actually was a way out of the jungle. Saying it repeatedly seemed to help. Usually, I managed to coast through these situations on confidence alone, but beneath the towering trees, surrounded by every terrible creature known to man, I was far from my element.

At least the snake is gone. I tried my best to keep quiet, but there was always something underfoot crunching, snapping, or squelching with every step. Silence fell over me in a slow wave, taking first the birdsong, then the distant howling of monkeys, and finally, the insects. The sound of rain falling died away as if the earth below had opened up to swallow the water whole.

Every step was an intrusion. The air was charged like it had been filled with significant electric power. The jungle was stagnant around me. I continued to walk, while everything else remained stationary as if frozen by some deity's remote control. I've disturbed holy reliquaries, resting places, nursing homes, you name it, but something was different about that moment. Every cell in my body told me I was in the wrong place at the very wrong time.

The Amazon rainforest is filled with ancient and not-so-ancient burial sites, so the idea that I had blundered into one was not that far-fetched. During a Paul Mansen special, I had learned that the Amazon rainforest played host to more ancient cemeteries and forgotten temples than most populated areas in the world. The rainforest hid everything until you were right on top of it and was a common resting place for the 'easily-disturbed dead.' As a great poet once said before having his brains bashed in: *They're the group of deceased I enjoy the least.*

When a person dies during a period of great turmoil—or really isn't ready to go—their bodies go into waiting. They're not alive, and self-awareness is a fleeting notion at best. If anything, the soul is lounging in a black void nearby, clueless. What makes them unique is their susceptibility to being raised by practitioners of the dark arts. Any necromancer with half a mind, some sheep's blood, and a two-dollar box of wine could manage.

For this reason, the easily disturbed dead were usually buried in places of excellent security. In the case of the Amazon, that meant booby traps and temples with more corpses than gold. I shuddered at the idea of braving a spike pit only to find a treasure of half-wrapped dead waiting to party.

By the time night fell, my legs were exhausted. The idea of camping on the forest floor was not ideal, but there weren't many options. Fortunately, the silence also meant an absence of bugs, though remnants of their reign remained in the form of itchy, swollen sores across my body. When my shirt's fabric shifted even a little, the itching would intensify and spread like wildfire. Every time I thought I was getting a reprieve, it would start up anew, somehow worse than before.

I considered climbing a tree to avoid whatever came out at night, but then I remembered the snake. In the end, camping on the ground seemed like the only viable solution. I trudged through the foliage, hacking with the now considerably dulled machete, looking for a small clearing. I had no such luck. The hanging vines only grew thicker and more challenging to cut through. The path continued to narrow as the trees grew closer together until it was difficult to swing the machete at all.

The sun slowly disappeared in the treetops above. As last light faded, I broke through the underbrush and into a clearing. Immediately, I set my bag down. I felt relief at the absence of weight, but it was swiftly counteracted by the fiery itching that sprung up where the straps had been digging into my shoulders. Trying to ignore it, I opened my bag and pulled out the tarp. Two trees at the edge of the clearing were the perfect width apart—my first luck all day. Using the last of my energy, I ran a rope line between them and laid the tarp over it. As far as shelters went, I could've done worse. The tarp kept the rain off my head, even if the ground below was soaked.

Dinner was a few rations that survived the crash—cold as there wasn't a piece of dry wood for miles. We had brought a cookstove, but, of course, it had been in one of the bags left on the plane. The bite from the centipede throbbed dully, but the pain had subsided, and the chills went away. It seemed that despite the odds, I had survived my first day and would live to fight another.

As I finished up a canned interpretation of mac and cheese, the rain stopped. The clouds parted, revealing a pale moon, and white light filtered through the canopy. Tree roots looked like bones reaching up from the forest floor, and the area took on a new, foreboding form. I sat with my back against a tree and looked up at the moon, trying to take my mind off where I was. A lump stuck in my throat. *It can't be.*

Suspended from the trees above was an empty parachute harness. *There has to be plenty of people who fell out of a plane here.* Even through a day of rain, the parachute still looked relatively new. It was the broken glass next to the fallen tree branches that killed my hope entirely. I had spent the day wandering in a circle only to come back to the exact same spot.

I spiraled, shouting at the trees around me, somehow hoping it would help my predicament. "There's no way I'm getting out of this place!" I kicked one of the trees. "FUCK YOU, JUNGLE!" I spat into the sodden leaves, hoping that somewhere, somehow, some ancient god would be offended and send a servant to off me and end my misery. "I'm sorry, James, but this isn't worth it!" My words cut off, and the silence was more solemn than it had been before. I tried to avoid saying the kid's name, but it slipped out every once in a while.

Despite the horrendous heat, I could feel the cold mountaintop where we had laid him to rest. Lopsang said we had given him a true mountaineer's send-off. All I could see was a young man's body, strapped to a sled, sliding over the edge of a cliff. I wondered where his corpse had ended up. Was it somewhere deep in a crevasse, haunted by the other spirits that dwelled there? I shook the thought from my mind and looked up at my parachute, clinging to my wits by a thread.

I'm not sure how long I stayed there—maybe a minute, perhaps an hour—but nature made no response. The vegetation stared back at me in stark judgment. "How the hell am I going to do this?" What I really needed was a drink to calm my nerves, but the shattered bottle in the dirt reminded me how far away that dream really was. Exhaustion overtook me, and I mustered what remaining willpower I had to drag myself back to the tarp. Using my gear bag as a pillow, I laid down and hoped that a solution would present itself by morning.

With the rest of the jungle blocked from view, I was almost able to conjure the illusion of safety. Within a matter of minutes, I was drifting off to sleep, the disembodied voice and other perils forgotten in favor of weariness. My eyes shut, and for a merciful moment, my surroundings disappeared…

4

———

LA MADREMONTE

The yeti's roar thundered through my body, shaking every bone, muscle, and sinew, threatening to tear me apart. I was in the cave, looking straight into the beast's dark eyes, watching the steam spew from its flared nostrils. Thick teeth and black gums grinned at me. I tried to move, tried to attack, but my feet were rooted in place.

James flew through the air, landing with a muffled thud in the middle of the cavern. I knew what came next; I had replayed the moment over and over again. If I could only move my legs, I could charge the creature and stop this. The yeti paid no attention, raised a massive, clawed fist to the sky, and slammed it into James's torso.

I watched the grisly scene play out as it had so many times in the last year. We eventually defeated the yeti, of course, we always did, but what came next was worse. I was holding James's battered body. Blood dribbled down his chin as his jaw worked, trying to speak.

"Save your breath, kid, we're going to get you out of here."

James's eyes went cloudy and cold in an instant, frozen over by a film of ice. The scene washed away, and we were outside the cave. James stared at me from the frigid toboggan Lopsang had strapped him to. "You b-better hurry up, Nick." The frost growing on his face cracked with every word. "If you die before you get to me, you're going straight to Hell."

My body was rigid, electrified by penetrating fear. A heavy blanket dripped over me, holding me in the moment. I knew on some level that James was right.

Lopsang reached out to push James's sled off the edge. "Don't let me die in a chasm, Nick," croaked James and then let out an otherworldly laugh. It enveloped the mountain, ringing in my ears and vibrating my bones.

"Stop it, kid! I'm on my—"

I AWOKE, screaming, with cold sweat trickling down my back. The jungle swallowed the noise whole. Silence fell over the camp. My breath came in ragged gasps, and my heart pounded painfully against the inside of my chest. Even in the vividness of my current living nightmare, there was no way to escape that cursed mountain.

Grabbing my machete, I moved the tarp back and stepped out into the clearing. It was still entirely dark, and the moon shone brightly through the trees; I couldn't have been asleep for more than an hour. Nervously, I watched the forest, hoping to hell that I wouldn't see anything. As if on cue, there was a flicker of movement. A green light illuminated my surroundings and just as quickly disappeared. I was about to chalk it up to hallucination when a whisper came through the rustling of branches.

"Estas perdido?"

There was no time to panic. I rummaged through the bag, looking for the book. If he had written about the beast, then he had found a way to kill it. I flipped through the pages as quickly as possible.

The underbrush stirred, and a quiet rustling filled the air. It was the sound of something being dragged across the forest floor. My hands were clammy in the muggy heat. Every beat of my heart was a gunshot trying desperately to escape my ribcage. Locating the correct passage was like defusing a bomb, the seconds ticking away before my untimely death. Attending to the words for even a second required the utmost patience and concentration. *It's alright, the beast hasn't killed you yet. Maybe there's a reason.* My fingers shook; the rustling grew so close that I dropped the book entirely. There was a muted thunk as it hit the ground. My spine tingled with the all-too-familiar notion that something horrible was standing right behind me. Perspiration beaded on my brow.

"Estas perdido?" the voice asked again, louder. Its raspy breath blew across the back of my neck. I could smell decay and sickly rot.

Gripping my machete, I whipped around with the idea of chopping the creature in half, but my hand faltered when I looked into its eyes. The weapon clattered to the ground. The creature stood, looking me dead in the eye, covered head to foot in leaves and vines. An ugly veil of moss and lichen hung across its face, obscuring most of its features. Unnaturally long hands like intertwining tree roots hung at its sides, ending in clawed fingers that raked the ground upon walking forward, leaves assimilating into its body.

It made a horrible clicking sound, cocking its head to one side, considering me. "Estas perdido?" The voice was now clearly that of a woman. It reverberated as if it were coming from the surrounding forest instead of the creature itself. The green light behind the veil intensified, growing to a fierce burn.

We both stared at each other, the creature's eyes piercing my own as if she could see through me. Its clawed hand rose slowly from the ground, snapping and creaking like a branch in strong wind. Vines spun around its wrist, rebinding the cracked pieces and strengthening them.

Rational thought became nearly impossible as fear filled every corner of my mind. *Alright, think about it. Nothing in this world is invincible.* I backed away slowly, trying to size up the creature. Its green eyes followed me. *Easy now. What is a six-foot-tall walking vine-monster afraid of?* The easy answer was fire, but I was shit out of luck for that. Given its composition's damp nature, I guessed a few matches would do nothing more than piss it off.

Going for the eyes seemed like the next logical step, but who knew what was behind that veil. I had become rather attached to my hands and never put them anywhere they might get chopped, bitten, or otherwise maimed. The creature's lack of an exact weak point was discouraging, to say the least. I was on its home turf and knew nothing about it other than the brief, drunken passage I had read.

As if sensing my stalling, the creature raised its hands to the veil and removed it slowly. Its face was worse than I could have imagined. A set of wooden teeth gnashed and creaked. They poked out in odd directions and shuddered as the creature inhaled. "Intruso." There was an uncomfortable air of finality to the word.

Sensing my impending doom, I went with an old-fashioned trick to buy time. "Sorry, I don't speak Spanish." I gave a mock bow, and at the low point, I picked up a handful of dirt in one hand and the tome in the other. On the way back up, I threw the dirt in the creature's face and bolted the opposite direction. My foot immediately caught on a tree root, and I went sprawling forward. At the last second, I regained my balance and charged ahead.

From behind, a shrill scream threatened to burst my eardrums. *Well, you know one thing about the creature. It's pissed.* I could hear a menacing rustle as if the jungle itself was chasing me. The creature's horrible wooden talons clicked and clacked, growing ever closer.

The eerie noises had done their job, throwing me off balance and causing me to lose focus. When I returned my attention to the task at hand—running for my life—I noticed that I was heading directly into my ramshackle tent. Had I not been in mortal peril, the level of clumsiness I was displaying might have almost been comical.

With hardly any time to slow down, I crashed into the tarp, sprawling into the dirt. The thin plastic material blocked the creature from view, providing me with a false sense of security. My illusion of safety was quickly shattered as a set of long claws tore the tarp in half, leaving me staring into the increasingly angry green eyes of the beast.

"That was expensive!" I yelled, hoping that irrationally berating the creature might buy me time. The harsh clicking noise from the creature's mouth returned, and I smelled the foul stench of old flesh. My guess was the last thing it had hunted had not gotten away. There's a special kind of stink that signifies a successful predator.

Grabbing the book, I stumbled to my feet and ran as fast as I could. My heart pounded loudly in my ears, but it was never enough to drive away the creature's horrible clicking from behind me. Every step was a contest between my balance and the many roots and rocks trying to send me sprawling to my death. *Why hasn't she caught me yet?* I was running faster than I previously thought possible, but I was far from in shape through various faults of my own. The horrifying notion that I was being toyed with dawned on me, but I tried to push it away and focused all my energy on running.

Each breath sent splintering pain through my chest. Every panting step threatened to collapse my weak lungs. I could hear the creature's ragged breathing behind me, keeping pace but never coming close enough to strike, when a low rumbling sound came to my attention. *I know that sound. Why do I know that sound?*

Thirty seconds later, I got my answer. The trees thinned out at an alarming rate, and the dirt path gave way to a cliff. Below it was the churning green-brown mayhem of the Amazon river. Jumping was suicide, but there weren't any other options presenting themselves. Mustering my last significant effort, I sprinted and leaped out of the forest and toward the water.

I hung, suspended in midair for a moment of glorious freedom until a series of needlepoints pierced my back. The creature reached out, hooked a clawed hand into the soft flesh of my shoulders, and pulled me back. Each needlepoint finger was agony, sending burning lightning across my already tortured skin. I cried out and tried to struggle, but exhaustion caught up to me, quelling the urge.

A dread sickness blossomed from within me as I was lifted into the air, hooked like butchered meat. The pain was excruciating. I grimaced, trying not to vomit as the creature's face came into view. Warm, damp breath blew into my face, and my eyes watered. My brain gave up. There was nothing left to do but try to say something cool before I died. I had always admired adventure heroes who kept their composure in front of mortal odds. Here was my chance.

Looking beyond the creature's face, I could think of nothing but the movie Predator. It wasn't much, but it was going to have to do. Wasn't like I thought anyone would hear it anyway.

The creature brought me closer until I was eye-to-eye with it. It clicked slowly, savoring the moments before my disembowelment. The pain in my back lessened as adrenaline took over. The creature opened its mouth and let out a piercing cry, its eyes narrowing to slits.

I took a deep breath, wishing I couldn't smell its last meal. *Here goes nothing.* I mustered the best macho voice I could. "You are one ugly mother—"

The creature dropped me, shrieking as if it had been burned. It clicked madly at a vibrating intensity and reached out with its claw, the fingers stopping inches from my face. Its eyes widened in anguish.

I didn't have much time to analyze the situation. In short, if it ain't broke, don't fix it. If swearing kept me alive, I would become a sailor. I spoke again, this time with a little bit more confidence. "You are one ugly mother f—". The creature's shriek cut me off.

I watched in delight as the creature backed away toward the edge of the forest. *You have got to be kidding me.* I thanked all those late nights where I had stayed up to watch R-rated sci-fi movies against my parents' wishes. I repeated the line, this time yelling and seeing it through. "You are one ugly mother fucker!"

The creature howled in pain, drowning me out. With one final stare, the monster melted into the forest. There was a moment of stunned silence. Sound rushed back in a wave. Unfortunately, with the noise came the insects, eager to land on my bloodied skin and find a fresh meal. I found it hard to care. The creature's presence had been like an ice bath, and with her gone, the world was a little brighter.

Still stunned by what had happened, I picked up the tome that had fallen to the ground in my struggle. With the book in my hand and the river in front of me, hope sprang eternal. Adrenaline kept me from feeling the creature's stab wounds on my back, and I opened the book to the page concerning La Madremonte again.

After stalking me throughout the day, the beast finally revealed itself when I settled in for the evening. Appearing directly behind me, it whispered in my ear and then tried to shred me to ribbons. Luckily, having spent a good deal of time with the people of Columbia, I knew that I had nothing to fear.

I had to scoff at this. Henry had been many things, but a brave man was not one of them. He was a drunk and a damned good shot, but brave he was not.

The Columbians will say it is best to avoid La Madremonte at all costs, but there is an exceedingly simple method for getting rid of it when encountered. Most prey, when confronted, is frightened into a form of paralysis. The trick is to insult the creature. Just about anything will do. La Madremonte is prideful and easily offended. And so, without gun, knife, or stake, I drove the creature back into the forest by merely calling it a series of increasingly vulgar names!

"Well, I'll be damned," I said, laughing. I closed the book and stepped out to the edge of the cliff above the river, careful not to get too close. The precipice I had tried to leap from was a good thirty feet above the water. Looking at it with fresh eyes, I was happy I hadn't made the jump. The turbulent rapids below looked far more dangerous than on first inspection.

I decided the best course of action was to follow the forest's perimeter until it got closer to the river's edge, then continue west. With renewed vigor, I turned around and started forward. There was a slight crackle of underbrush, and my heart froze. I looked down to see a large, brown snake slithering toward me. Unfortunately, instincts took over. I flinched backward, and the world fell out from beneath me.

5

____

THE RIVER

The fall happened in slow motion. I remember smacking my head on the muddy slope as I crashed down the steep banks leading to the river. Rushing water enveloped me in momentary cool relief, contrasting the oppressive jungle heat. I floated, suspended in the churning void, thankful to be alive. Then, I was dragged down and shoved into the world's most violent washing machine. I thrashed, trying to avoid whatever rocks might lay below but succeeding only in getting pulled further into the current.

I grew disoriented as the water sucked me down, spinning me until I no longer knew which way was up. Opening my eyes, I could only see the river's green gloom and the dark rocks at its bottom. As I flailed through the current, a pain shot through my leg, and my forward momentum stopped. I tried to kick free and found that my foot had wedged itself painfully between two rocks. The water tugged viciously as I struggled to free myself.

I dislodged my foot from the bottom with a painful scrape and was pulled back into the wash. I could feel the cloud of warmth as blood flowed from my wound. Trying not to think of the creatures that might be able to follow my scent, I made a fresh bid for the surface and managed to breach. My head popped above water long enough for me to gasp a desperate lungful of damp jungle air. Ahead, white foam broke around submerged boulders. A last-ditch surge of adrenaline hit me. *Ah, shit.*

I tried to put my feet downriver to protect my head. The water accelerated, and I was pulled down, becoming the equivalent of a human pinball, ricocheting between rocks. Each agonizing collision was a sharp reminder that I was both still alive and in a great deal of pain. I heard nothing but the roar of water around me and my own grunts with each fresh bruise nature gave me. I opened my eyes to green-white bubbles. Blind, I tried my best to conserve my breath and let the river take me.

The water moved in a cycle, pushing me to the surface where I could catch a breath and then dragging me down so far that explosive pressure assaulted my eardrums. *Well, at least I'm not going to die of dehydration.* The thought was absurd, but to my oxygen-deprived brain, it was nothing short of high comedy. I laughed, losing some of my precious air.

As I oscillated between the surface and death, I found myself thinking back to the snake that had sent me on this wretched journey. I hated it with every fiber of my irrational being. Through my fuzzy-brained logic, I made many vows against the world's endless supply of reptiles, most of which involved prolonged dismemberment.

The torture continued for what felt like hours but was only minutes. Then, the water calmed, and I was able to kick my way back to the surface. I bobbed up and down, catching glimpses of the banks on either side. They were too steep to climb. *Nothing wrong with a little river float.* I stretched out in my best imitation of a starfish and let buoyancy take care of the rest. The distant roar of the rapids was almost calming. I floated, listening to it, but quickly grew confused. Rather than dying away, the cry was growing louder.

I flipped over into an awkward dog paddle and looked ahead. The river ended in a sudden frothing edge where it met a misty skyline. "Oh, fuck you, jungle." Summoning what little strength I had left, I kicked and sputtered, making my way toward the river's edge. The banks now resembled cliff faces, but anything sounded better than heading over a waterfall. Every muscle in my body screamed as I pushed them to their absolute limits.

My hand scraped along the edge of the muddy bank, and I grabbed for anything to pull myself up. With numb fingers, I gripped a strong-looking root and hoisted myself out of the water. I was halfway out when the slimy mud that had been holding my lifeline in place gave way. The root slipped a few inches, and it was all it took for me to lose my grip. I fell, and the warm water smacked my back, sending a bolt of pain through my already abused body.

The roar of the waterfall was omnipresent. I tried once more to put my feet downstream, but the current was too strong. It tugged at me, pulling me over the edge. Then, for the second time that day, I was falling. My body spun head over heels, becoming one with the rush of water. I closed my eyes and waited for it all to end. There was a muted impact as I hit the pool below, and what remained of my breath left me in a rush. Stars sprang up before my eyes, and I found myself floating in space. The water was dark and peaceful. *Not a bad way to go,* I thought, surrendering to it. It had been a long day.

My face broke the surface of the water, and I felt the evening breeze. *Huh, no rocks.* Apparently, living through the experience was still an option. With leaden arms, I turned myself over and pushed towards the edge of the river. It took all the effort I had left to even breathe, but when I took that first lungful, I knew I could survive. The shore wasn't far, and it only took seconds before the tips of my toes touched the silty river bottom. I half-registered that, luckily, I hadn't been tossed into a shallower portion of the pool and stumbled to the muddy river's edge. A thousand muscles I had never used screamed at me for ignoring them. I walked far enough away from the river where I wouldn't get pulled back in and collapsed face down in the mud.

For a while, I laid there, panting, taking stock of my life. *Jungle, never again. Never again am I coming back to the god-damned jungle.* I listened to the river's gurgling and quickly realized it was the only sound I could hear. There was no birdsong, no distant animals making their way through the treetops, only water passing by. Fearing La

Madremonte's return, I mustered the last of my energy and jumped to my feet, striking a defensive posture.

I looked up to the riverbank in the pale moonlight and fell backward as I spotted five ghostly faces staring back at me. I scrambled backward, trying to get away, but quickly found a crude spear inches from my throat. The man holding it spoke in a language I didn't understand and inched the weapon closer to my skin. Four other men quickly joined, all clutching ugly weapons that appeared to be constructed of scrap metal.

"Hello, there," I ventured.

The first cocked his head, quizzically. His eyes were black like a shark's, in sharp contrast to the white streaks of paint on his face.

"Who might you be, and what have I done to offend you?" I knew there wasn't much use in talking, but I didn't have many options.

The man's eyes widened in what looked to be surprise, fear, anger, or a mixture of all three. A line of psychologists will tell you that I've never been great at picking up emotional cues. I was close to letting my guard down when the man held the spear above his head, preparing to lunge for a killing blow. He let out a loud war cry. I winced, shutting my eyes against the inevitable.

"Woah, woah, woah," came a voice from the forest's edge. A man ran out from behind the trees. Under the moonlight, I couldn't tell much aside from the fact that he didn't look like the others. He wore the same face paint, but his hair was lighter, and his skin was pale. "Jerry, what are you doing?" the man yelled in a thick Scottish accent.

The man holding the spear pulled back and turned to face the newcomer. "Wanker," he said, pointing to me and making a kill motion.

"You don't know he's a wanker!" The man ran up, put a hand on the weapon, and moved it away from my throat. My would-be attacker slapped the newcomer with the flat edge of the spear and said something that sounded aggressive in his native tongue. The other men murmured in agreement.

"I'm pretty sure he's not a devil." The Scottish man turned to me. "You're not, are you?"

I looked at my hand in the moonlight. "Not unless I drowned in that river." With all I had already experienced, waking up as an undead was certainly a possibility. Necromancers made a quick job of raising corpses when they needed a friend.

The Scottish man turned back to the others and argued with them in their language. Then, stopping, he turned around to me with wide eyes. "Hold on a minute…you," he faltered, "you speak English?"

The men behind him stirred restlessly, still white-knuckling the handles of their spears.

I nodded slowly. "And you're not from around here, are you?" I wasn't sure what I had stumbled on to, but for the first time since jumping out of the plane, I couldn't believe my luck.

The man laughed heartily and grabbed my shoulders with callused hands. With a mighty jerk, he lifted me to my feet, sending pain shooting through my limbs. All the bruises that covered my body cried out at once, reminding me that jumping headfirst into Amazon rapids had been a terrible idea.

Whether the man noticed or not, he made no move to ease my discomfort. Instead, he circled me, pushing me back to a stand whenever my legs faltered. He muttered to himself like a jeweler appraising an incredibly valuable stone. At last, he came back around in front of me. "Nah, you've got to be a hallucination. The latest batch must have gone bad. I knew I should have checked the stills…"

At that moment, my legs gave one final wobble and completely collapsed beneath me. I fell backward into the mud, knocking the wind from my lungs. "I'm very real," I gasped, "and I'm in a lot of pain." I motioned to the small puddle of blood that had formed beneath my foot. Even looking at it brought a new wave of nausea.

"Oh, I'm so sorry." The man put a hand around my shoulder to lift me and keep the pressure off my foot. "I didn't see you were injured. Forgive my skepticism, it's…" he trailed off, looking at the trees around them. "Do you have any idea where we are?"

"In the middle of a hellish jungle somewhere along the Amazon river?"

"Aye. So, you're real then." The man shook his head, still unbelieving.

The pain continued to creep up my leg, and I grew woozy. "Not to be a party-crasher, but I don't suppose you have any medical supplies or know how to fix this?" I motioned to my leg and nearly collapsed.

The man looked down. "I can do you one better," he said, shouldering more of my weight and taking the pressure off my foot. He spoke some words to one of the other men, and after a brief argument, he came to support my other side. The man who had held a spear to my throat was still watching with an aggravated stare.

"Follow me, friend, and I'll show you one of the best parts of this cursed place."

6

MODERN DAY CASTAWAY

Albert looked at Nick intensely over the top of some frothing concoction that made his eyes water. Through the dim lights of The Haven, it was difficult to tell whether he was impressed or skeptical. Luckily, Albert wasn't one to hold his tongue. "Alright, Nick, I think we've had enough of this. A Scotsman in the middle of the Amazon rainforest? Do us all a favor and let this poor young woman go. She doesn't need to hear your tripe." He belched as he said the last word.

Marcus was still half asleep but had moved to a closer booth to hear the story clearer. For Marcus, that was about as attentive as he got. Jimmy continued watching television behind the bar, occasionally muttering some unheard advice to the characters.

"Believe me," Nick said, finishing his glass and twiddling his fingers, "if I was going to make up a story, I would make it more believable." He looked around, hoping for some form of support.

"Oh, don't sell yourself short, Nick," crowed Jimmy, turning away from his soaps. "I seem to remember you and your young apprentice telling some pretty tall tales. What was that about the lake monster and a boat full of chocolate?" Jimmy laughed heartily and turned back to the television.

"I have pictures of the bloody mess we made after killing that beast." Nick gave his date a placating look. Luckily, despite the patrons' constant derogation, she still seemed to be paying close attention.

In fact, a hint of a smile crossed her face. "Sounds like an intriguing story for another time." She winked and drank some more of her half-empty glass.

Running out of time here, Nick thought, desperate to get the conversation back on track. "I've got a Polaroid for you back at my apartment, Jimmy. If it's real, you buy us all a round next time I'm in."

"Probably forgery anyway," muttered Jimmy, waving him off.

For a bunch of monster hunters, they sure are skeptical. Nick wanted to be angry but couldn't. When the tables were turned, he was equally as caustic and derisive. A week earlier, Albert had told a story about stalking a vampire on the London Underground and even had fresh bite marks to prove it. Nick had told him to stop covering for another lousy date and come out with the truth. *What goes around comes around, I suppose.*

"Alright, if you're all so convinced that I'm spinning a yarn here, maybe I should stop telling the story." He looked to his date and flicked his eyes toward the door. It was already getting late, and going somewhere that wasn't filled with critical drunks seemed like a more pleasant way to spend the evening. Maybe they could even go to B's Diner.

His date raised her eyebrows. "Oh no, Nick. You're not getting out of this that easy." She motioned to her glass. "I haven't finished my drink, and you still have to impress me." She sat back in her chair, folding her arms and wearing a devilish smile.

"Yeah, ya idjut." Marcus's words morphed together as if they were being poured from a blender. "Might be a loada crap, but 's interesting." He slumped in his booth and flicked his wrist in the air, telling Nick to go on.

"Fine." Nick let out a melodramatic sigh. "Where were we?" He motioned for another drink, and Jimmy brought him a glass full of clear liquid. Nick picked it up, took a sip, and nearly choked. "Jesus, Jimmy, what is that?!"

"Water." He chuckled. "Finish the glass, and I'll bring you a pint of the good stuff."

Nick looked at the glass begrudgingly and drained it in a few quick gulps. "Thanks, Mom."

Jimmy gave him the finger.

"So, the cannibals were surrounding me from all sides, advancing with their flaying knives…" Nick continued.

"What the bloody hell are you talking about?!" roared Albert, suddenly alert and present.

"Oh, was I not there yet?" Nick looked to the ceiling as if in deep thought. "Maybe another drink would make me remember."

Jimmy poured a pint.

"Ah, that's right, I think I remember now. I was walking into the jungle with the Scotsman…"

HAD THERE BEEN anyone else in that awful place, we would have made an odd sight. The Scotsman still wore pieces of what might have at one time been a business suit; I looked like I had drowned on my way to a fancy party. If it wasn't for the cadre of men surrounding me with spears, the scene could have been a typical Saturday night. Our progress was slow, but luckily with the aid of the two men, we were able to make our way through the underbrush.

A small path was carved between the roots, vines, and dense trees. To the untrained eye, it would have been difficult to notice, but as I had spent my last day searching for any semblance of a trail, it might as well have been a freeway. The men who weren't helping me stand had fanned out on either side of us, relaxed but keeping a watchful eye on the trees. It was difficult to see much. Even with the pale moonlight filtering through, I could barely see twenty feet in front of me.

My head ached, and every piece of my body burned with the torture I had been put through. The journey passed by in a series of agonizing blurs, swimming before me much like the river. I had to close my eyes to keep from vomiting. When I tried to speak, nothing came out.

The Scotsman broke the silence. "I don't believe I caught your name."

"It's Nick," I managed through a terse grunt. "Yours?"

"Callum. Pleasure to meet you. I'd shake your hand, but I'm afraid you might collapse." He looked me up and down as if reassessing my condition. "You're looking worse for wear, best we be careful with you." He laughed and looked to the other men, one of whom followed suit with a little too much gusto.

"Cheerful fellow," I said, a little uneasy at how quickly the sound had become maniacal.

"He doesn't know what he's laughing at," whispered Callum.

The man continued to laugh as we walked, gripping his spear with fanatical firmness. He turned back, looking back for some sort of acknowledgment, and some of the other men started laughing as well.

"Great, now he's got them all going." Callum sighed. "He does that because he thinks it'll make us feel more comfortable. I've tried telling him, but…" The man cut him off with another raucous guffaw.

I switched topics, willing to try anything to distract me from the maddening, itching sensation burning my leg. "So, Callum, how long have you been out here?"

"Oh, let's see." Callum held up his free hand in calculation. "Probably coming somewhere on ten years now, but you really lose track of time." Melancholy dropped into his voice. "It could be worse. I could be like the other passengers…"

I was tempted to ask about the fate of said passengers but thought better of it. "Ten years?" I asked. "How have you been able to survive out here for ten years?" Managing two days had been hell for me. Ten years seemed like a lifetime.

"Well, as it turns out, I'm a lucky man." Callum crossed his chest. "When I first crash-landed here, I thought it was a curse." He made a gesture to the trees and vines surrounding us. "It's hot, humid, and about everything on the other side of those trees is trying to kill you."

"So I've noticed," I said with a laugh I immediately regretted. The man on my right laughed so loudly that each chuckle sent tiny, painful needles shooting through my injured ribs.

"Real sod, that one," muttered Callum, looking at my wounds. "Looks like you've been through the wringer. My first few nights were rough, too, no doubts there, but I didn't decide to go for a swim…"

"It wasn't exactly a decision," I admitted.

Callum shrugged and continued. "I spent my first evening in the busted hull of my airplane with naught but the dead for company. Lost everyone else on board: my co-pilot, the rich bastard who paid us to fly out here, and his entire investment group. Must have been an interesting board room meeting back home…" Callum spat. "The rich bastard, he deserved it, but some of the others weren't so bad.

"Now, I was a damned good pilot, mind you, but the storm we flew into came out of nowhere. Clear skies, the weatherman said, clear skies at takeoff. Clear skies right up until the storm blew in and shit-kicked us right out of the sky. Within five minutes, I lost engine one. I tried to bring us down safely, but the storm was too much. Last thing I remember was coming through the clouds and then *WHAM!*" He jolted as if experiencing the crash again. "The trees were right there to meet us, and the plane was pooched beyond repair. Tree branch went right through the cockpit, impaled my co-pilot, and gave me a nasty little scar. Rest were dead by the time I came to."

I grimaced. "It seems we've got more in common than I thought." The memory of falling through a similar storm was still fresh and brought a renewed wave of pain to my limbs.

"I'd say we do. I saw your plane headed down in the storm. Fireball streaking across the night sky."

"That would be Lopsang…" *Hope he's having better luck than me.*

"Pardon?"

"My pilot."

"Take it he didn't make it?"

"He had me ditch before we landed. I've seen him survive worse. Hell of a pilot." Talking up Lopsang's piloting skills seemed far more manageable than explaining the fact that I had been traveling with a near-immortal demi-god.

Callum nodded gravely. "I'm sure he is." He mumbled a short prayer under his breath. I couldn't help but find it odd that someone had been able to retain so much faith given the circumstances.

"Well, like I said, at first glance this place might have seemed like a curse, but I've actually done quite well for myself out here. A few days after I crashed, this tribe found me." He jerked his head toward the men fanned out around us. "At first, they were downright hostile, but they came around shortly after I showed them the most efficient way to strip my plane bare." Callum motioned to the strips of metal hanging from his ears, which I then recognized as pieces of some sort of control board.

"Memento?" I asked.

"You could say so. I couldn't bear to let them take the whole thing. That plane was a part of me for fifteen years." Callum went silent, looking out at the forest for a while. "Anyway, after a while, they accepted me. I help them out with my skills in mechanical engineering, and they give me protection. It's not home, but it'll do." He smiled, proud of his accomplishment.

The thought of living in the jungle, surrounded by death and fetid humidity sounded like a worse fate than hell. Glints of metal caught my eye through the trees up ahead. The dim moonlight made it impossible to see anything beyond large silhouettes. "What's that?" I asked, pointing forward.

"That's my plane."

The forest cleared, revealing a dirt path running between pieces of scrap metal. Like a scene out of an apocalyptic movie, strung together were various airplane parts, ranging from a small cockpit all the way to a commercial airliner fuselage. They had been placed in what loosely resembled huts. As we walked farther, I could see the entire village. Every building was made of wreckage, with some still bearing recognizable logos from their past lives. "Wow…" was all I could manage. "Am I having a fever dream?"

Callum laughed heartily as the man on my right joined in.

"No, Nick. This is my home."

"Is all this your plane?"

"Oh, course not. There have been quite a few to go down out here over the years—plenty more before I even arrived. The villagers didn't know what to do with them. I've gathered that this is sort of a hotspot. There's at least one crash a year. We always check for survivors, but you're the first I've seen since I landed here myself." A child bustled past us wearing oversized khaki shorts and a pith helmet. "You'd be surprised what we find out there." Callum chuckled. I could not help but feel uneasy wondering about the fate of the other crash victims.

Luckily, there wasn't much time to think. A group of men dressed in various ripped suits and Tommy Bahama shirts approached. Each carried a weapon and had assortments of metal decoration dangling from their body. Almost immediately, I found myself at spearpoint again. Our escorts quickly disappeared to join the other side of the confrontation.

"Woah, easy there, boys," said Callum. One of the men jabbed their spear forward as Callum spoke some words in the native language. A terse argument broke out between them. The conversation oscillated between Callum's placating tones and the shaking of spears.

"I… uh… don't suppose you have anything metal on you?" asked Callum, turning his attention back to me. "They're not keen on outsiders, but scrap has sort of become a currency around here. If the chief were here, things might be easier."

I rummaged through my pockets, surprised anything had stayed in them through my trip down the river. All I found were a few pieces of change and plenty of river mud. "This is all I've got." I extended my palm with the filthy coins in it.

The man arguing with Callum dropped his spear immediately and walked over to paw through the coins. His attitude shifted from skepticism to excitement. After a minute of examination, he looked up at me and spoke in a language I couldn't understand.

"He wants to know if he can have one."

"Sure, take any one you like." I'd never traded my life for a quarter before, but it seemed like a pretty good deal.

Callum translated, and the man took one of the coins in his hand, holding it up to the moonlight. He clapped me on the shoulder and then ran off to one of the huts to hide his new prize. The other men soon noticed the short supply in my palm and ran up to meet me. Each took a coin and left smiling.

"Well, that was the easiest negotiation I've ever done."

"Good thing you had those on you, or it might not have gone so well," Callum said uneasily. "Either way, it seems like you're allowed in now. So, Nick, welcome to New Glasgow."

7

NEW GLASGOW

As Callum led me through the town, I was amazed. Both he and the villagers had been busy in the ten years since his crash. The makeshift street was lined with huts no more than six feet in height, but their size grew as we walked farther. In many cases, the wrecked bits of aircraft had been expanded to stand multiple stories. A porch swing made from the wing of a World War Two bomber croaked in the evening breeze. In fact, the whole village creaked like an uneasy windchime.

At the end of the street stood the largest of the buildings, constructed primarily from the nose of a commercial airliner. It was nearly twice as tall as any other structures and looked surprisingly undamaged for having presumably crash-landed. It shone under the moonlight, despite vines and creepers growing up the base. If I had arrived in daylight, I would have seen the tireless team of villagers charged with its upkeep.

"There's the chief's domicile," said Callum, following my gaze. "Don't even ask me how we got it here. Took us well over a week, and we pissed off most of the jungle along the way. Nearly started a sizeable tribal war with some of our neighbors over it. Lucky for us,

I'm a negotiator. A couple of shouting matches and we agreed we'd keep the nose and they'd keep the hull. That's politics for ya."

"Tribal war?" I asked, only half paying attention while trying to process the surreal scene around me. The level at which Callum had adapted to his setting was incredible. I had nearly died after two days, and here this man was thriving. A sense of shame grew within me.

"Ah, they're not much anyway. It's mostly a bunch of spear waving, some trading, and then de-escalation—nothing like the wars at home. Every once in a while, one of the spears gets thrown, but so far, no casualties. Lucky thing too because there's not many of us out here."

Callum continued to lead me down the street. The only thing keeping my agony at bay was pure fascination. I caught glimpses of people staring at me through passenger windows in the metal huts, but if they noticed me looking back, they'd duck out of sight. Wind-chimes made of spare parts hung on almost every porch, contributing to the constant ambient noise of metal on metal.

As we neared the end of the street, I noticed a large cylinder set in the ground. Fuel lines spiraled out at odd angles as the smell of burning wood wafted from beneath. Through a tiny window at the top, I could see liquid frothing and boiling. "What on Earth is that?"

Callum puffed out his chest. "That is a building that took over four years to construct. There were a lot of terse discussions with the chief over it, but in the end, we pulled it off."

The building was incredibly complicated, especially with the parts on hand. "Is it some sort of fuel storage?"

"Oh, heavens, no. It's a distillery."

My heart might as well have leaped from my chest and somer-saulted down the lane. I grabbed Callum's shoulder, half for support and half for emphasis. At the simple word, my knees had gone weak beneath me. "Say it again."

"We've got a distillery," he remarked through a chuckle, clapping me on the shoulder.

It took all I had to stand. "They've got a distillery," I muttered to myself in disbelief.

"I'll warn you, it tastes worse than a jungle rat's sweaty ass, but you'll be drunker than Baron Foulkes during a cessation hearing." Callum waited expectantly as if he had told one of the best jokes he had ever thought of.

"I'll be honest with you," I said, trying to be gentle. One must never upset a host who is the sole provider of alcohol for hundreds of miles. "I've got no idea who that is, but I'd be willing to talk about it over a glass." I couldn't help grinning like a schoolboy who had been given the rest of the day off, albeit one that was also slowly bleeding out. *Maybe this place isn't so bad after all.*

"I think after a day like today, you've earned it." Callum smiled. "But first, we need to get you some medical attention. As much as I love carrying you around, it'd be good to get you back on your own two feet." He looked me up and down. "Plus, you're bleeding over the whole village, it's a real mess…"

Reluctantly, I agreed. "Alright, bandages first, distillery second."

Callum chuckled. "Whatever you say."

Together we hobbled over to one of the larger huts. Callum rapped delicately on the door. There was no answer, and he knocked a little harder. From inside, I heard muttering and someone bustling around. A glass bottle broke, and I was about to ask if everything was alright when a squat, wrinkled old woman opened the door. She looked pissed. A candle flickered in her right hand, giving her the gaunt appearance of a crypt keeper. Callum spoke to her in a friendly tone in the native language.

She slapped him upside the head and spoke some angrier words. I couldn't be sure of what they meant, but from context clues, I had to guess it was something akin to 'Why would you wake me up this late, asshole?'

"She's a little grumpy," said Callum. He motioned to my bleeding leg.

The woman's eyes widened as if noticing that Callum was propping up a second person for the first time. She bent down, looking closely at my leg, examining every inch. I was about to ask how bad it was when she jammed a finger in the wound, causing me to cry out in pain. Tendrils of fire lanced out from the injury. The woman didn't falter, moved her finger around a bit, took it out, and tasted it. She spat blood onto the ground and gave Callum an angry look.

Callum shrugged as if to say: I told you he was in a bad way. The woman glared at him and motioned for us to come inside.

"What the hell, lady?" My fists balled up. It had been a while since I had fought an old woman, but most old women didn't dig their dirty fingers into my injuries.

"Be thankful," whispered Callum, "she wouldn't invite us in if she didn't think she could save the leg."

The thought of losing it had not even occurred to me; I quickly shut up and hobbled inside. A wave of heat and the smell of woodsmoke blasted me in the face. Apparently, "Hotter than Hell" was a thermostat setting for these people. Small piles of sticks burned in the corners of the room, wafting through a circular chimney set in the middle of the roof. The smell was sweet, overpowering, and nauseating all at the same time.

"She's a little odd, but trust me, she's your best shot." Callum laid me down on the remains of an airline seat that had been converted to a bed. The woman walked in small circles, talking to herself and looking to the ceiling as if for guidance.

"You sure we can't get a second opinion?" I asked.

Callum laughed uneasily. The woman came over and pushed him toward the door with short, hard shoves. "She wants me to leave, Nick. Something about bad luck." He moved obediently towards the door.

"Don't leave me here," I said, trying to hide the desperation in my voice. Suddenly the distillery seemed all too far away. My stomach tightened. I didn't like doctor's offices, much less when they were filled with smoke and wound-poking.

"I'll come back and get you when she's finished, don't you worry!" Callum hurried out.

The woman opened a blind to ensure he was actually leaving and just as quickly shut it. She muttered under her breath and waved her hands through the smoke. It might have been the pain or the smoke inhalation, but shapes danced in the candlelight's long shadows.

"You going to wrap the wound?" I asked, hopefully. *This is the best chance I've got?*

A skeletal face formed in the smoke, fixing its empty eye sockets on me. There was something familiar in that face, but before I could recognize it, the smoke dissipated into a vague cloud.

Great, black magic. I had dealt with the dark arts on numerous occasions, but I always preferred to be the practitioner instead of the patient. Being unable to understand any of the incantations, I wasn't sure whether I would end up possessed, cured, or some horrible combination of the two. Dark magic has a fine line for error, among even the most accomplished of its users.

The woman continued about her muttering and bent down to look at my leg. Thankfully, her fingers stayed out of my wound for the follow-up examination. Instead, she went to a small crate and pulled out a bottle marked with three 'X's. She took a swig for herself, and then without warning, she poured the rest of the bottle onto my leg.

I might as well have been doused in acid. If I could have raised my head, I'm sure I would've seen steam coming off the wound. I did my best to remain lucid, but the room wavered and shifted before me. The pain coursing through my leg was immeasurable, and I was sure she had set it on fire. I could feel the woman's hands around my wound, but the world was beginning to go black. Through the ether, I heard a voice call to me, high and cold.

"You're looking well, Nick. See you soon."

The voice was horribly familiar. I tried to focus on the sound and place its owner, but the world was growing dark around me. "Who are you?" I murmured, the words sloughing out in a jumbled mess.

The voice didn't call back. I tried to sit, and a black circle closed around the edge of my vision. The room spun. I blacked out.

8

CAMPFIRE TALES

When I came to, I was sitting in a plush chair on the edge of the street. The sun had sunk low on the horizon, casting the entire village in a fiery orange glow. Around me, I could hear children playing, and the sounds of conversation drifting through the air. Beyond that, the jungle was active, full of birdsong; monkeys howled from their perches in the canopy.

I blinked, trying to bring everything into focus. It took a minute to remember what had happened; I immediately jolted forward to look at my leg. The motion was dizzying, but the relief at seeing a crisp bandage around my still-attached ankle was enough to keep nausea at bay.

"Good morning, Sleeping Beauty." Callum walked up carrying a travel thermos and put it in my hand. "Drink this, it'll help." He plopped down in another cushy chair next to me.

I unscrewed the cap of the thermos and sniffed. "This doesn't smell like alcohol." I took an experimental sip. Sweet, cold nectar ran down the back of my throat and brought life to my parched body. Without further thought, I downed the rest of the container, realizing how thirsty I was.

"It might not be alcoholic, but you're going to need the energy.

Chief came back this morning while you were asleep. Sounds like we're going to have a big party."

"How long was I out?" I asked.

"Only a day. Count yourself lucky. That wound was full of river water and god-knows-what. But you'll make a full recovery."

"And here I assumed I'd been out drinking again." I moved cautiously and winced at the extreme soreness in my limbs, then closed my eyes, letting the sun's warmth seep into my skin.

Callum shifted uneasily. "There's one more thing…"

I opened my eyes to find his face had gone pale. "We found this in the river this morning." Callum looked reluctant. He passed me a leather-bound tome.

"Well, I'll be damned," I said, turning over the familiar pages. "Henry really thought of everything." It appeared that not only could the book repel water, but it had a way of finding its way back to me. I didn't want to begin to think about the complexity of the spells needed for such a parlor trick.

"You recognize it?"

"Sure, I do. It's mine." Truth be told, I was relieved. I had carried that damn book with me on every expedition, and Henry would have risen from the grave if I had lost it. "Don't know how it found its way out of the river, though." I immediately flipped through the book's pages for the entry on La Madremonte. When I reread it, I couldn't help but laugh out loud.

"What's so funny?" Callum's friendly demeanor had been replaced with a suspicious edge.

"It's an entry on the nasty beasty that I encountered before falling in the river. La Madre—"

Callum shushed me quickly. "Don't talk so loud. Do you want to bring her down on us?"

I couldn't help but laugh again. "Well, now that I know her weakness, I'm not too worried about it." I skimmed through the page, ensuring that I had read it correctly.

Callum sat silent, watching me.

"Oh, lighten up, she might be a little scary, but also vain. Here, take a look." I held the book out to Callum.

He cocked his head quizzically.

"Ignore the naked drawings. Henry was a bit odd, to say the least."

Callum chuckled despite his apprehension. "The beast fled at the mere utterance of insults?" he read aloud.

"The legends never stop getting weirder," I muttered.

"Best we don't mention any of this to the rest of the village. They don't take so kindly to this sort of thing."

I scoffed, remembering the healer who had mended my leg. "What about the old crone?"

"Oh her? She's good with tricks. Nothing to your leg other than some good old-fashioned bandages and tree sap."

Didn't seem like traditional healing. I thought back to the skull that had materialized in the smoke and the voice I had heard. There was something so familiar about that voice. "If you say so. We'll keep this our little secret then." I winked and put the book down at my side. "Maybe we could get something to cover it."

Callum nodded. For a few minutes, we both sat in silence, listening to the village's bustling sounds. "What exactly is it you do, Nick?"

I sighed. The explanation was never easy and would be difficult even for a man living the plot of an adventure movie. "That's a conversation that's going to require a few cups of the good stuff." I waited expectantly.

Callum was still on edge. "Alright, but I want to hear all of it. And don't put any of your fancy spells on me…"

"I'm not a wizard…"

Callum eyed me suspiciously.

"I promise. Too many dusty old books and dusty old men. Never really was my thing." This was mostly true. Wizards have all sorts of rules and regulations in their community; I'm more of a dabbler in the dark arts than anything else.

The sun set, and Callum brought me to a small firepit out behind the distillery. Like most of the other meeting areas, it was flanked with repurposed airplane chairs. Reflexively, I reached for the seatbelt as I sat down, only catching myself after Callum had noticed.

"It's a bit odd, isn't it?" he asked.

"I'll say. How does one get used to this?"

Callum popped open a hatch in the back of his chair and pulled out a glass bottle and two cups. "Oh, humans can get used to anything when they have to." He poured a murky drink and handed it to me. "Cheers."

We clacked the glasses together, and I took a swig. It took all my effort not to cough and splutter, but I wasn't going to waste my first drink in days. Callum was right—it did taste worse than a jungle rat's ass, but the fuel-like nature beyond the flavor told me it would serve its purpose. I swilled the liquid and took another drink. The booze wasn't top shelf, but it made me feel better. The jungle, and all the dangers awaiting within, seemed momentarily far away.

Callum took a seat opposite me. The fire crackled between us, sending red sparks floating into the evening sky. In the village, sounds of preparation echoed off the corrugated steel walls. "So, tell me, what brings you to South America in the first place?" His tone was friendly, but it was clear that he would not let this line of questioning go.

"It's a long story, but the simple version is that I'm here looking for a friend."

"Odd place to find a friend."

"Well, it's an odd sort of friend." Unbidden, images of a cave high in the mountains flashed before my eyes. I saw James's body crumpled in the chalk circle I had created while his blood ran out in a pool around him.

Callum remained silent, waiting for me to continue.

"My friend," I started, finding the story much harder to tell than expected. "My friend died." Saying it out loud made it feel real all over again. Sure, the Amazon was terrible, but at least it had provided an escape from the responsibility I carried for his death. Searching for courage, I continued. "We were on a climbing expedition about a year or so back. Things went bad. I made it out; he didn't." The climb down without James had been one of the hardest things I had ever done. The thought of it made me sick.

"Why come all the way out here to pay your respects if he died in the mountains?" Callum's face was filled with genuine confusion.

I weighed my options, decided Callum wasn't one to bullshit, and came out with the truth. "I'm not here to pay my respects. I'm here to bring him back."

The fire sputtered momentarily, sending a massive plume of sparks into the sky as a strong wind blew through the village.

Why does that always happen?

Callum's face darkened. "Bring him back?" He paused. "Remember what I said about dark magic? People around here are nervous enough already with the book they found." He made the motion of the protective cross over his chest.

Where did people pick that shit up? The act of crossing one's chest did approximately jack in the presence of evil. I tended to blame movies for the idiotic practice, but the moment didn't seem right for a lecture, so I held my tongue. "Actually, it's got nothing to do with black magic." It had more than a little to do with black magic. "Mostly, it's a matter of finding a path into the Land of the Dead." At least that was true.

Another strong breeze caused the fire to sputter.

"It does that a lot around here, doesn't it?" I asked, surveying the village.

"Not usually." Callum looked up to the canopy and sat in silent thought. "Even if I believed you about the Land of the Dead, and I'm not saying I do..." He eyed the fire carefully, waiting for another gust of wind. When that never came, he continued. "I still don't see why you'd have to trek to the South American jungle to get there."

Callum seemed uncomfortable with the topic, but I was beginning to feel a little buzzed and plowed on. "As it turns out, death is a tricky business. From what I've read, a soul goes to rest in the same place it was born, mostly."

"Mostly?"

"Well, there are some exceptions, usually around demonic intervention, but the records of those are few and far between." I had never had to deal with a demon personally and counted myself lucky for it. "Originally, I thought I was going to have to find a portal near Akron, Ohio to the American Land of the Dead, but after a little digging, I found that James wasn't born there."

Callum looked confused. "Slow down. American Land of the Dead? Don't tell me the deceased still adhere to national ties."

"Well, not exactly, but suffice it to say the Land of the Dead is split into regions depending on the culture surrounding death. I've never been, but I imagine the American Land of the Dead is full of cow skulls, tall men in dark robes, and motorcycles with skulls for engines."

Callum sputtered, trying to conjure the image.

"It's all conjecture at this point. Most of the people who go in and successfully return become heavy drinkers. Their accounts are nothing but unreliable depictions of fiery lakes and demons that rip sinners to shreds." I paused, thinking it over. "Sounds more like Hell to me, but I wouldn't be surprised if the two were connected." I had never put much stock in the biblical unless it was a useful deterrent against the beast of the day.

Callum resumed his silent watchfulness.

"There's an American author, can't remember his name now. He talks about a world beyond ours where souls are stuck in waiting. Not like a traditional limbo, but more akin to a second plane, like our own. He believed that there were several conduits to enter through around the globe and that going through them was surprisingly easy. It was getting out that was the hard part. I had to assault a very rich ma——"

Callum cut me off. "Look, Nick, you seem like a nice enough fellow. Weird, but nice enough." He ran a hand through his tangled hair. "I really don't want to get the village involved with any of this." There was no anger in his voice, only a determined finality. "The chief has talked about dark magic users beyond our borders and creatures that go bump in the night. I've never seen any of it myself, but I don't want any part of it."

Even though it was the sensible thing to say, it still stung. "You'll probably live longer with that attitude." A bitter taste crept into the back of my mouth, and I could feel the high whistle of mountain air ringing in my ears. *Can we not do this now?* Asking my own brain to lay off had never worked in the past, but it was worth a try.

"The first night I crashed, I heard whispers," said Callum. "There's evil out there, and I'm happy to stay as far away from it as possible."

"I understand. I won't stay long." It was still a little disappointing that we weren't going to get deep into the politics of the dead, but there would be other opportunities. Still, the idea of going back out alone was not a welcome one. "Is the passage upriver safe?"

Callum gave a hollow laugh. "Not even by jungle standards. There's another village about ten miles away, but the chief is skittish about going there."

"Why is that?"

"Black magic, the dark arts, you name it. They wear the skulls of the dead for ornaments, and rumor says they feast on human flesh."

"Got it. Well, can you spare any guides to help get me around?"

The idea clearly caused Callum pain, but he nodded. "There's a group of hunters headed that way tomorrow. I don't know how far they'll take you, but at least past the rapids."

Toward the center of the village, the sounds of celebration swelled.

I drained what was left in my tumbler, coughing and spluttering. It was easy to see why Callum had stayed. The village certainly had its quirks and wasn't a life of luxury but going back out was terrifying. The thick trees surrounding the town were an impenetrable wall hiding untold dangers. There was more than a small part of me that wanted to stay in safety forever.

"If you're keen on going upriver tomorrow, you might as well live it up tonight." Callum cocked an eyebrow. "You've never seen a party like this, I can assure you."

"Could be my last night on Earth. Might as well make the most of it."

UPRIVER

It must have been a good party because the next thing I remembered, I was awoken by a group of men with spears in the early morning dawn. Through my blinding headache, I opened my eyes, wincing at the brightness and cursing the sun for having the gall to rise so early. Somewhere in the distance, tools banged on metal, each hammer blow bringing a painful reminder that I had spent the previous night drinking what was likely jet fuel.

Despite the unpleasant remnants of the evening's festivities sloshing around my newly sensitive skull, I wasn't doing terribly. A man spoke to me in harsh tones that I had to assume meant 'Get up, asshole, we're late.' The stiffness of my limbs made even crawling to a standing position a feat. I wanted to blame the rapids, but the old crone's magic had worked too well. The evening had been joyous—at least I think it had—but the toll I paid was as clear as day.

Satisfied that I was awake, the men motioned for me to follow. Together, we walked down the middle of the street; someone passed me a cup and I drank it. It was more of the fruit juice Callum had given me the day before, and I wondered if I would ever experience anything so good again in my entire life. The farther we got down the street, the louder the sounds of metal on metal grew.

Eventually, I was able to make out the source of the commotion. Men and women were stripping sheets off the sides of their houses and carrying them down toward the river. I thought about inquiring but realized no one would understand me. They seemed to have a basic grasp of Callum's words, but the few times I had tried, all I received were blank stares.

Callum came out of one of the small houses, face painted white —well, whiter than usual—and carrying a steel hunting spear that matched the other men's. When he emerged, they all cheered, lifting their weapons to the sky.

Callum returned the gesture, with less vigor.

"I thought you were staying here," I called.

Callum hurried to join the line. "All that talk about evil out there, I couldn't possibly let you go alone." Up close, it was easy to see he hadn't slept well. Dark circles shadowed his eyes, and a nervous sweat beaded on his brow.

"And?"

"And they were starting to dog me a bit about never going out with the other men. Besides, you'd be bored out of your skull without me to translate."

The group kept their eyes trained on me, murmuring amongst themselves. "Fair point. Do they…know why we're going upriver?"

"I don't think so," answered Callum. "I think they're impressed that you drunk the chief under the table last night."

I raised two fingers to my temples, the source of my hangover now evident. "Ah, this makes a lot more sense now." Sure, I drank a lot on most occasions, but I was a fiend when challenged to a contest.

Callum said something to the men in their native tongue. They all laughed and cheered. I looked to him for an explanation, and he shrugged. "Like I said, they're impressed. Now, let's get some food before we head out. Going upriver isn't going to be an easy journey, and if we're going to die, it might as well be on a full stomach."

Callum tapped one of the men on the shoulder and said something. He motioned to me, and we stepped off the main path toward a longhouse full of activity. From inside, I could smell the sweet aroma of bananas mixed with woodsmoke. The other men continued to move toward the river.

"It's not a five-star meal, but the coffee isn't half bad." Callum led me inside where a few men and women were cooking pans filled with a light-yellow mash. He walked over to one of the pans, scooped some of the mixture out, and put it on a plastic plate prominently displaying the Delta Airlines logo.

I took the plate with about as much enthusiasm as I could muster. The goop didn't look delicious, but I was starving. Before Callum could even hand me a fork, I dug in with my fingers, scooping the mash into my mouth. To my surprise, it was plantains. They tasted better than I could have imagined. Then again, anything beat the cold military rations Lopsang bought on surplus. I couldn't remember much of the night before, but something told me I had forgone a proper dinner in favor of more drink.

Callum returned, laughing at my haste, and handed me a plastic cup of coffee. "Don't drink that too fast, it's hot as hell." Sure enough, even in the heat, the cup was steaming.

Callum ate a few mouthfuls of plantains and motioned to the door. "Better get going. They are really excited to show you the improvements to our boat."

"Improvements?"

"Well, to be honest, they weren't sure our boats could hold you. I might have told them some stories about how fat Americans are. Part of it got lost in translation."

I couldn't tell whether to be offended or laugh. I settled on silently sipping my coffee. "Lead the way."

We picked our way down the path and came to a riverbank near where I initially washed up. The men were retrofitting two small boats with what appeared to be armor plating.

"We expecting trouble?" I asked.

Callum laughed, but it was hollow. "It's the jungle, Nick, there's nothing *but* trouble."

The thought of going back into the fetid hellhole I had so recently escaped was one I would have preferably avoided. We made our way down to the beach. The men stopped their work and stepped aside, proudly revealing their handiwork. I wasn't sure they'd float at all, but I figured the villagers knew better than I did. From the path behind us, a steady stream of men and women joined us on the beach. It seemed that everyone had come to see the hunting party off.

"Now comes the hard part," said Callum.

"What's that?"

"We have to portage the boats above the rapids."

Sure enough, the men were already lining up on both sides to carry the boats.

"And it's going to be a bitch with all that metal they added." Callum chuckled, then walked to a position alongside one of the boats where he prepared to help lift.

One of the men looked to me and motioned to a small bag on the side of the boat. After some finger waving and repeated pointing between him and me, I ascertained that it was for me. He passed me a surprisingly light spear, despite its full metal construction. The bulk of the upper shaft was a flat blade that contracted to a single point, making it equally suitable for throwing and slashing. Given that everything in the wild was trying to kill me, I was willing to take all the protection I could get.

Following Callum's lead, I lined up. There were twelve of us in total—six men for each boat—and when we hoisted the metal hull onto our shoulders, I found it surprisingly easy to carry. A thirteenth man scouted ahead and led us down a barely cleared path. Before long, we were back in the dark, dank shadow of the trees, stumbling over roots and vines.

After the first half-hour, sweat poured down my back. My limbs burned with exhaustion. It did not take long to remember why it was I had hated the jungle. The insects were incessant, letting off a constant dull buzzing that perpetually felt like it was next to my ear. There was plenty of laughter when we passed a bright green snake and I nearly dropped the boat. I was still raw from my previous experience in the canopy.

Even with someone who knew the way guiding us, our progress was slow. Previous hunting parties had cleared a trail, but the jungle was continually growing. That meant occasionally stopping to clear the way or doubling back to make sure we were on the right course. Frankly, I had no idea how they kept it straight. The whole forest looked like nothing more than an endless sea of green to me.

To distract myself from the soreness in my limbs and the weight of the boat, I struck up a conversation with Callum. "How do the villagers avoid getting lost?"

Callum repeated the question to one of the men holding his boat. They all laughed. "He says it's impossible to get lost if you know what you're doing. I know how that seems, but for them, this is a morning walk in the neighborhood."

"Don't suppose this neighborhood has a liquor store?" I had filled my flask with some of Callum's still, but it was unreachable with my spear in one hand and the boat in the other.

"If only."

One of the men spoke to Callum again.

"He says that this is an old hunting trail. They're following the path left by their ancestors. So long as they don't step off it, they can never be lost."

The overgrowth beneath my feet didn't resemble any ancient path I had run across, but their ease made some sense. The group's numbers would ward off most predators, and if they had a set route that they could see, it would be difficult to go off course. *Amazing. A few days out here and I've already learned more than from every Paul Mansen documentary combined.* I nearly laughed at how absurd those old films seemed now. *Maybe he was using a green screen the whole time.* From my experience with his brother, Rick, it wouldn't have surprised me.

After walking for an hour, we came back to the river. A sickening sense of familiarity came over me as I looked in the distance and saw the rapids gurgling in the distance. Before that was the muddy slope I had fallen down. The thought of the snake made me angry again. *Beasts from Hell.*

The men put the canoes down on the bank of the river and flipped them over. We all set our bags inside and boarded. Callum spoke with one of the men and switched places with him so we could ride together. He barely had a chance to sit down before we were pushing off the bank and paddling upriver.

The purpose of the wide-tipped spear became apparent as the men dipped it in the water to paddle forward. I followed suit, grateful for anything that took us farther away from the rapids and the tangled roots of trees on the bank. I had been expecting at least some form of cool river breeze but was disappointed. The water did nothing to chill the air and instead reflected the midday sun back to us, intensifying the heat.

Paddling upriver was difficult work. Luckily, in the afternoon, we stopped to eat some smoked meat and drink fresh water from the canteen. Even in the shaded fronds of the jungle, the heat was still too much for me. The men conversed with each other, and Callum occasionally joined in. I was alone. Rather than try to insert myself, I pulled out the tome and read.

Part of what kept me alive was knowing what dangers lay ahead. While Henry was a coke-addled, unsavory charlatan, to say the least, his writings were helpful. I flipped right past the giant image of the river snake, Yacumama, and instead settled on a passage about Encantado—Amazon river dolphins that could sometimes take human form. I was halfway through a story about Henry encountering one of these creatures at a particularly wild party when I realized the conversation around me had stopped. I looked up and found all eyes had drifted to me.

"Uh, Nick, what did I say about the book?" Callum asked, nervously.

I shut it slowly. "Oh, come on, no harm ever came from reading a book, right?" I put the tome back in my bag and covered it, noticing the eyes on me as I did so.

"Maybe we should get back to the river then?" The muscles in my neck tightened at the thought of a spear being thrust between them.

"I think that would be best." Callum muttered some reassuring words to the crew, but they still seemed on edge. In either case, we were soon back on the river but with none of the playful chatter from before. Instead, we all rowed silently, watching as the endless miles of dark green forest moved by.

As we worked our way farther upriver, a fine mist clung to the surface of the water. It was thick, making it look as though we were rowing through clouds. The men whispered nervously to each other but never stopped paddling. They were single-minded in their task, aside from the occasional glances back at me or to the bag containing Henry's tome.

As we continued, the mist grew thicker until it was at the rim of the boat. "Is this normal for this part of the river?" I asked Callum.

"No," was his only reply.

The entire crew remained silent, watchful, nervous.

Soon, the mist was waist high and obscured both sides of the river. We were paddling into a uniform wall of white. *Impossible to get lost in the jungle… right.*

Fear had only crept into the corner of my mind when one of the men spoke the last word I wanted to hear. It was only a terse whisper, but it might as well have been a shout to my mind. "Yacumama." I had barely processed what the word meant when there was a massive splash off the front of the boat. Waves rocked us from side to side, and I watched as a serpentine ripple split the calm water ahead.

10

———

GIANT, SHITTY RIVER SNAKE

I barely had time to think. My mind was able to process the ripples and understand precisely what they meant, yet I couldn't spur my body to any meaningful motion. I picked up the flask from my side and downed half of it in a solid gulp. If I was going to get eaten by a giant, shitty river snake, I was going to be good and drunk for it.

"What the hell is that?" asked Callum, shaking.

"Yacumama!" shouted one of the men, pointing his spear at what was becoming a roil beneath the water's surface. Two yellow orbs blinked open in the murky depths. Through the surface of the river, I could see the dark shape shooting towards us; my body went numb. In that moment, gripped by primal fear, I would have instead fought the yeti again.

I had enough time to think: *This is not a fight we can win.* Then the creature burst through the surface. In an elegant motion, a huge, serpentine head lifted above the boat, river water pouring off it in great rivulets. It looked us over with two orange, glowing eyes. Black, terrifying slits ran down the center, cementing my worst fear. The water pouring off its diamond-shaped head and dripping from its jaws created a peaceful pattering sound on the river below. The

66

Yacumama swayed back and forth, surveying the boat, flicking a long black tongue out to taste the air.

A man on the other boat aimed a spear at me, yelling what I can only assume was a curse. I had enough time to see my life flash before my eyes, but the aggressive movement also caught the creature's attention. In one horrifying, swift motion, the snake's jaws opened with lightning speed, revealing rows upon rows of teeth. Ragged flesh hung between them, and the stench of decay was overpowering.

Several men jumped to the back of the boat just in time to avoid the strike, but one was not so lucky. The creature's jaws closed, engulfing the boat in a single snap, and pinning the man's torso to the metal. His screams echoed through the mist, ending quickly with a massive crunch and a gurgle as the force of the bite tore him in two.

The boat creaked and groaned under the pressure of the serpent's jaws. The metal the villagers had attached made a valiant effort of delaying the inevitable, but the bow snapped. The other men jumped in the water and started swimming toward what they no doubt hoped was the shore. Through the mist, it was impossible to tell. The serpent dipped its head, pulling the remains of the man and the boat below.

Callum and I remained frozen. The only man left on our boat saw his chance for a clean break and took it. He jumped in the water and swam. "Stay in the boat," I said to Callum, "and paddle like your life depends on it." He didn't argue, and together, we rowed. My arms burned almost immediately, but I pushed the pain down, digging for what little reserves I had left.

Where the serpent went under, red bubbles frothed to the surface. Then the river fell still. Chunks of shredded meat floated up; I tried not to look. As always, I found myself wishing I had done more of the required reading. The best bet for fighting the creature was to go for the eyes. In my life, I have fought plenty of horrible monsters, and none of them have ever shrugged off a dagger to the eye.

By the time we could see the trees materializing out of the fog, we were only twenty feet from the bank. My heart thumped loudly in my chest, and each ragged gasp for air sent needles through my lungs. *God damn, I need to hit the gym and get a decent drink.* I continued to row with a vigor I reserved for life or death situations and cramming in a beverage before last call.

Ahead of us, the first man had reached the shore and was urging the others on. To my right, a serpentine ripple cut the surface of the water. With a whip-like motion, the Yacumama's tail shot out and swung around, knocking the man offshore and back into the river. His body hit the water with a sickening smack.

"Move, dammit!" I yelled, hoping to spur him to action.

It was too late. The water welled around the man in the instant before the serpent's jaws broke the surface and snapped shut. Blood and bits of men sprayed our boat and the swimmers below. Red streaks coated the creature's massive teeth. The Yacumama's body extended a full twenty feet out of the water. The head was similar to an anaconda with two thin black stripes leading down the back.

Before I had time for further assessment, the creature's head turned back toward us. I held a hand out to Callum, and we both stopped paddling. My hope was to avoid being noticed. The last two men were nearly toward the shore when the serpent dipped its head almost casually and speared them both on sets of jagged teeth. It didn't even bother to eat them, instead shaking their bleeding corpses off, sending them flying back into the water.

"Any ideas, Nick?" asked Callum, his voice shaking.

"Go for the eyes?"

"Aren't you supposed to be an expert in this kind of thing?" he hissed.

The serpent turned its attention to us, waiting. It swayed back and forth, assessing its prey.

"The last time I had to fight something like this, I had chocolate and a shit ton of dynamite." Anything explosive would have done, really. Nothing solves a problem like a good powder keg to the gullet.

Callum swore. "Got it. The eyes then."

"Wait until it strikes. You're only going to get one shot." I tested the weight of the spear in my hand, hoping it would be enough. The creature's bright yellow eyes glowed down at us. If it blinked, even the scales on the eyelids would have been enough to stop a spear. *This is going to be close.* "Come on then, big boy. What are you waiting for?" I yelled across the water.

Callum looked sideways at me.

I shrugged. "Works most of the t—"

The creature opened its mouth and let out a mighty hiss, blowing the putrid stench of its gut across the water.

"Sorry," I said, fanning the air to get the smell away. "Can we cut the pillow talk and get to it? I've got a man to see about the Land of the Dead." I raised the spear. "Swift jab to the eye and swim to shore."

He nodded, and at that moment, the creature's head shot forward with blinding speed. I jumped to the side, narrowly avoiding a fang. The boat sloshed through the water as the beast shook it back and forth. Seconds passed like minutes, every detail taking on significance as it often did when close to death.

Each individual scale on the creature glinted. The elongated body constricted with effort as it continued to shake the boat. Callum was hanging on for dear life. The snake's nostrils flared as it breathed in short spurts. One yellow, glowing eye stared straight at me, and with no hesitation, I jammed the spear into it. There was a soft pop as it broke the outer layer and white ichor spilled out, followed by black blood that gushed from the wound.

"Callum, jump!" I yelled as the boat was thrown into the sky. Rearing from pain, the creature recoiled, pulling us into the air. I watched as Callum was sent toward the middle of the river. Blood shot from the creature's eye and coated me. If I hadn't been so terrified, I might have vomited.

The serpent lifted the boat above the fog, and I saw greenery spread out in every direction for miles. For a peaceful moment, we floated on a cloud, sailing above the tree line. Then, as quickly as it had risen, the boat dropped out from under me as the creature plunged back into the river. I tried to right myself midair, but I hit the water somewhere between a pencil dive and a belly flop. White spots blotted out my vision as the air was knocked from my lungs, and I was pulled beneath the murky surface.

I sank down through the churning maelstrom and listened to the sounds of the creature thrashing. Broken from my brief paralysis, I kicked toward the surface, wondering with each passing second when a tail would whip up to drag me down. When I finally got my head above water, I heaved a sigh of relief. The shoreline was less than twenty feet away. Callum was swimming somewhere behind me, but I didn't dare to glance back.

The creature hissed angrily, a piercing sound that engulfed the river. I could smell its breath and knew time was short. Ignoring my fatigue, I churned my arms. Those were some of the longest seconds of my life. Each movement could have been my last, and when my hands finally scraped the shoreline, I recoiled in shock. Keeping my eyes toward the shore, I scrambled to my feet across the muddy bank, trying to get as far away from the river as possible.

Beyond the edge of the river, the earth grew in uneven mounds with young trees sticking out at odd angles. I looked back toward the river and saw Callum swimming towards me. Behind him, the snake was swinging its head, sniffing for prey.

"Nick, help!" gasped Callum between strokes. The Yacumama moved towards him. The terror in his eyes was plain to see. He wasn't a good swimmer and was moving slower than I would have liked. I knew with a quick mental calculation that rescuing him would only put me in more danger. The pit of my stomach sank.

"Nick, please—" the last word was choked off as the creature's tail wrapped around Callum's mid-section and lifted him out of the water. He struggled violently, beating his fists against the creature's hard scales. "Help," he choked out. "I don't want to—" The breath went out of him.

The Yacumama turned to look at me with its good eye, mockingly.

"It's going to be alright, Callum." I picked up a spear one of the men had dropped on the shore, but I knew the fight was over. There was a chance I could hit the creature's eye from a distance, but the spear was better protection than my machete. I lowered the weapon, my heart feeling like an iron lump.

The Yacumama pulled Callum under. Sparse bubbles broke the surface. There was a familiarity in the creature's eyes—a menace I had known before but could not place. The snake's mouth opened wide, revealing its teeth and hissing. Then it dove, leaving nothing behind but ripples in still water.

Callum never floated back up. The only remnants of the attack were the two dead men the Yacumama hadn't seen fit to eat and Henry's tome, which had made another miraculous escape. I picked up the book and backed away from the scene, trying to ignore the wave of guilt and terror washing over me. *Wish I had a drink right about now.* The thought of Callum's distillery redoubled my regret. *He could have stayed safe in that village forever. It wasn't home in the traditional sense, but he had built a life there.*

Wanting to do something, anything, to ease my pain, I walked into the mounded earth of the forest and found two sizeable sticks. Binding them together with vines, I made a crude cross and carried it toward the river's edge. "I'm sorry," was all I could manage. I was about to put the cross in the ground when a green glow sprang up from behind me.

"I wouldn't do that if I were you," said a hollow, echoing voice. I turned slowly, bristling at a distinct chill in the warm jungle air.

"The dead that are put to rest here don't generally leave." The source of the voice was a woman, glowing green and pointing a spectral spear at me. Her throat had been cut, and several stab wounds broke her leather armor. Behind her stood a veritable army of men and women, all armed to the teeth and very much deceased.

"Ah, looks like I'm on the right track…" I fumbled for my flask, which had somehow survived the fight, but found it empty.

The woman laughed, hollow and distorted as if it were echoing through multiple dimensions, which I suppose in a way it was. With each sound, her form shifted, revealing the skeleton beneath the rough pale skin. "You look like a man who could use some help from the dead." Her lips parted into a smile, revealing rotted teeth and ragged flesh. The army behind her joined in the laughter, filling the jungle with the same uneasy sound.

"I don't suppose any of you have a drink?" I asked.

PART II

FRIENDS IN LOW PLACES

1

———

SAVIOR OF THE DAMNED

"Aztec warriors?" Jimmy had come out from behind the bar and was standing next to the table.

"And conquistadors, and—"

Jimmy cut him off. "Aztec warriors next to the Amazon river, Nick?" His tone was growing testier by the second.

"Is there a problem with that?"

"Only if you've ever looked at a map."

Nick was growing indignant when Jimmy cut him off again. "Aztecs lived primarily in central Mexico, Nick."

"Right," Nick replied, trying to drink from a beer glass that had gone empty. He looked to his date, who was luckily more interested in her phone than hearing him questioned for the hundredth time that night. *Better not be tweeting about this,* Nick thought. It was more for her sake than his.

"The Amazon is three-thousand miles away from Mexico!" exclaimed Jimmy, growing hot in the face.

"Ah, I see." Nick considered that none of this seemed particularly important, but Jimmy was the bar owner, and he wasn't ready to get thrown out yet. He was also holding out hope for another round or two of drinks to help finish out his story.

"What made you think they were Aztecs?" roared Marcus, violently rejoining the Land of the Living.

"I don't know. Lots of feathers, spears…" If he was honest, Nick had seen a bunch of warriors and used the only heuristic he had: bad action movies.

Jimmy slapped a palm to his head. "Christ, Nick. They were probably Incan. Aztecs didn't know how to make spears."

"Right, Incan." Nick gently lifted his glass and set it back on the table with a hollow clink, hoping Jimmy might take the hint. "Basically, the same thing, right?"

Jimmy was steaming. "They are not the—"

"Since when do you know so much about Incans, anyway?" asked Marcus.

"I did my dissertation on them!" Jimmy pointed a shaking finger to the plaque hanging behind the bar.

"Wait a minute. That's real?" Nick had seen the degree many times, but he had a similar one in his flat from "Harvard!". It was expected that any hunter worth his salt would have a fake degree to demonstrate a base level of cunning.

"I've told the story of my trip to Peru ten times." Jimmy leaned on a bar table for support.

"Peru." Nick turned the word over. Something about it seemed right. "Is Peru near the Amazon?"

Jimmy looked as though he were about to bubble over with rage but stopped himself and took a deep breath. Decades ago, he would have verbally sparred with Nick until dawn, but it wasn't great for business. "Yes, Nick, it's where the headwaters—"

"Yup, I was in Peru then." It made enough sense and was the path of least resistance.

"You can't jus—"

"Next round is on me!" exclaimed Nick, trying to shift the spotlight off Jimmy's pointed criticism. His date was losing interest quickly, and her drink was draining faster than he liked.

"Nick," Jimmy cut in again, but Marcus stood and put a heavy, sweaty hand on his shoulder.

"The man says drinks are on him." He pointed a finger at a sign above the bar. "Rule number three. You wrote them."

Above the bar was a small wooden placard with a list of hand-scrawled rules. Number three was simple: "Thou shalt not question the one who says 'Drinks on me.'"

"Damnit," muttered Jimmy as he wandered behind the bar to pour fresh glasses. "No one gives a shit anyway," he mumbled to himself, cursing as he prepared the drinks.

Marcus raised his eyebrows and looked at Nick. "Testy, isn't he?"

"Don't say it too loud…"

"I heard that," called Jimmy from behind the bar. "Don't make me call your kids and tell them where you are, Marcus."

Marcus's eyes went wide, and he slunk back into the booth behind Nick's table.

Nick's date yawned, unfazed by the conversation. He wondered if she had heard any of it. "Well, where were we?" he asked her, hoping for some sign that the date wasn't completely sunk.

Before she could answer, Albert lifted himself from a corner booth and shouted: "We were talking about some bullshit ghosts that never existed!" Though staggering drunk, his words came out clear as a bell.

"Thank you, Albert." *At least someone is listening.*

Albert gave a short salute and slumped back onto the worn vinyl.

"There I was, in Peru, surrounded by warriors from across the ages, held at spear point."

It took me a few minutes to understand what I was seeing. Adrenaline was still pumping hot in my veins from the fight with the Yacumama. While my life is made up of a cavalcade of curios and oddities, staring at a glowing legion of the undead was new. *Never a dull moment.* We watched each other in silence. Insects buzzed through the air, paying the dead no mind. Eventually, satisfied that our meeting couldn't get any weirder, I spoke. "So, who are you lot then?"

The woman at the lead chuckled with that same unearthly echo. Every time she did, the air grew a little cooler. "I'm Eztli." When she smiled, the scar on her neck opened, revealing the torn muscle and sinew beneath the surface. "Ez for short."

"Right, of course, Ez for short," I mumbled to myself. *Because that makes sense.* Something wasn't quite right, but I was having a hell of a time putting my finger on it. The undead legion, sure, I could understand that. I'd seen weirder in the crypts of Paris, but... It hit me. "How are you speaking English?"

Ez looked surprised. "Am I?" She moved her bony fingers to her lips and smiled again. "Maybe it's just your perception." She winked at me.

Something was stirring in the back of my pea brain, and I couldn't believe I was feeling it toward a dead woman. After another look at her rotting flesh, I was quickly reminded that things would never work out between us. "Right, makes sense." Again, weirder things had happened. "So, Ez, how can I help you?" Spirits walking out of the forest holding weapons always have an agenda.

"And here I thought you were the one who needed help." She motioned to the jungle around us. "Poor pale devil out in the forest all alone."

There was a chorus of laughter. Some of the men behind her licked their lips hungrily, and I wondered whether I should chance the swim.

Cannibal warrior ghosts? I wondered.

"Only kidding." She waggled her spear at me.

"Of course, I knew that," I said with an uneasy laugh. My breath came out in a mist before me. "Neat little trick here with the air-conditioning." If I hadn't been walking the edge of a spear, I might have stopped to enjoy the reprieve.

Ez looked at me, quizzically. "Air conditioning?"

Right, different time periods, I reminded myself. "It's cold," I amended. "Although, I guess you wouldn't feel that..."

Ez was looking at me strangely, and I sensed a danger brewing beyond the border of her confusion.

"Anyway," I started with all the awkwardness of a high school suitor picking up his prom date, "now that you mention it, I could use a hand." There was no running into the river, and something told me ghostly spears were just as deadly as their living counterparts.

"You are a strange man." Ez returned to her playful demeanor. "But I've never seen a man fight the Yacumama like that." Her eyes drifted to the river behind me. "We are in your debt." She gave a slight bow, eyes never leaving me.

I wasn't sure why, but somehow things were going my way. Without booze, I came to my natural instinct for questioning my good fortune. "Did the Yacumama…" I struggled to find the right words.

"Kill us?" Ez asked. "No. It was a guardian on our burial site, preventing us from reaching the afterlife." There was a chorus of groans and jeers from behind her. "Thanks to you, it was blinded long enough for us to walk free. Now we can march on the halls of the dead and finally claim our eternal rest."

"Halls of the dead," I mused. "Any chance those would be in the Land of the Dead?"

Ez cocked her head at me. "You fight smart but talk dumb."

"Right, silly. Of course, they are. So, when are we leaving?"

There were mutters from behind Ez, but she held up a hand and silenced them. "What's a man like yourself with so much life to live want with the Land of the Dead?"

My skin prickled, reminding me that I was soaking wet and the air around us had practically frozen. "I need to find a friend," I answered. "It's a long story, but if you can get me to an entrance to the Land of the Dead, we can call it even."

"What do you say?" asked Ez to the men behind her.

"I say we gut the white devil and string him up!" yelled a man whose head had been crushed in on one side. "No offense," he muttered to the conquistador standing next to him.

"Isn't that why you got buried here in the first place?" replied Ez with a smirk.

The man grumbled something that sounded like: "Worth it."

"I think you'll do best to stick close to me," Ez said to Nick. "If you can survive the mortal perils along the way, I will take you with us to the Land of the Dead."

"Fantastic." I couldn't believe it had worked, and while my luck was running, I figured it was smart to press it. "But one more thing before we go."

"What's that?"

"Any chance some of you were buried with booze?"

2

————

BAD COMPANY

As luck had it, a few of the undead had been mercenaries in their former lives and weren't above robbing their own graves. After all, I had saved them from the tyrannical river spirit keeping them from the afterlife. After a few minutes of digging, I had two bottles covered in dirt and desiccated remains. Under the circumstances, I could have done much worse. I brushed away the filth around the top of the bottle and lifted it to my lips. The first sip tasted like absolute piss, as fifty-year-old rum is bound to, but it did the trick.

A familiar buzz twisted its way down my spine, and I was nearly my old self again. A few gulps after that, tentative mental ease slipped over me. I walked to Ez, who was chatting with a few conquistadors—an odd sight, to say the least. After waiting awkwardly for a break in the conversation, and growing emboldened by the alcohol, I interrupted them. "So, where are we headed then?"

Ez looked to me and then to the bottle in my hands. "Maybe you are a warrior, after all." She chuckled. I never got used to the sound it made echoing across multiple planes of existence. Even the most joyous laugh from a ghost was the stuff of nightmares. "We're going to march west."

"West. Good direction." *I already knew we were supposed to be going west.* "And what's west?" While I was thankful for the company, I wanted to get to my journey's end as soon as possible. It had been a miserable few days, and the comforts of modern civilization were calling.

"There's a great power to the west, I can feel it in the air." The conquistadors at her side nodded in agreement. "Maybe a day or two at most."

"Great power meaning the Land of the Dead?"

"Only one way to find out." Ez had lost her interest in straight answers. She made a motion with her hand, and the ghostly procession marched forward. The silvery-green figures moved through the woods as if they weren't even there, passing through trees and underbrush with eerie ease. It didn't take long for me to realize I would have a hell of a time keeping up.

I pulled out my machete, scuffed and worn from the previous days' toil, and prepared for another afternoon of hard work. *Last time I ever complain about Lopsang's exercise routines,* I thought, wishing that I had participated more instead of drinking from the sidelines. I swung my machete in a wide arc, tearing through vine and leaf alike. Despite my effort, the jungle was thick and progress was slow.

Ez turned around, and my face reddened. "Let me help you with that." She pointed her spear forward, and a pitch-black jungle cat made of mist jumped out of the end. Ez looked at the creature fondly. "Darling, would you take care of this?"

The creature growled and leaped forward into the foliage. Wherever it touched, everything withered and died. Vines shriveled, contracting to gnarled, desiccated tangles. The few creatures that were fool enough to stick around turned instantly to pearly white skeletons. The cat continued to run, clearing a path far into the distance.

"That's a neat trick." I knew black magic when I saw it and was beginning to question why the warriors hadn't made it to the after-life already. Over the years, I had dabbled with black magic more than a few times but had never seen anything like what she was able to do. "Remind me never to cross you."

"You won't get a reminder." She used the same playful tone, but it was clear she meant every word of it. I needed to tread softly. *The dead are always looking for company*, I reminded myself and kept a respectful distance from the other mercenaries in the group. This was partly for safety and partly because, honestly, they grossed me the hell out.

Ordinarily, the dearly and not-so-dearly departed make at least some effort in presenting themselves; top hats to cover gunshot holes, tight suits for evisceration, the usual. The undead legion I traveled with made no such effort. I saw stab wounds, gaping slash marks that ran up the length of their bodies, and all manner of blunt-force trauma. None of them seemed to want to do anything about it. They were perfectly comfortable in their uncomfortable decay, and so, it was left to me to keep my stomach from churning.

The first day's march was uneventful, aside from the macabre company. By nightfall, I was exhausted, and even the thought of murderous skeletal warriors couldn't stop me from falling into a dreamless sleep. Rest unmarred by nightmares was a feat I rarely achieved, and if it hadn't been a spear to the ribs that woke me, it might have almost been refreshing.

I opened my eyes to red light from the morning sun and a rotting corpse staring at me with a spear at my neck. In a panic, I smacked the weapon away and jumped to my feet. I came up with a short stick and a handful of dirt. The dead man looked at me and laughed. The motion shook his jaw so much that it threatened to dislodge entirely. "Still alive," he called. "Don't worry. If we wanted you dead, you wouldn't have seen it coming." He winked as if it was supposed to be a reassuring sentiment and walked off to join the others.

"What the hell?" The words came out like sandpaper, and I realized how thirsty I was. I rolled over, looked past my canteen, and grabbed one of the bottles instead. Waking up to a homicidal dead man was enough to make me want a few morning nips to get started on the right foot.

"Sorry, we had to check," said Ez, striding over. "No point in waiting around if you had passed on."

"Right, how efficient of you." I rubbed the sleep from my eyes, wondering how much longer before they would have looted me and moved on. "Quite the alarm clock he is."

"He had the dullest spear," she mused.

"Right." I took a deep swig from the bottle, wincing as fire ran down my throat. "Thanks, I guess."

Ez looked to the bottles as if she was going to say something but didn't. "We need to get moving. You slept through the night, and the power source is near."

"Of course, the power source," I said, standing up and moaning at the severe pain in my limbs. *One of these days that's going to hurt less,* I promised myself. I picked up my bag and slung it over a shoulder. "The power source that's going to lead us to the Land of the Dead, right?"

"One would hope." Ez didn't provide further clarification and instead set off again. Not wanting to argue with the armed dead, I followed the trail of decay in her wake.

The day started off without incident, but shortly before midday, things got weird. At first, it was odd patterns in the foliage, vines twisted into elaborate braids, and occasional stones that looked as though they had been intentionally stacked. Then, I caught on to something bigger and out of place.

I stopped, noticing a tree off the main trail. The bark had four deep grooves gouged in it, revealing the white wood below. Not too far off our path, the untamed jungle had been tamped down. I knelt and examined the dirt. Large paw prints were clearly visible in the soft earth, and a tattered piece of cloth was tangled in the under-brush—a knot formed in my stomach.

The temperature lowered as Ez walked up behind me. "What is it?" she asked. "A jaguar?"

I laughed. "Not unless jaguars need pockets." One of the cloth tatters clearly had a pouch sewn into it. "I don't think we're that lucky. If my guess is right, it's something much worse." I wanted to be wrong, but only the improbable remained when all the other logical solutions were gone. "How it would survive out here is beyond me."

"What are you talking about?" Ez tapped her foot impatiently.

"You ever hear of a werewolf?" I asked.

Ez looked at me, confused. "A werewolf?" She turned the word over like it was a strange piece of meat.

"Half wolf, half man, and one-hundred-percent son-of-a-bitch." Werewolves weren't an easy opponent when I had the proper gear, much less when I was down to a machete, a spear, and some elderly booze.

"Whatever it is, my men and I can surely handle it."

I looked around at the troupe. "Don't suppose any of your weapons are silver?"

"We would never use such a treasure for weapons, why?"

"We better get moving then, because all your men are going to do is piss it off, and there's only one person here it can actually kill." I pointed a finger at myself and hoped to hell that I was wrong.

"You have a lot of confidence for a nearly dead man."

"Well, it won't be nearly if that creature gets a hold of me." There was only one way to block out the incredible sense of impending doom I was facing—heavy drinking. I drained the bottle, tossed it in my bag, and pulled out another. The sharp edges of the world were replaced by wavy lines, and the thought of being brutally mauled by an eight-foot-tall walking carpet grew distant.

In my inebriation, I did what I do best: talk. As it turned out, the warriors were chatty when asked about their past lives. Through these conversations, I learned they were some of the worst characters imaginable—essentially, the equivalent of Peru's death row inmates—but at least they were personable. The man who had woken me with a spear to the ribs had become exceptionally cozy. Well, as cozy as the mutilated remains of a warrior can be. We walked, and he regaled me with stories of battle, all inevitably leading to the death and disfigurement of anyone he ran across.

"Those days were glorious. We would run through a town like a plague, burning the houses to the ground and killing anything that had the nerve to come running out." He laughed as though it were a fond memory of a little league game rather than a depiction of mass slaughter. "Of course, that's what landed us in that shithole in the first place." He motioned behind us where, many miles away, the burial site stood.

"Who put you there?" I asked. Shame still festered in the back of my brain for the men who died in the fight with Yacumama. Every time the thought came up, I drank a little more, and it got farther away.

"Some prick of a king." The man spat. Gobs of ghostly flesh flew from between his jagged teeth, disappearing before they could hit the ground. "Decided that it was time for a change in the Incan empire." He rattled his spear, and the gold around his neck shook. "Went on a campaign, capturing any mercenary he could find."

The man's eyes grew more distant. "I was hiding away in the mountains, but they found me all the same. Took a team of six men. They bound me and carried me three days to the river's edge with no food or water. I swear that nearly killed me." He ran a hand over his jaw, producing an eerie clicking sound as he popped it into place. "They had a list of all the crimes we committed. Never know how it was they got it, but they did. Every single misdeed I had ever done was there."

I didn't want to think of a tribunal for all my crimes. We'd all die of natural causes before they were finished reading the charges. My throat tightened as Callum's pleading eyes flashed before me. I could hear him begging for help, and it took a deep gulp of rum that threatened to destroy my taste permanently to get it to stop. Rationalizing that there was nothing I could have done, I tried to focus my thoughts on the man's story instead.

"We were punished according to that list," continued the man. "They did their best to keep us alive until the end too." He held his ghostly palms before me, their flesh ragged, blistered, and black. "Started by burning our hands with a hot iron poker. Not all at once, mind you." He held up his charred fingers for emphasis. "They'd give us 'breaks,' the kind men that they were.

"When there was nothing left of our hands, they'd move to our feet. Agony is all I remember after that. Death was not swift, and even when it did come, it was not a release. We were bound to our burial sites, never to leave. Our ancestors were forever out of reach, and the peace we had earned was nothing but a memory."

For the first time, I wondered if wounding the Yacumama had been the right thing to do. If this lowly grunt had committed unspeakable crimes, I couldn't imagine what had landed Ez there. Practitioner of dark magic buried in a tomb she couldn't escape from; those were two strikes. As a personal rule, I never wait for a third.

"That was until you came along anyway." The man clapped a hand to my back, and I actually felt it. A cold wave shot out from the spot and quickly dissipated. I held my revulsion in. "Anyways, what's your stor—" The man stopped, eyeing the edge of the path ahead.

Cold air blew around me in a vortex as I stepped through the ghost in front of me. Disgusted, I swatted at my clothing, trying to get the sensation off like a bug, but stopped short. The entire marching line had halted and drawn their weapons. All eyes were facing forward.

My buzz kicked into high gear, and I picked my way through the undead marauders to where Ez stood. "What are we looking at?" I asked, the words slurring almost beyond recognition. The trees wobbled and deformed, making strange, humanoid shapes. *Stronger booze than I thought.* "Maybe we could look at some different trees? There's a lot of them, and these ones are freaking me out."

Ez put a hand out in front of me, bringing another wash of cold air. "Quiet. Looks like we're going to have a fight…"

3

THE LOST EXPLORER

Men and women emerged from the forest, painted green and black. Even beyond the foliage, it was hard to see how many of them there were. Some carried traditional weapons: spears, swords, the lot, while others wielded staffs ornamented with bones and spikes. I sidled over to Ez. "Those are black magic users. You probably know, but I thought you might need a second opinion."

"You don't know when to stop talking, do you?" Ez raised her spear and pointed it at the nearest aggressor. "Stop right there," she commanded. "We are on our way to the rest we have earned and will massacre anyone that gets in our way."

"Strong argument." I backed away slowly, glad to be on her side.

A man wearing a headdress made from the remains of a jaguar stepped out of the forest. In his right hand, he carried a smooth, black staff topped with a human skull. The skull's eyes had been ornamented with green gemstones that glowed dully in the afternoon light. "I do not wish to impede your passage, but you are treading on our grounds," he said, planting the staff in front of him. "If you wish to continue, you will have to stand tribunal."

A collective angry murmur sprang up from the ghosts around me.

"Sorry," seethed Ez. "We've heard that word before." She made a hissing noise and motioned toward the man—one of the ghostly warriors charged without hesitation.

The man hardly flinched, lifted his staff, and stamped it on the ground. Green light shot from the skull's eyes, striking the ghostly warrior in the chest. Fire spread rapidly from the point of impact, burning away the apparition almost instantaneously. I saw the warrior's eyes go wide in the last second before he was simply gone. The air was still, as though no one had been standing there a second earlier.

Ez cursed. "What did you do?"

"He attacked me, and I defended myself." The man planted his staff and pointed the eyes directly at her. "Now, I'd urge you to put down, dematerialize, or dissolve the weapons in your hands before I have to use this again."

There was something about the vocal cadence that was condescending and familiar at the same time. I crouched, attempting to get a better look at the man beneath the mask. It was no use. Then the apparent truth hit me. "He's speaking English too," I whispered to Ez.

"One of our finest warriors was vaporized, and you're worried about the enemy's language?" Ez was holding the spear in a firm grip.

"He was already dead," I pointed out.

"Nick?" asked the man. "Nick Ventner, is that you?"

Ez shot me a look.

"That's never good." I don't like being recognized on my home turf, much less in the middle of the Peruvian jungle. Whoever it was had bad intentions, and the occasions I left my acquaintances with fond memories were few and far between.

"That *is* Nick Ventner." The man pulled back his helm.

"Well, I'll be damned." I did nothing to hide my astonishment.

The man behind the mask was none other than the fabled lost explorer, Paul Mansen. "Nick, why don't you have your"—he paused, looking for the right word—"friends here put their weapons down. We can all head back to the village and have ourselves a little chat." The imposing wizard shtick was gone in an instant, replaced by the bravado that had landed him such a lengthy run on National Geographic.

"Well, gee," I started, stifling a hiccup. "That does sound nice, but you're awfully armed, and last I checked, you weren't pleased with me." Paul had threatened to kill me after I wrecked all his gear on a Mojave Desert shoot. It hadn't been my fault, but most people would rather believe in a rowdy drunk than a dust devil. When he disappeared shortly after that, I had considered it my lucky break.

"Oh, come on now, Nick. Ancient history. Besides"—he lifted the staff, causing the jeweled eyes to glow again—"I could kill you. It's much more painful for the living than the dead."

Mansen had a point. I looked to Ez, trying to get a read on her. The only thing I was able to interpret was fury. "Look, Ez, he's making a lot of sense here."

"Coward," she muttered, tossing her spear to the ground where it vanished instantly. The rest of her ghostly entourage followed suit.

"See? That's more like it." Mansen whistled as more men and women materialized out of the trees behind us.

"Hey, what the hell is—"

"A little security." Mansen waved his hand dismissively. "Come on, it's a short walk, and I'm sure you've got more than a few questions for me."

Presumptuous little bastard, aren't you? "The legendary Paul Mansen, performing black magic in the jungle… Yeah, you could say I've got questions."

"Wonderful. Let's discuss it over a drink."

My heart leaped.

"You do still drink, right? Sort of your thing, isn't it?" There was a cold fire in his eyes.

I plowed through the implication at the thought of booze that didn't come from a tomb. "You know me so well, Paulie."

"Don't call me that." Mansen whistled again, and the men and women around them started moving. "This way."

4

THE DARK VILLAGE

"Paul Mansen disappeared almost ten years ago!" roared Albert, standing at the booth like he was in the middle of a speech. Somewhere during Nick's recounting of the dead man's story, Marcus had begun snoring and Albert woke up to take his place. Nick wondered if they had managed to work out a schedule for their alternating naps and criticisms.

"I know that, Albert. I was as surprised as you were." Nick looked at his date. Her eyes still glowed in the dim blue light of her phone. If the story about Paul Mansen wasn't going to get her attention, he wasn't sure what would. Everyone who owned a TV in the nineties had heard of Mansen's adventures. Hell, they were still showing re-runs in the late-night slots.

Albert lumbered over until he was eye-to-eye with Nick, who could smell every heinous chili-covered potato snack he had eaten that day. "Look, Nick, I like your stories"—he let out a quiet belch that threatened to peel Nick's skin away with its foul stench—"but she's not even paying attention." He made a loose flapping gesture with his right hand and leaned on Nick's shoulder for support.

"Don't you think I know that?" Nick whispered. Both men looked to his date to see if she had picked up on the sidebar. If she did, she made no indication and continued to scroll with a lazy finger.

"So, what's the point in lying?" Albert spluttered and raised the volume of his voice to the level of a minor god. "YA SACK OF SHIT." He slapped Nick's shoulder and stumbled to the ground with convulsive laughter. When he struck the floorboards, the whole bar shook, and Marcus woke from his uneasy slumber.

"Huh? What did I miss?" He wiped at his nose with an already filthy sleeve.

Albert was still rolling on the floor at the hilarity of his own joke. Nick didn't really understand it, but then again, Albert had always been a bit of a mystery.

Nick's date was brought to attention by the sheer lunacy of the situation. His heart leaped. It was the first sign of interest she had shown in thirty minutes. Hoping to recapture her attention while she was still reeling from the shock of Albert's outburst, he resolved to continue. "You didn't miss much, Marcus. Paul Mansen is alive and well, hiding in the Peruvian rainforest with a village of dark magic users."

Marcus snorted. "First bit of sense you've made all night. Always thought he faked that disappearance. Too much pride to go quietly."

That you believe? Nick was shocked but didn't want to jinx his luck.

Albert stopped rolling as if all at once he remembered how disgusting The Haven's floors were.

"So, Paulie led us back to the village…"

As it turned out, we were far closer to the power source than I had thought. From the point of our capture to the village was no more than a twenty-minute walk, made less strenuous because the jungle was cleared. Nearer to the town, rocks were laid in the dirt, forming a rudimentary cobblestone path. "Really like what you've done with the place."

"One does what one can." Mansen's air of presumption and condescension reminded me all too much of another 'friend' I was glad to be rid of. It had only been a year since Manchester's fiery demise, but some wounds never truly healed. "Now, I want you to listen closely," said Mansen with the cadence of a schoolteacher. "When we get to the village, no funny business."

"I wouldn't dream of it." I raised my hands in mock surrender. Mansen's men were on edge and lifted their spears at my sudden motion.

"Yes, you would, and I'm telling you, don't." Mansen snapped his fingers, and the spears lowered. "Your compatriots are going to stay at the village entrance while you and I go have ourselves a talk."

I had only just gained my warrior spirit entourage and was loath to part with them. "Is all that really necessary?"

Paul cocked an eyebrow. "For you? Yes. Every time someone seems to finally have your number, you manage to slip away. Not this time." Mansen ran a hand roughly through his hair. "No, you're going to come with me, we're going to talk, and then I'm going to turn you over." The idea of letting someone else handle my judgment clearly pained him.

It was my turn to cock an eyebrow. "Turn me over, eh?" *First good news I've had all day.* Even without a flair for dark magic, Mansen was a formidable opponent with a fierce temper. His grudges were also the subject of legend. If rumors were true, he had used an intern as bait for a vampire nest just because the kid had taken the last everything bagel from the snack table. Given my proximity to his brother's death, being judged by anyone else was preferable.

"Yes, Nick, turn you over. While I've got some pressing questions, it seems I am not the only interested party."

"Popular guy." Ez chuckled.

"It would seem that way." I should have left it there, but the opportunity to taunt Mansen a bit was too tantalizing. "So, what's it like being someone else's errand boy for a change?" I had never seen Paul without a full camera crew and an army of production assistants begging to kiss his boots.

Mansen swore under his breath. "Contrary to popular belief, I was never lost, Nick. I simply grew tired of the likes of you and dedicated myself to a new calling. I teach no more and have instead become a student."

That explains the staff. "And let me guess, you're out here getting an anthropology degree?"

"It's no secret that you've delved into the dark arts yourself, Nick. You forget that the dead love to talk."

It was a fair point that I had no response to. The dead were vocal and loved the chance to gripe. If he had managed to communicate with the other side, there were plenty of people willing to commiserate in his hatred of me. The idea of an undead group text composed entirely of my decomposed rivals, enemies, and past apprentices gave me pause.

"Don't worry, you'll have a chance to chat with them yourself before too long."

"And here I thought we were going to have a *friendly* chat." I assessed our escort, seeing if any of them looked especially weak. Despite our constant, monotonous march, the guards were still at full attention. I got the impression that one false move would leave me in more pieces than I was comfortable with.

"Our chat will be as friendly as you make it, but there's time enough for that soon. We're here."

We rounded a corner and faced a black wall constructed entirely of impaled skulls on thick spikes rising from the dirt. In the center was a large gate, with black runes etched into its surface. I couldn't read them, but they shone with a sticky, tarlike substance on closer inspection. It oozed between the runes through deep grooves in the door, making its way slowly to the dirt below. All the plants within fifty feet of the structure were dead and withered, providing a sharp contrast to the verdant green of the trees beyond.

A native man stepped up to a guard post on the wall and mounted a high caliber machine gun, pointing it directly at us. He yelled something in a language I couldn't understand, but the mere presence of a weapon that could fire so fast unnerved me. Spears, swords, and serpents I could handle, but guns are quick and often kill by mistake.

"And here I thought you'd want to stay true to their culture." I tried my best to keep my movements smooth and non-threatening. There were far too many people in proximity who wanted me dead. Sure, we were headed to the Land of the Dead anyway, but I wanted to get there on my own terms.

"We only use the spears for hunting. Modern-day explorers require modern-day solutions." Mansen waved at the guard and whistled. The man called out and walked out of sight, leaving the gun mounted. A moment later, the wooden gates creaked open, scraping along the dirt.

From somewhere inside the village, the salty-sweet aroma of cooking meat wafted out to me. I was repulsed at the idea of what it might be, but hunger was a strong impulse. A painful knot took hold in my stomach, reminding me that it had been days since I had eaten anything decent. *Wouldn't be the first time.* Beyond the wooden gate were rows of single-story buildings leading up a slight incline. At the top of the hill stood a tall multi-leveled hut, adorned with all manner of skeletal remains and grisly iconography.

I looked up as we passed beneath the gate and was unsurprised to find more sharpened spikes pointed straight down. *Booby traps, potential cannibalism, dark magic. Feels like I've been here before.* A scream echoed across the village and choked off. "Lovely." Thoughts of being slow-roasted alive overrode my attempt at maintaining calm. Questions raced through my mind with no hope of stopping them. *How did they get so many heads for that wall? What are a bunch of dark arts users doing in the middle of nowhere? Do friendly chats involve free drinks?*

A group of guards emerged from alcoves embedded in the backside of the gate.

Mansen greeted them with a friendly wave. "Take this group into holding. I'm sure the high priestess will be intrigued by the magic that binds them." He locked eyes with Ez. "I'm not the only one with a staff like this, so I suggest you behave. The high priestess has a soft spot for the intelligent undead and might help you—if you're lucky."

"Sleep with both eyes open," hissed Ez. "You can't hold us

forever, and we've gotten good at waiting." The long cords of rotting muscle twitched and pulsed beneath her flesh.

Mansen didn't flinch. "I'm sure you have, but I'm afraid this is all out of my hands. If it's any comfort, you're getting a better deal than your friend here."

Before Ez had a chance to retort, a man dressed in full armor came hustling down the street. Hollow clanks echoed through the village with each of his heavy footfalls. Two ancient swords were slung across his back and a pistol hung loosely on his belt.

I was sweating through what little remained of my clothes and couldn't imagine adding more layers. "Now, that's dedication. Where's your armor, Paulie?"

"Quiet, or I'll have to skip our little chat and deal with the consequences later."

The armored man stopped inches from Mansen. "High Priestess wants him now."

My hope swelled at the thought of avoiding Mansen's chat. "And I'd love to see her, shall we go—"

Mansen held out his staff and pointed it right at me.

The armored man drew his pistol. "She says, she gets to see him first."

"Well, go back and tell her we had an agreement. Who knows what will be left of him when she's done?"

The armored man shrugged.

"Go and tell her that I'll bring him along shortly."

The armored man looked to Mansen and then to me. "She's not going to like that."

"That's my problem, not yours."

The armored man holstered his pistol and repeated: "She's not going to like that." Then, he turned on his heel, clanking off toward the large hut at the center of town.

"Sounds like we're going to need to have our little chat now." There was no time for protestation. Mansen's grip was firm, and I had no desire to be vaporized. Having watched it twice before, the experience looked wholly unappealing.

Mansen led me to a squat building that had been nestled right against the village's outer wall. Black curtains covered the main entrance, blocking all light from the outside world. Once inside, the darkness was absolute. I could hear Mansen bustling around but couldn't see anything.

"Let me guess. Trying to understand the perspective of a bat?" It wasn't unheard of. Some vampire enthusiasts thought the key to transformation was knowing the soul of the creature they wanted to embody. They were a bunch of idiots, but I didn't think that highly of Mansen to begin with.

A pinprick of light illuminated as he struck a match. He moved around the room, touching the flame to an array of candles, casting our surroundings in gloomy orange light. "You and I both know there are some arts that are better kept to the shadows." He motioned to a few cushions on the floor. "Have a seat, Nick. Our conversation is going to be much shorter than I would have liked."

I wasn't arguing. It had been a long day of walking, and any sort of padding was better than damp dirt. Mansen crossed the room and opened a small wooden cabinet, revealing several glass bottles filled with varying shades of brown alcohol. My throat went dry, and my palms grew sweaty. Ancient rum did half the job, but the thought of a proper drink practically sent me into convulsions. I gripped my right hand with my left, trying to stop it from shaking.

"Here's how this is going to work. I'm going to ask you a question. If you answer, I'm going to give you a drink." He poured a glass and came to sit down across from me. Between us, a candelabra of black wax burned, giving off a noxious scent that I hoped wasn't human-derived.

"Seems fair enough." I would have told him where to find the blood of Christ himself if he asked. The withdrawals barreled down on me like a freight train, and I was willing to do anything to avoid it.

"Good. What happened to Manchester?"

My throat tightened. "What do you mean?" I had told few people the true story of what happened on the mountain, and those I did had paid me handsomely for it.

"Again, Nick, the dead love to talk. I heard he's been making quite a ruckus in the underworld, and word is you sent him there."

I let out a protracted sigh. What happened to Manchester had been his own damned fault.

Mansen shook the drink in front of me like a master offering their dog a treat. "Come on, we're short on time, remember?"

"Manchester was never good at interpreting ancient riddles," I explained. "We were in the mountains chasing a beast unlike anything I have ever faced."

"The yeti?" asked Mansen, clearly intrigued.

"Yes, but that's not what killed him. We had been working together for about a week when we came to the gates of an ancient society."

Mansen scoffed. "You and Manchester working together?"

"I know, trust me, it was strange for me too. In any case, he got a little too confident and decided he wanted to push my team and me through the gates at gunpoint. Use us as fodder for whatever traps lay beyond." It had been a smart move. I never went through ancient doorways first as a rule. "My apprentice went through and nothing happened. Harvey assumed it was safe but didn't realize James had gone through unarmed. When he stepped between those guardians, brandishing the pistol he so loved, they melted him."

"Melted him?"

"Yes, hot fire shot out of their eyes, the whole nine yards. Melted him from the middle out. Painful way to go, really." I reached for the cup and drained it in a single gulp. Since returning, I had never told the story sober. I'm not sure I could to this day. "That was more like half a drink. A spot more would help my storytelling."

Mansen remained silent, thinking over Manchester's fate. "He was one of the greats, you know?"

"That's a matter of opinion."

A flicker of annoyance crossed his face. "I still admire him to this day." He poured another glass.

"You should get some better heroes." I didn't want to think about the reckoning Manchester had planned in the underworld for me. Whatever it was, there was no way it was going to be pleasant. "Next question," I said, reaching for the drink.

Shouting started outside the hut, and I heard the familiar clanking of armor approach. "Looks like your friend is back."

Mansen eyed the door and drained his glass. "Fine, one more question then. What happened to my brother, Nick?"

My heart stopped. If he knew about Rick, I was in more trouble than I thought. Outside, the commotion grew louder and closer to Mansen's door.

"I know you were there, Nick, what happened?" The volume of his voice rose, and he stood. In the darkness, his shadow towered over me.

I tried to find the words that would describe Rick's death without self-implication. Sure, I had been by his side, but Rick's undoing was his own fault. Why can people never understand that? Still, it was plain to see that nothing I had to say would ease Mansen's fury.

"I heard you goaded him up that mountain. Heard you missed your shot when that man set himself upon my brother. Heard you watched as he was ripped to shreds." Angry tears welled in Mansen's eyes, and I lost all hope of another drink.

A woman burst into the hut, sending brilliant beams of sunlight into the darkened interior. I went temporarily blind, trying to adjust to the brightness. Mansen spoke defensively in another language and received a stern reply. The argument only continued for a few seconds before a set of muscular arms were looping under me. I was hoisted to a standing position and pulled back into the street. My vision cleared, and I saw a small army of guards, led by the armored man.

Mansen stormed out of the hut. "I want to hear you say it!"

"Your brother's death was his own fault." It was the cold, hard truth. Rick had taken on a mission he was not prepared for and had gotten killed as a result. "I told him to turn back, but he refused."

"Liar!" shouted Mansen. "I hope you enjoyed that drink, Nick, it will be your last."

Ez and her men were still being held outside the hut, and she caught my eye. "Good talk?" she asked.

"Just like old times." We were marched up the street at spearpoint. Black smoke rose in an ugly column from the top of the large hut in the center of the village. "I assume that's where we're headed?"

Ez nodded. "Smoke started a few minutes ago."

"That's never good."

"No."

Drums started up, beating in the distance, heavy and loud. In the same instance, flaming torches sprang up in a ring outside the building. From hidden vantage points inside their huts, the villagers began chanting. At first, I couldn't understand them, but their voices became more apparent. They spoke a single word, over and over again: "Tribunal."

5

TRIBUNAL

The drums grew louder as I was marched through the entrance of the hut. Polished human remains were scattered about, making the inside look like home to some foul beast of legend rather than a priestess. The entryway was lined with skeletons garbed in gold and riches, standing sentinel over anyone who dared enter. Their vacant eye sockets had been filled with colorful gems that reminded me too much of Mansen's staff. Above, flames burned in mighty braziers hanging from the ceiling.

I tried to keep my mouth shut, but nervousness got the better of me. "Does anyone else think that's a little hazardous?" From what I could surmise, a hut made primarily of wood and a fuel-based light source that close to the roof was asking for an accident. The flames licked up the walls toward the ceiling, but by some act of luck, or more likely magic, the wood never caught. "I'm sure you all have faith in your incantations, but this is—"

My escort smacked me with the butt of his spear and pushed me out of the entryway into the main room. Once more, the décor focused dually on the theme of human remains and fire. Unlike the entry, the ceiling was tall enough to house several levels of seated balconies running in a circle. Despite myself, I was impressed by the cavernous nature of the room. Drummers sat upon the highest level, beating a continuous, aggressive rhythm. In the balconies below were masses of hooded figures, crowded around, looking down with great interest.

Well, this feels all too familiar. I've been captured by more than a few cults. After a while, they all start to blend together. On the most recent occasion, I only made it out due to semi-divine intervention. The mere presence of drummers and so many damned skulls indicated that my odds of surviving were long.

My escort pushed me into the center of the room so that I was standing on a circular indent in the floor with a line running through the middle. I hate trap doors. They usually hide a bootlegger's stash in America, but it's never anything so nice with cults. I stamped my foot down and heard the tell-tale hollow thunk. There are few times I hate being right, but that was one of them.

I tried to sidestep my way off the door, but a spear shot out and pushed me back into the middle. "So, it's like that then." I scowled at the man who had prodded me. He smiled, revealing teeth that had been mostly replaced with gold. "Bones and gold. If it weren't for all the dark magic, I'd say this was El Dorado." The man held his threatening smile. "My humor is lost on you." The drums grew in intensity, filling the room with their chaotic booming until, all at once, they stopped.

The room fell silent. I could hear anticipatory whispers from the hooded figures above, and my skin prickled. To my left, a set of doors I hadn't seen creaked open, cutting the silence in two. I steadied my breathing, readying myself for a fight. In general, secret doors in front of chanting crowds usually hide monsters. Instead, a regal woman in flowing dark robes walked out.

Bangles of dark metal ran from her wrists to her elbows. Small daggers hung from her ears, their sharp edges glinting in the dim light. Whether for show or function, they exuded dazzling intimidation. From above, the crowd began chanting in a foreign language, the sound rough and reverent. The woman held her hands out in a warm gesture, reveling in the noise. She continued to move toward the center of the room until she was only ten feet from me.

Despite my fear, I stared at her, transfixed by her slow, graceful movement. Her gaze slid down from the crowd to meet my eyes, and she lowered her hands. The crowd's chanting stopped, leaving the room in an anticipatory quiet. I was naked under those eyes, unable to hide anything, and unable to move. The second part was mostly due to the spear-happy guards.

"Now, we begin tribunal." Her voice was soft but magically amplified to fill the whole room. It was a simple trick but an effective one. She walked away to a chair that, aside from the cushion, was constructed primarily from an oversized rib cage and intertwined spinal columns. To top it off, two cat skulls adorned the arms of the throne. The eyes had been filled with obsidian, causing them to glitter and shine in the firelight. She ran a hand over one of the heads, whispering quietly and caressing its smooth surface.

"So, Mr. Ventner, is it?" asked the priestess, sitting down.

"That's me. Who do I have the pleasure of addressing?" Flattery never hurt anyone who was standing on top of a trap door.

"You may call me High Priestess." She waved a hand, and the torches lining the room shrunk, darkening the place further.

I wasn't impressed by the act of creating a magical dimmer switch, but I let my eyes go wide with wonderment. I was also a little drunk, so the performance might have been less than adequate. "Your majesty?" I asked.

"That will do fine, too."

"Is all this really necessary?" There was a simple rule about trap doors; the longer you spent on top of them, the more likely you were to fall through. My mind wandered with horrifying possibilities. *What are they hiding down there? What if it's a spike pit, or worse, all the missionaries they captured before me? I can't hold out against conversion for the rest of my miserable life.* I was about to ask her to kill me when she spoke again.

"You've trespassed on our lands," she boomed, and then almost as an afterthought, she added, "and you've upset our dear pupil, Mansen." There was a twinge of a sarcastic smile behind the last point. "Yes, I'd say tribunal is necessary."

"Right." It took all my effort not to laugh at the mention of

Mansen as a 'dear pupil.' "Well, I'm terribly sorry about that, but Mansen's misery is his own problem. He's been misinformed as to the death of his brother."

She cut me off with a sneer. "I'm a busy woman with little patience for lies. Mansen has demonstrated himself trustworthy, and you, on the other hand, are an outsider that has proved more than a little dangerous."

There was a murmur from the crowd surrounding me. "Mansen is a piece of—"

The woman didn't wait for me to finish. "I think we can end this tribunal quickly so that we may all get on with the evening's entertainment."

"Isn't there a part where I get to tell my side of the story?" I shifted my weight, edging away from the center of the trapdoor. As before, a quick spear reminded me that it would be a poor decision.

The priestess let her hand fall to a lever I had failed to notice. "Feisty, aren't you?" Keeping in theme, it was constructed from a femur. "Ordinarily, we'd let you share your point of view, but Mansen has informed us of your gift with words. I'm sure given enough time, you could talk your way off that platform, but I'm afraid we're going to have to keep this chat short."

"I've been having a lot of short chats today," I muttered, bending my knees so I didn't break my legs when I landed. Assuming, of course, it wasn't a spike pit.

"Lucky for you, I have a soft spot for tricksters."

My heart leaped.

"Nick Ventner, you will prove your worth in the arena. If you live, you will be released, if you die, well, no need to release you then."

My heart plummeted back to Earth.

Arenas were not my specialty. I was about to make a counterpoint when she pulled the lever, and the two halves of the trap door fell out from beneath me. The world above disappeared, and the drums resumed. As I fell, I heard the clack of the trapdoor shutting above me, and then there was complete darkness.

The chute tilted gradually as I slid down its muddy interior. The ride didn't last long, but in my disoriented state, it was an eternity. I was still reeling from the 'tribunal' ruling when I shot out the end of the tunnel and into a poorly lit cell. When I finally hit the ground, I was happy to find that spikes didn't pierce through my feet. Instead, my ass hit the stone floor first and sent a fresh wave of pain through my spine.

"No doctor is ever going to believe all this," I moaned from the floor. My back had already started to cramp up, and I guessed it was going to have to endure a little more torture before it finally got some rest. Gingerly, I rose to my feet and got the lay of my surroundings. I was in a small stone cell with iron bars. A single torch burned in the hallway beyond the cell door, illuminating a long, dank corridor. The only furnishing was a trough that had been dug into the side and wasn't draining much of anything, leaving a sickening smell that threatened to kill me before I got my chance to fight.

The ground beneath me shook with thunderous footsteps. I made a silent prayer to whatever deities might have been around at the time. *Please, friend, whatever I fight, make sure it's not that.* As if in response, the cell shook again. As usual, it seemed the gods had sent me straight to voicemail. Not knowing how long I would have to remain in the cell, I resigned myself to a stretch. If I died in the arena due to a strained muscle, there were more than a few people in the afterlife who would never let me live it down…

6

———

THE ARENA

Time passed at a snail's pace. The cell was hot, and the moisture in the air grew more disgusting the longer I spent there. I longed for the ethereal chill that had accompanied my murderous ghostly companions. Without any view of the outside world, it was impossible to tell the time of day or how much time had passed. I slumped into the corner farthest from the rancid trough and thought through my plan.

There were few scenarios where I survived a one-on-one fight sober. I had killed many beasts, sure, but most of the time I was heavily armed and pleasantly drunk. As it always seemed to, a hangover pulsed through my temples, sending bright motes of pain flashing behind my eyes. *This is not going to end well.*

I was raised from my misery and self-reflection by a grinding clank as another heavily armored guard unlocked my cell. "That time already?" I asked. The less time I had to wait, the better chance I stood.

The guard responded with a grunt and swung the cell door open. He motioned with a spear to the hallway. I didn't need to be told twice. Thankful to be rid of my dingy confinement, I walked out, trying to work the soreness out of my muscles. Between days on

106

end being abused by nature and spending hours reclining on a stone floor, the constant pain that had taken hold in my body was immense.

I was escorted at spearpoint through a long tunnel, which sloped up at the end, presumably counteracting the fall I had taken. "What kind of arena are we talking here? Is this more of a Thunderdome or a Gladiator type situation?" I knew the guard couldn't understand me, but inane chatter calmed my nerves.

The reply I got was a non-committal grunt.

"Interesting. A mix of both, you say? Well, I'm excited to see how you've managed to pull off that aesthetic." There wasn't much time to continue our conversation. Before I knew it, I was being pushed into another small room, and a heavy wooden door slammed behind me. If I had a dollar for every door I've been forced through, I'd be out of this damned business for good. A deadbolt scraped into place, filling the room with a sense of finality.

A slat slid open midway up the door, and a pair of eyes looked in at me. "You prepare to fight now. Lucky you didn't wait longer."

Before I had a chance to respond, the slat shut again, leaving me alone. I looked around the room and found it lined with various weaponry ranging from swords to tridents. *Where did they manage to get all these?* There were several racks of armor, all crusted black and far too large for my frame. Upon closer examination, most of the armor still bore remnants of their previous owners. Given the state of repair, the plate wouldn't have provided much protection anyway. Walking into an arena without protective gear was a gamble, but I hoped it would give me an edge with speed.

On the far side of the room was an iron gate, and beyond it, a dirt ramp led upward. There were no other exits, meaning that was the path to the arena. Even looking at it made my heart flutter. I walked circles around the room, testing each weapon, trying to find anything close to balanced, but none of them measured up. The longer I went without choosing, the more nervous I became. I like to think my combat proficiencies lie in improvised weapons that often end with a bang. I'm decent enough with a blade, but I'd take a sack of holy powder over a sword any day.

What's worse, none of the implements appeared to have any sort of magical element to them. I would have given anything for even an enchanted pebble. I've done dark deeds with magical stones, but unfortunately, my captors were wizardly cheapskates. There were plenty of staffs, but they appeared to be nothing more than showcases of shoddy woodwork.

From somewhere above, the drums started again. My heart hammered in my chest. It was time. A tremor crept into my knees, nearly sending me to the ground. *Keep it together, Nick.* I reached out and picked up a trident, but it slipped through my sweaty palms. *You've only got one shot at this. Combat was always decided in a single moment. Letting it slip would mean my life.*

Behind me, the iron gate that had been blocking the tunnel rose. I vomited what was left in me onto the dirt and was disgusted at my bile's bright orange coloring. The sound of iron against stone was deafening. When it stopped, the drums outside somehow seemed louder. *What happens if I don't go out?* As if answering my thoughts, the slat in the door opened again and a gun barrel poked through. "Time to fight," said the man. There was an audible click as he turned the safety off.

"I'm going, I'm going." I picked up the trident I had dropped and a shield. "I'm going to die here," I whispered aloud. I've got a great habit of encouraging myself when I need it the most. I walked up the steep tunnel at a slow pace, hoping that my opponent would die by some miracle before I reached the top. Above, I could hear the pounding of drums and the anticipatory chatter of a crowd that grew to a steady roar as I ascended.

The tunnel ended abruptly, and I stepped out onto the sandy floor of an arena. Red stains still covered the ground where the last combatant had taken their final breath. The place smelled like blood, death, and roasted meat. A gout of flame leaped out from the side of the arena. With a quick scan, I spotted small, black holes in the walls, no doubt filled with spears to keep fighters in the center. There were also some dubious indentations in the stonework, concealing other deadly implements.

Might as well give them a show. I stepped out into the center of the arena, squinting at the bright light from above. Seated in circular stands on all sides were hundreds of men and women, looking on with a hunger for blood sport. Above the seats were deep grooves set into the stone and filled with multicolored flames that lit a domed ceiling. I wondered if we were underground or if the building was nestled somewhere deeper in the trees. The drumming stopped, and the audience grew quiet.

The high priestess stood high above the spectators on a mighty pedestal opposite me. "My friends, you have come here tonight to see judgment." It electrified the crowd, causing them to cheer louder. "Today is your lucky day. We have the famous monster hunter, Nick Ventner." Hisses and boos filled the stadium.

"So nice to see you all again." *At least Mansen gave them an accurate description.* I smiled at the audience and took a deep bow. *Fake it till you make it,* I told myself, hoping the principle would apply to combat skills.

"It seems only fitting that a monster hunter should fight our own monster, don't you think?" Across the arena, another gate opened. The crowd stamped their feet, and the dirt shook with their collective enthusiasm. I tightened my grip on the trident. A thousand scenarios ran through my head of what might be coming out of the gate.

They've got a giant scorpion. Not sure how they got it here from Egypt, but it would explain the sand. I had never seen a giant scorpion, but the thought of the stinger was enough to make my throat go dry. *Maybe it's the undead?* Undead fighting pits were common in the circles I rolled with. Generally, they didn't present much of a challenge, but the margin for error was much lower with saliva that toxic.

At last, the gate fully lifted, and a figure stepped out. He wore a long, ragged cloak that hung down to cover his face. The man took his time walking to the center of the arena in a casual saunter, arms swinging at his sides.

I slammed the trident against my shield, hoping to intimidate him.

The figure laughed and lifted his hood.

You've got to be kidding me.

The figure revealed himself to be a smiling, confident Mansen. "I'm sorry our chat got cut short earlier, but this will have to do." He shed the rest of the ragged cloak, revealing a tense, muscular body covered in scars—a far cry from the trim television host he had been in the past. "I'm going to enjoy this." He had no weapons or armor.

On any other day, if someone had told me I would fight Paul Mansen, I would have bet everything on myself, but something was off. His confidence radiated, slapping me in the face and highlighting my own inadequacy. I gestured to Mansen with the trident and locked eyes with him. "And here I thought I was going to be fighting a monster. Sure, metaphorically maybe, and you're a bit of a dick, but—"

A grinding noise from above stopped my taunting. I looked up to see the top of the dome opening. White light spilled out from a tiny iris into a pinpoint on the sand before Mansen. I only realized my predicament a few seconds before the ceiling widened enough to reveal a full moon. "Oh no," I said aloud, taking a few steps back. "What have you do—" I didn't have time to finish.

Mansen stepped forward, the white light striking his pale skin. "You see, Nick," he said with an unearthly snarl, "I never got lost." The skin on his back bubbled and boiled in the moonlight, ripping down the middle to reveal grey fur. "I came here to protect those I love." His jaw shot forward, bones creaking and snapping to form an elongated snout.

"That's sweet and all," I said, backing away farther and trying to think of a plan, "but you know we could have helped you back in the city, right? Being a werewolf isn't a death sentence, Paul! Hell, there's a Werewolves Anonymous meeting down the street from me." I had spoken at it a few times in exchange for free donuts. Lovely kids, really. It was only the rogue werewolves that needed to be kept in check by people like me.

"Make your jokes," he growled. "They can't save you here." His deep voice gave way to a final howl, and the audience erupted with cheers. He reached a gnarled hand to the sky, fingers extending to claws, and ripped the remainder of his human skin away. The tattered shreds of Mansen were scattered across the sand, leaving only the beast. He stood three feet taller with loose foam that slathered from his jaw. "When I'm finished with you, they'll have trouble finding pieces big enough to barbecue."

Ignoring the cannibalistic implication, I ran through my options. There weren't many. I didn't have much time as Mansen bared his teeth and charged me, running on all fours. Each footfall shook the ground, vibrating my bones. At the last minute, I tried to roll out of the way and almost made it. He slashed with a claw and raked it across my back, sending blood spraying onto the sand. The force of the blow sent me flying to the side. I landed on my shield, bashing my jaw on its edge and loosening more than a few teeth—the clash of metal on bone rung my head like a bell. The stadium blurred. The crowd cheered and stamped their feet.

"Sure, what's another concussion between friends?" My words were slurred, punctuated by blood dribbling between my lips. I stood, woozy, my jaw full of pain. The world had gone foggy, and I realized it was going to be a quick fight. I dropped the shield and hefted the trident in both hands. *This isn't going to kill you, but it's going to hurt like a bitch.* "Here, boy!" I called with a whistle. "Who's a good boy?" If there's one thing werewolves hate most, it's being treated like dogs. Usually, I never taunted one without silver on hand, but I wanted him angry, acting on impulse.

Mansen recovered from his initial charge and pawed at the ground restlessly. I was preparing to hurl another insult when he surged forward without warning. This time, I planted my feet and put the butt of the trident against the ground. When he tried to snap at me, I plunged the three tips into his sternum and side-stepped. Mansen stumbled as the prongs sank into his chest, and the weapon stuck.

A smart combatant would have let go, but at the moment, I was frozen, hands still gripping the shaft of the weapon. Mansen stumbled forward and shook violently, slapping wildly at his chest. The motion yanked me off my feet and sent me flying. Before I could brace myself, I smacked into the floor of the arena. Sharp pain lanced through my mouth, and there was a loud click as bone struck against bone. I mumbled something that might have been a curse but was muffled by my already swollen jaw.

Blood from my mouth dripped onto the sand, where the greedy earth drank it up. I poked around experimentally with my tongue and found an empty socket where one of my molars had been minutes earlier. I could hear Mansen struggling with the trident in the distance and knew it wouldn't impede him for long. I've never been one for giving up, but I'll admit, the odds were far from in my favor.

"Do you have any idea how expensive these are to replace?" I looked around and saw the white tooth poking out of the bloody dirt. Snatching it up, I stood. The arena spun before me, and my head was about fifty pounds too heavy. Concussions really are one of nature's fucking miracles. Through blurry vision, I watched Mansen pull the trident from his chest and snap it in half. It looked like a bloody, oversized dinner fork. He tossed it to the ground and snarled. At the same time, his wounds sealed up, and before I could blink, they were completely healed.

"Now, that's just cheating." I spat more blood. Electric pain shot out from the messy site of my dislodged tooth. I doubled over, trying not to fall again.

"Don't tell me the fight's gone out of you already. We were just getting started." Mansen chuckled.

The crowd booed, and I held up my free hand to flip them off. Simultaneously, the solution to all my problems came to me in a moment of agonizing brilliance. I held out my palm to examine the tooth and saw the small, metal core running through the middle. I thanked whatever paranoia had caused me to have all my fillings done in silver. Never say an anxious mind can't have its uses.

In my distraction, I had forgotten to move. Mansen, growing bored, rushed and sent me sprawling to the ground. My back slammed against the earth, and all the wind went out of me at once. Stars flashed before my eyes. I thought of all the mild-mannered, chastising doctors I would have to see if I managed to escape. *Time enough for their criticism later*. I gripped the tooth in my fist, thankful to find it hadn't fallen out.

Mansen's hulking form was on top of me before I had a chance to recover, his snarling jaws a mere foot away from my face. Hot, stinking breath made my eyes water. I closed my fist around the tooth, hoping that the back-alley dentist had been worth the money I paid.

A deep voice resonated through the arena. "Finish him."

"Really?" I wheezed, trying desperately to regain my breath. "Could you get on with it? I've got a hell of a headache."

Mansen stepped off me, relieving the pressure on my chest. Then, he gripped me with a claw and hoisted me into the air. I looked right into his eyes, hoping to reach the man behind the beast. "You know, you look just like the creature who killed your brother." Mansen let out a howl, and in the same instant, I punched my fist into his mouth. Hot, sticky werewolf bile coated my fist as I let go of the tooth.

Instinctively, his jaw closed on my wrist. My mistake was immediately apparent. If he broke the skin, I was as good as dead. Sure, being a werewolf wasn't a death sentence, but being a werewolf famous for hunting and killing monsters? I wouldn't last a day. Mansen's jaw flexed as if trying to close, but I could already feel the silver heating up in the back of his throat. My fingertips began to burn.

Mansen's jaw went slack, and his eyes opened wide with dread. The grip around my waist loosened, and I fell flat on my back. For half a second, I was convinced I'd never be able to stand again. Between my jaw and my already tortured back, every nerve in my body lit up to let me know I was doing myself serious harm.

Meanwhile, Mansen backed away in a panicky shuffle. Smoke rose from his nostrils. I looked into his eyes again and saw understanding dawn in them. He belched smoke, blowing the acrid smell of his burning insides right at me. I coughed and kicked with my feet, trying to get as far away as possible.

I couldn't get far enough. Mansen's throat glowed red hot like an iron straight from the forge. The hairs on his neck curled and caught fire, the skin beneath them bubbling with heat. His face contorted in a mix of agony and surprise as the fire spread. *This is going to be gross.* The end was abrupt and far worse than my wildest expectations. The creature that had been Paul Mansen exploded in a shower of half-cooked blood and gore.

I closed my eyes and tried not to gag as a wave of the foul stuff coated me. Murmurs of disgust rang out from the lower levels of the arena. My guess is no one told them they had bought tickets for the splash zone. *Maybe next time they'll sell some ponchos at concessions,* I thought, lying back on the dirt. Nausea swept over me in a wave, but I kept it down, knowing the pain of vomiting would be far worse.

After a few minutes of silence from the crowd, I raised a shaking hand and wiped the gore off my face. Lycanthropy could only be transferred from a bite, but I was still careful to keep the blood out of my eyes. Who knew what unknown diseases were lurking? I managed to stand and lifted a fist in the air like the champion I was. "Are you not entertained?!" I yelled to the crowd, my possibly broken ribs screaming in response.

The crowd remained silent, still sitting in their seats, clearly waiting for something more. I was a little insulted. After a show like that, I expected at least a few half-hearted cheers if not a downright standing ovation. The priestess followed suit with the audience, not moving from her seat and instead lazily lifted a hand. The drums on the edge of the arena started up again, and another gate opened…

7

―――――

ROUND TWO

I scrambled across the arena to pick up my broken weapon, the tips still covered in black werewolf blood. It was substantially lighter with half the shaft broken off but must have looked ridiculous. The gate rose to reveal a dark tunnel across the arena, much like the one I had come from. I spat blood and winced as the exposed nerve endings in my gums shrieked in protest. My jaw seized, and I did my best not to show the agony I was in.

The crowd stamped their feet rhythmically and chanted a rough, guttural verse in their native tongue. "You've had your appetizer, Mr. Ventner," boomed the priestess. "But now it is time for the main course. I present our champion, never defeated in the arena. The Nagual!"

The crowd went silent as a squat man emerged from the tunnel, covered head to toe in bones. His headpiece was made of three jaguar skulls, giving him the appearance of a ghostly Cerberus. Slung across his back were two broad swords that glinted in the moonlight as he passed under the iris. The Nagual wasn't a tall man, but I could feel the deadly menace he carried with each approaching footfall.

"Nagual," chanted the crowd in hushed tones. "Nagual, Nagual, Nagual."

The man stepped into the center of the arena and stared at me; black circles painted around his eyes completed the image that he was one solid skeleton. He reached back with a gloved hand and pulled one of the swords off his back. A gout of flame burst out from the wall to my right, dismissing any notions I had about keeping my distance.

"Look, Mr. Nagual!" I shouted, hoping he could hear me. "I've just killed a werewolf." The guts still covered me head to foot. Each step I took sloshed and squirted small streams of the creature's black blood onto the sand. "So, if you wanted to call it a day and get out of here, I'm sure there's a bar somewhere in this village where we could have a drink and talk this over." For good measure, I threw in a grotesque smile, still full of my own blood.

The man was no more than twenty feet away, and the air between us was electric. Finishing some mental assessment of me, the Nagual advanced, spinning his sword in a tight arc as he went. I tried to keep my distance without getting too close to the stone walls behind me. My movements were a delicate dance between the options of being barbecued or diced.

The Nagual's movement was slow and methodical. His eyes never left me. Despite my best efforts to maintain distance between us, he was still getting closer. We were only ten feet apart when the man stopped in his tracks and laughed.

"You sure you don't want that drink?" My hands shook around the trident, making it difficult to keep straight.

The Nagual continued laughing.

Despite my better instincts, I was insulted. "Look, pal, I just killed a—"

The Nagual cut me off. "I can't believe it. Seconds from death and still begging for a drink." The man dropped his blade in the sand. "Almost a week in the jungle, I have to say, I'm impressed."

In an instant, I recognized his voice. "You've got to be kidding me."

The man reached two hands up to the bony jaguar helm and

slid it off. Sure, the makeup and ornaments made him look like he was in a death metal band, but standing before me was Lopsang. Aside from the getup, he seemed normal, like he had only just stepped out of the plane. Perks of being a demi-god, I suppose. He was even at ease with the idea of being the leading entertainment at the end of a magical, gladiatorial spectacle.

"Lopsang, how in the hell—"

He didn't wait for a response and instead ran to embrace me, lifting me off my feet. The crowd cheered, no doubt thinking this was a new technique for dismemberment. My bruised ribs sent stabs of pain all the way through to my back, completing the image.

"Easy there, fella," I spluttered. "Good to see you, too."

The crowd's cheers quickly died when I failed to explode in a shower of gore or fall crumpled to the arena floor. As it turned out, public displays of brotherly affection didn't play well with audiences hoping to see blood sport. Who knew?

Lopsang put me down and backed away. "Dear god, you look and smell like shit."

"I just had a run-in with an old friend."

Lopsang cocked an eyebrow. "Should I be worried?"

I shrugged. "Not if you know where the bar is."

MARCUS INTERRUPTED me with a loud belch filled with bits of a half-deboned chicken wing. The Haven was not known for its food, and there was a reason. The fact that he had placed an order meant they were in for a long night. "Who in the hell is Lopsang?" Marcus asked.

"You met him about a year ago," replied Nick.

"He was the pilot at the beginning of the story," answered Nick's date, lazily.

Nick's eyes widened. *So, she is paying attention.* Her gaze had not drifted from her phone.

"Riggght, the pilot." Marcus sniffed deeply, clearing his nostrils. "You say I met him?"

After some thought, Nick supposed it was reasonable Marcus wouldn't remember. "Drinking contest. Didn't end well for you." Marcus had collapsed onto a bed of shattered bottles, not two booths from where they were currently sitting. There was still a dark stain from Jimmy's poor attempt to clean up the blood.

"That's right." Marcus paused in brief remembrance and then bellowed: "HE CHEATED!"

"No, he's a...he's got a strong constitution." Nick found it easier not to explain Lopsang's demi-god heritage. With his compatriots as drunk as they were, the questions would no doubt turn lewd before he could get back on track. Besides, it wasn't like anyone was going to believe it anyway. "He beat you fair and square." It had by no means been either fair or square. Lopsang could drink an army of mortals under the table without so much as a buzz. If he ever got drunk, it was because he allowed the alcohol to affect him.

"Bullshit," muttered Marcus.

"Did I hear you say you murdered Paul Mansen?" asked Nick's date, unexpectedly alert and listening. Her phone was face down on the table, and her drink was empty.

That's the part she's asking about? Usually, the questions were around Paul being a werewolf first, and my involvement with his death second. "After he viciously tried to rip me limb from limb? Yes, I killed him, but it was far from murder." The implication that Paul's death was anything other than an act of survival left a bad taste in his mouth. Nick had killed his fair share of monsters, metaphorical and literal, but never for pleasure.

Hoping to change the subject, he attempted to launch back into the story. "So, anyway, there I was, reunited—"

"*The* Paul Mansen?" asked his date again. "Brother to Rick Mansen?"

Nick ran a hand through his hair. "Yes, you a fan?"

"Not particularly, but your story is getting harder to believe by the minute." She picked up her phone with one hand and shook her empty drink with the other. "And I'm not impressed by lies."

"Look..." Nick stopped, unsure of what exactly he wanted to say. "Don't tell anyone about this, alright?" His brain was fuzzy, but something told him that admitting to killing Paul Mansen might have been an incorrect play.

His date looked up again with deeply sarcastic eyes. "Don't tell anyone the story of how a drunk went to Peru, survived a plane crash, took down a plethora of mythical beasts, and shacked up with a bunch of murdering ghouls before killing a famous television host?"

"Hey, they weren't ghouls. Ghosts are a completely—"

She interrupted. "Yes, I *was* listening." She tapped furiously on her phone. "Now I'm calling a ride." She turned the phone around, so it faced him. "Looks like you've got fifteen minutes to wrap this up, and it better be one hell of a finale."

Nick's heart sank, and he motioned for another drink. Jimmy shook his head and gave him the finger, all without looking up from the TV. Nick turned to Marcus.

"Don't look at me," he slurred. "You've got fifteen uninterrupted minutes. Go, boy, go!"

Nick swallowed hard. A good story was never told quickly, and it appeared he had already lost his intended audience. *Ah, what the hell?* If she didn't believe him, it wasn't going to work out between them anyway. "Well, I'll do my best, but if you leave on a cliffhanger, it's your own damned fault."

The woman had returned her attention to her phone and didn't look up.

Nick sighed. "Right, well, getting out of that arena took some doing, but in the end, we were able to get a meeting with the high priestess herself."

8

YET ANOTHER BLOOD SACRIFICE

Lopsang and I made our way out of the fighting pits together. The crowd's silence quickly turned to boos and jeers. Lopsang tried to explain the situation to me, but I couldn't understand anything past the throbbing pain in my jaw. I was reminded of one of the many reasons I had decided against following the family business of dentistry.

Luckily, an old woman in flowing dark robes was waiting at the bottom of the tunnel. "Tell me she does healing," I slurred through my severely swollen mouth.

"Yes, she—"

"Great." I walked up to the woman, thought about pointing out my wounds, and instead made a sweeping gesture to my whole body. If I was a car, an appraiser would have totaled me. Luckily, dark arts practitioners don't believe in the concept of 'too far gone.' In the end, the worst-case scenario is accidental necromancy, and that's more of an impressive feat than a mistake.

The woman looked me up and down and pulled out a small bottle filled with black fluid. It was topped with a silver skull and the label had long-since been smudged off. "Silver." She pointed to the bottle topper and handed it to me. I uncorked it, gave the liquid a sniff, and drank it without question. If I was in pain before, nothing compared to the unbridled agony of that mixture hitting my empty tooth socket. The world went white in an instant and I passed out.

When I came to, I was lying on the tunnel floor, and the woman who had given me the potion was gone. Lopsang stood above me, waving a hand frantically and shouting in my face. I couldn't hear what he was saying, but he certainly looked agitated. I turned my head and saw a retinue of guards running down the tunnel towards us.

Lopsang turned to face them and put on a charming grin. Sounds came back to me in light bursts. I could hear Lopsang trying to negotiate with the guards and saw some terse sword-waving on their part, but to this day, I have no idea what he said. Either way, the negotiation ended with what looked suspiciously like a high five. Next thing I knew, Lopsang was hoisting me to my feet.

"Good news, I got us a meeting with the high priestess." He huffed, out of breath. "How are you this heavy after a week of starving?"

"How are you this feeble after spending a week as a prizefighter in a cannibal village?" I countered, the words growing sharp in my ears.

"Yes, well, most of my fights were less blood sport than good sleight of hand."

I shuffled to get out of Lopsang's grip and walk on my own two feet. "Sleight of hand?"

"I'll tell you more about it later." He jerked his head toward the guards, who were waiting for us to follow.

"Right, meeting with the high priestess. She's a fan of mine."

"So I've heard." Lopsang clapped me on the back, and we followed the guards out of the arena and through a narrow maze of twisting stairs. In less than fifteen minutes, we were back in the tribunal room. I made sure to sidestep the trapdoor in the center as we passed by, heading toward the double doors the priestess had entered through. The guards ushered us in, then left to wait outside.

Much like the rest of the village, the room looked like a converted mausoleum. Long candles burned in every possible alcove, their licking flames ever-so-close to the wooden walls, threatening to burn down the whole damn wicker village. Bookshelves lined the room, and in their empty spaces, skulls glared down at us. My mind spun from the sheer lunacy of finding Lopsang shacked up with a group of dark magic users.

I looked around at the room, wide-eyed, trying to take in the whole macabre aesthetic. Meanwhile, Lopsang was entirely at ease. When the high priestess emerged without a sound from behind us, he did not jump. I, on the other hand, was still on edge and knocked over a shelf full of steaming glass decanters in my fright. Clouds of smoke erupted from the floor, forming dancing skeletal shapes in the gloom.

Lopsang grabbed my shirt and pulled me out of the way.

The high priestess chuckled as the ghastly shapes evaporated into nothingness. "Lucky you didn't knock over that one." She pointed to another equally precarious array of glassware. "We might have been having this conversation through a séance." The imposing voice she had used at the tribunal was gone, transformed into a silky-smooth tone that bordered on condescension.

"You just leave that stuff lying—"

Lopsang put a hand on my shoulder and squeezed. "Easy, Nick, she's a friend." He released me and moved to kneel before the high priestess. I followed suit but stumbled at the last second and crashed to all fours.

The priestess laughed. "You let Adela heal you? Her potions are effective but will leave you off-balance for a bit."

"Should have put that on the label." I brushed myself off and came up to a proper kneel.

"Indeed." She touched a hand to Lopsang's forehead, and he stood. I waited for her to do the same to me, but she instead backed away. "Quite the anti-spectacle you put on out there."

"This is the man I was telling you about." Lopsang motioned to me.

"Yes, I suppose he does fit the bill. You can stand." She pointed a long finger toward me.

I rose. The high priestess looked different from our last

encounter. There was dark paint around her eyes, dripping down to the corners of her mouth like black tears. The ornate headdress was gone in favor of a simple black band around her head.

"It's time for me to be on my way," said Lopsang with apparent regret.

The priestess lowered her gaze. "And here I was hoping your fabled friend would be lost forever and you could stay here." She shrugged. "You were one of the best fighters we've ever had and will be missed." She bowed and motioned to the door as if that settled the issue.

I'm not one to look a gift horse in the mouth. The second she said we could leave, I was headed for the door. Lopsang had less caution. Rather than taking our escape for the incredible boon it was, he asked for a favor.

"There's something else we could use your help with before we go."

The priestess raised an eyebrow. "There's always a catch, isn't there?" She walked over to a long bookcase and ran a finger over the ancient spines. "You're looking to find the Land of the Dead."

"How did you—"

"Your companions were talkative." Her finger came to rest on a thick volume with crisscrossing gold inlay on the spine. She pulled it out, revealing a cover embossed with a silver skull on the front and crossbones leading to the edges. "Not an easy thing to cross over to the Land of the Dead. You'd need permission from The Psychopomp." She brought the book to a low wooden table, set it down, and motioned for us to sit.

As I moved closer, I understood. "That's one of the books of the dead." Saying it out loud seemed silly.

The priestess put a hand to her mouth in mock surprise. "He knows how to read. Miracles never cease."

Lopsang looked at me sideways.

I shrugged. "Oh, come on, Lopsang, you've seen me do a bit of dark magic before." Granted, he had asked me never to do it again, but he had still seen it. "Besides, every hunter worth their salt has heard legend of these books. Most of the creatures I'm hired to kill are mentioned at least once or twice."

The priestess looked at me with disgust.

"No offense." I held out my hand in a placative gesture that led to a terse silence. Rather than trying to hold out through the tension, I ended it. "So, how did you come across this one-of-a-kind treasure?" I really didn't care. What I wanted was to get my hands on it and pour through the pages while drinking my way through my apartment's liquor cabinet. There was enough information in that book to set me up for a lifetime of care-free monster hunting, and possibly an easy buck off wealthy tourists of the occult.

"It took some time to find it. Around seven hundred years ago, a conquistador stole it from the Incans. Luckily, he and his men found the jungle quite difficult to pass through. They entered on a fine day in summer and never returned. Twenty years ago, one of my teams happened upon the new owners and relieved them of it."

"As always, it seems the Book of the Dead brings death," I muttered. The silver on the cover glinted, catching my eye. My hand moved on its own accord to grab it, and I had to force it back to my side.

"Indeed, it does." The priestess lifted the cover, and a strong wind whipped through the hut, snuffing several of the candles.

Lopsang looked around nervously. "Do we really need to open that right now?"

The priestess clucked her tongue as she flipped through the pages. "You're trying to get into the Land of the Dead and need permission."

"It's not going to raise anything evil, is it?" Lopsang recoiled slightly. Turns out, even demi-gods don't fuck with things that come back from the Land of the Dead.

"I knew I should have never shown you those movies." Watching the classic monster flicks had been part of our year of 'training' leading up to the expedition. "Calm down, O'Connel, the cursed mummies come out of the Egyptian Book of the Dead, right?" I turned to the priestess for confirmation.

She shrugged. "Sure, but there are far worse things than mummies in here."

"Not helping." I leaned closer, trying to take in whatever I could from the pages as she flipped past. "Think of it like a supernatural phone book, Lopsang. We're simply looking up an address and giving them a quick call to let them know we're coming."

"I'm not a child, Nick." Lopsang's fear had bubbled over to anger.

Just like old times.

"I hate to say it," admitted the priestess, "but your friend is right. You can't go knocking at the gates to the Land of the Dead. More likely than not, you'd end up a permanent resident." She stopped flipping through the pages and came to rest on an image of a massive dog-like creature guarding a gate. "There we go." The page was covered in a dense foreign script. As I looked at it, the words melded and shifted until I could read them in plain English.

"That's a nice trick," I said, moving closer to the book.

Lopsang edged away and folded his arms.

"It wouldn't be much use if only some could read it," said the priestess. "Now, this," she pointed to the dog, "is Xolotl, the traditional guardian of the Land of the Dead. But I don't think he's been guarding the entrance for some time. It's more of a rotating position these days." The priestess stood and walked over to the crystal decanters. "With any luck, someone will still pick up the phone." She selected one with a smoky froth bubbling inside.

"We brewing a potion?" I asked.

"*We* are not doing anything." The priestess continued around the room, grabbing dried ingredients that hung from the ceiling and piling them into a wooden bowl. A pair of rats squealed from a cage in the corner, writhing over one another and trying to back away. I knew it was going to be a bad day for the furry critters.

"Lopsang, you'll probably want to look away." I didn't much want to see it either, but curiosity compelled me.

The priestess moved the cage and pulled one of the rats out by its tail. "Don't worry, this is Rasputin, he's used to it." She stroked the rat's head and put him in the bowl with the other ingredients.

"So, what do we do? Call and ask for permission?" I asked.

"Something like that." The priestess set down the bowl and pulled a dagger from her belt.

"Is that really necessary?" Lopsang asked. In a swift motion, she swiped the blade into the bowl, severing the rat's head and ending its life.

My stomach turned.

Lopsang's eyes were wide with horror. As if noticing, the priestess winked and pointed a finger at the cage that held the other rat. There was a soft pop, and a second rat appeared in the cage. "Good boy, Rasputin." She turned to Lopsang. "If you want to enter the Land of the Dead, I suggest you get a little more comfortable with its core principle."

Before Lopsang had the chance to answer, she uncorked the bottle of white liquid. Little wisps of fog spilled over the bottle's edge. They cascaded to the floor but never lost density, instead remaining solid and dropping like slow water. The high priestess poured the bottle into the bowl, and almost immediately, a white cloud burst from it, enveloping the room in opaque mist.

The floor disappeared from beneath me, and with it, my sense of gravity. I was floating in space, the cool mist running around my body in tiny rivers, tracing my outline. Had I not seen the blood sacrifice needed to generate the effect, I might have been at ease. "Lopsang?" My voice was swallowed up immediately, dying before it became more than a murmur. I squinted, trying to make out my surroundings, but there was nothing. The floor was gone, and the walls were gone, leaving only empty space and that thick whiteness.

From the ether, a cold, high laugh echoed.

My heart froze in my chest. "I know that laugh…" These words rang out clear as a bell, shocking me to shivers. "Lopsang, is that you?" I knew damned well it wasn't.

The shadow of a man emerged from the white mist, tall and wearing a wide-brimmed black hat. His silhouette was pure darkness against the fog, and there was no mistaking the swagger in each step. "It's been a long time, Nick."

9

———

OLD FRIENDS

It was hard to make out through the haze, but there was no mistaking him. I had watched Manchester die, but as he stepped through the mist, it was clear that I would never truly be rid of him. His face was entirely obscured in shadows aside from his eyes, which glowed a bright blue from beneath his hat's brim. Looking closer, he seemed almost precisely as he had in the moments before his death. Every inch of his coat was burnt to a crisp, dropping flakes of black ash with each step he took towards me. His hat, which was ordinarily trim and pressed, was ragged with holes and tears running through the brim. This was not the Manchester I had known. Something told me he was far worse.

"High priestess?" I called. "Lopsang?!"

"They can't hear you, Nick. I only take calls from people I want to speak to, and I've been waiting a long time for this one."

"Look, I had no idea—"

"That I would get melted? Save it. I'd say it's water under the bridge, but I'm one to hold a grudge." His eyes glittered in the darkness. I tried not to look directly into them. You never know what you'll get from eye contact with a spirit. I've seen strong-willed hunters possessed by less. "Don't worry, Nick. I can't harm you here.

In fact, I'm not really here at all. So, think of this as a friendly chat." He twirled the white mist around his fingers idly.

"I've had a few too many of those recently."

"Yes, dear Paulie told me about your unfortunate encounter earlier…" Manchester sighed. "Yet another great explorer dead by your hand. What's that put the tally at now?" He held his fingers out and made a show of counting them. "Seven?"

Even in death, Manchester still had the power to piss me off. "If you're counting that bumbling idiot Rick, what happened to him was his own damned fault. My hand had nothing to do with it. If that moronic brother of his has been spout—"

"Temper, temper. Let's be civil, seeing that we are old friends and all." He circled me, flakes of ash always trailing his long, black coat. I tried to get a better look at his face, but the shadow followed him wherever he walked. "There's quite a lot of people who are unhappy with you here, Nick."

"Oh? And where is here anyway?"

Manchester clucked his tongue. "You've always been good at deduction…when you're not at the bottom of the bottle that is."

"Well, unless the wires got crossed when the priestess made her call, you're sitting pretty in the Land of the Dead."

"Brilliant, as always."

"But by my mark, you were born in some backwater Midwest town that should be wiped off the face of the earth for nurturing you." I found strength in my anger as it obscured my fear. "So, that would put you a couple thousand miles off course. Shouldn't you be cozying up to the grim reaper right about now?"

"Very good, Nick." Manchester clapped his hands in sarcastic applause, each motion sending puffs of ash into the air. "But, as we both know, death is somewhat of a fluid state, especially when you're friends with the great Nick Ventner." His words were acid, dripping through whatever false bravado I had mustered and rotting it to nothing. "Even the gods of death have their grudges."

"This is what you get for pulling six demons out of a choir boy." I spat. "I knew I needed to stop doing favors for the church." While I was concerned that capital 'D' Death might have a personal interest in me, Manchester's position was a more pressing matter. If he was in the same realm as James, getting the kid back was going to be harder than I thought. I made a mental count of all the people I had wronged in South America. The list got long quick. "So, clearly your plan is going fine. Why take the call? Why not surprise me at the gate like the good friend you are?"

"Can't I check-in? It's been a while since that cursed mountain, and one could say I've missed your…" He paused, searching for the words. "…special breed of antagonism." Manchester smirked and walked forward until we were only a foot apart. A light fell on his face, revealing a horrible patchwork of burnt blisters and scars. His jaw barely hung on by a few pieces of baked sinew, and I could see clear through to his throat. "Not a pretty sight, is it?" he asked.

"I won't lie, you've looked better, Harvey."

Manchester laughed, and the sound echoed through the space around me. "You don't possess the capacity for change, do you?" he asked.

"If it ain't broke—"

"It's a shame, really. You know, finding your apprentice wasn't easy. I traveled all up and down the great lifeless deserts of the American Land of the Dead." He ran a hand across his jaw. "But after all that time, he was down here, hiding out in South America."

The mention of James set my blood boiling. "You're a real piece of shit."

"Again, with the temper. And here I thought we were going to work out a deal." Manchester's eyes never left mine.

"What have you done with him?"

"Relax, Nick. He's already dead, remember? You're the one that got him killed." Manchester bared blackened teeth. "Such a long list, the people you've carelessly thrown into the afterlife. I imagine it gets tiresome trying to remember them all."

Anger rushed through me, hot and furious. "I am going to bring him back. The only people I leave for dead are pricks like you."

Manchester put a hand over his heart. "Oh, Nick, you wound me. What makes this one so special? I don't remember you throwing yourself into danger for any of your other countless pupils."

Most of my pupils had gotten themselves killed from their own idiocy. The truth was James was the only death I felt responsible for. Even thinking about it, I could feel the rope slipping between my fingers. The angry hulk of the yeti flashed before my eyes like a burning reel of film. I'll never forget the stench of its breath or the earth-shattering sound of its roar. "I'm coming for him."

"Yes, you've said that. I'll be sure to let your other students know. They're all so fond of you still." Manchester watched my face with exquisite pleasure. A ticking sound came faintly from his wrist, and he lifted it to check a watch that was miraculously still running. The minute hand moved slowly backward. "It seems we're out of time, dear friend."

"Why the hell did you take the call?!" I shouted. James was within my grasp. We were almost there, and this prick was the only thing standing in my way.

"Because I wanted to watch that last light of hope in your eyes die as I told you you'd never see your apprentice again."

My heart sank like a leaden weight deep in my stomach. I thought of the horrible, stinking slog and the people who had died along the way, all to be stopped by some asshole with a grudge. My hands shook. "You're going to get yours, Harvey."

"I already have, remember?" He moved closer to the point where we were almost touching. "This life of yours does nothing but create death. No amount of booze is going to change that. *If* you were smart, you'd turn around now. Head back to that shithole apartment in Midway and drink away the memory until you've found someone new."

I lashed out to strike him, but Manchester disappeared before my fist could connect.

"That's what I thought. Be seeing you, Nick," he called from the ether.

"Alright, my ride is here," said Nick's date, matter-of-factly. "As much as I love hearing about your dead friends coming back to haunt you and your many potentially murderous flaws, I'm going to call it a night."

Nick raised a hand to motion for a drink, but Jimmy was already bringing it. "You were listening after all," he mumbled.

"Pleasure meeting you, everyone," said the woman as she walked out of the bar. There was a blast of cold air as she stepped out; it died with a whisper when the door closed.

Nick hung his head to the table, trying to keep the room from spinning. A morose, moping notion covered his brain like a wet blanket. Manchester had been an asshole, but he wasn't wrong. It seemed that wherever Nick went, people died, and in more than a few cases he had been responsible. No matter how far away he got, he could still feel the man's dark implication clinging to his skin. *Nothing really changed, did it?*

"Hey, cheer up now." Jimmy slid a tall glass of something green and glowing across the table.

Nick lifted his eyes from the stained wood and looked up at the glass. "Where did you get that?" Jimmy didn't serve glowing drinks for kicks.

"I always keep a private stash in the back."

Smelling the top-quality booze, both Marcus and Albert woke from their slumber and sniffed around like truffle pigs. "What's that?" asked Albert, eyeing the glass suspiciously.

"That is Witch's Brew; illegal in most circles, but a damned fine drink." The trick with Witch's Brew was that it removed the symptoms of drunkenness but not the root source. You could be blind drunk but feel clear as a bell, and the next minute you were keeled over dead. If only someone had warned Poe, he might have lived to write a few more stories.

"Don't say I never did anything for you." Jimmy winked at him.

Nick reached for the glass and brought it toward him.

"Wasn't there a woman here a minute ago?" asked Marcus, slumping onto the stool she had recently occupied.

"Shut up, Marcus," replied Nick.

The door to the bar opened, and Nick looked up hopefully.

Lopsang strode in, removed his jacket, and hung it on a rack. He looked at Nick. "Weren't you supposed to be on a date tonight?"

Nick groaned and took a gulp of the Witch's Brew. The ice-cold liquid dripped down his throat like molasses. Right as he thought it might come back up, the drink did its work. Invigoration spread through his limbs, and the horrible spinning sensation that had been plaguing him for the last half-hour was gone. In its wake, only pleasant warmth remained. "You just missed her."

Lopsang walked over and clapped Nick on the shoulder. "How many times do I have to tell you? The Haven is no place for a date."

Nick spoke the last line with him in unison. "I know," he replied, taking another sip of the Witch's Brew. "We weren't supposed to stay here, but I got caught up telling a story."

Lopsang sighed and motioned to Jimmy for a beer. "Not the yeti again, I hope."

"Land of the Dead." Marcus belched the words like some horrible dive-bar version of Alice's caterpillar.

Lopsang surveyed Marcus with a mix of curiosity and pity. "He's looking more upright than the last time I saw him."

Marcus smiled, taking it as a compliment.

"So, you gon' finish the story or wat?" asked Albert.

"I don't know." A chorus of groans from his drunken companions cut him off.

"You know how much they hate to end a story early, as much as they might protest to the contrary," said Jimmy as he brought Lopsang his beer. "You start something in my bar, you better finish it."

"Where were you at?" asked Lopsang.

"Manchester." Nick uttered the word like a curse.

"Ah, explains your attitude."

"Oh, shut it."

"Want me to tell it instead?"

Nick considered the idea for a minute and thought better of it, as Lopsang would gloss over all the good bits and his heroism. Better Nick finish the story himself. "Right, well, there Lopsang and I were, out of options, stranded in the middle of the jungle."

"With a book detailing how to get to the Land of the Dead," Lopsang reminded.

"With a stupid book," corrected Nick.

"And an army of ghost soldiers willing to help us get there," Lopsang added.

"And a bunch of undead pricks who thought *he*," Nick jabbed a finger at Lopsang, "was a god!"

Lopsang smiled to himself.

"It took us fourteen days—"

"More like five."

"Lopsang, I'm having a hard day. Can I tell the story, please?"

Lopsang made a zipping motion across his mouth and dropped the imaginary key in his beer.

Nick laughed. "Idiot. How will you drink with your mouth locked shut?"

Lopsang reached for the key.

"Don't answer that!"

Marcus and Albert peered into the beer glass, looking for an actual key.

"Fine, Lopsang, we'll skip the journey and get straight to the destination. No one wants to hear about your romantic encounter with an Encantado anyway."

"Hey!"

"Oh, alright, romantic is a strong choice of words, but it did nearly drown you."

"Nick, I am—"

"So, there we were, deep in the jungle, dying of heat, and cursing James for not being born in a milder climate..."

PART III

THE LAND OF THE DEAD

1

NONE SHALL PASS

Our traversal through the jungle was made far easier by the powers of our ghostly companions. Traveling with beings who knew the area meant fewer encounters with the many dangers lurking in the trees and an overall shorter trip. While the priestess had let me copy the relevant pages from her Book of the Dead, they didn't exactly serve as a map.

The book's logic was circuitous and focused only on the parts the writer found interesting. There had been plenty of images describing what the temple might look like, but as far as instructions on how to get there, it only read: *Head east until you find the temple.* I supposed for those who were already dead, wandering forever to find eternal rest wasn't all that bad, but as a member of the living, I was quickly bored.

The heat was amplified tenfold by the heavy metal breastplate and frilled shirts Lopsang and I had been dressed in. The idea was for us to look like a pair of conquistadors lost on their way to eternal rest. Manchester made it perfectly clear that we weren't getting in on his watch, so we fell back to the oldest trick in the book: disguise. In theory, it had been a great plan. In practice, it was like being trapped in a metal sauna filled with my own evaporated juices.

On the first night, I stripped off as much of the costume as I could, being sure to leave it close to our undead friends. No creatures would come near them, and the last thing I needed was some horrible creepy-crawly taking up residence in my clothing. Lopsang and I built a fire, more out of comfort than necessity. With all the spirits resting in one place, the air was noticeably cooler but by no means cold.

I pulled my breastplate up next to the crackling flames and sat, reflecting on the journey so far. The days blended together, forming a single line of images in my head. There had been horror, joy, and more drunkenness than expected. Above all, I thought about Callum. I tried to focus on James, but the face of the friendly Scot continued to pop in. 'Your fault,' the face mouthed.

Lopsang pulled his breastplate up beside me, and I jumped. "You alright, Nick?"

"Yeah, fine." Callum's face faded away.

"Well, good, because I think you owe me a story or two."

I laughed. "I'm not even sure where to start."

"Well, the last time I saw you, you were falling out of a burning plane."

"Fair point." I tried my best to recount everything that had happened in the few days we had been apart. I told him about La Madremonte and wandering in circles through the forest pursued by a homicidal green snake. When it came time to talk about New Glasgow and the Yacumama, I almost couldn't do it. A lump stuck in my throat at even the mention of Callum's name, but eventually, I got through the tale. "He didn't deserve that. No one deserves that." I could still see the life being squeezed out of Callum as the Yacumama dragged him beneath the water.

Ez sidled up to the fire. "But you wounded the creature enough to let us walk free. Those men lost their lives so our spirits can finally rest."

I sighed, fighting back guilt and shame. Trading the souls of a few good men for a band of murderers and thieves wasn't a fair transaction in my book. Callum's loss hadn't been for the spirits; it was to help right another one of my many wrongs. The memory of the serpent's single good eye looking at me across the foggy river was clear as a bell. *Is this what memories are like without booze?* "Well, after all that, I hope it's a damned good rest," I finished, hoping to change the subject.

Lopsang looked at me with concern, but Ez spoke before he had a chance to question me. "It will be a glorious rest. In our culture, warriors are rewarded in death."

"Gold? Gems? Booze?" I asked, hopeful that we might be able to acquire some of the latter.

"Of course, there's that, but the greatest honor of all is being spared The Nine Trials."

Lopsang leaned in. "I've read about those. Wind made of knives, mountains that are constantly shifting, trying to crush you into oblivion. And here I thought our myths around death were harsh."

Ez nodded. "The Nine Trials are no joking matter. They're meant to encourage one to fight in life. Without them, the Aztecs wouldn't have gotten as far as we did. The promise of an easier afterlife pushed us beyond ourselves in combat. In war, there were many times when I wanted to give up, go home, and forget it all, but I knew that if I did, Xolotl would be waiting for me with judgment at the gates."

There was a chorus of agreement from the other soldiers.

"Xolotl?" I asked.

"He guards the entrance to the Land of the Dead, weighing our deeds and judging who is worthy of entrance."

"Ah, a psychopomp," I muttered.

"A what now?" asked Lopsang.

"Almost every culture has one, they just call them by a different name. In Greece, it was the ferryman, taking payment in coins to help souls cross the River Styx. In America, we've got some bony bastard riding a pale horse. Around the world, the dead have one thing in common..." I eyed my company, realizing I might have gone a step too far.

"And that is?" Ez's eyes glittered in the firelight.

I took a deep breath, hoping I hadn't made the inadvertent decision to join her skeletal crew. "No matter where you go, the dead are always confused. The psychopomp is there to help ease that confusion and get them moving to the next plane."

Ez nodded. "It's true. You can prepare for death all you want, but no matter what, in the last few seconds before it comes, we all feel the same thing."

"Fear?" I asked.

"No, surprise. I was a warrior; death was coming for me every day. Even when we were being tortured, I thought I would have the chance to claim my revenge. I plotted and schemed, but when that final darkness came, I couldn't believe it. I kept thinking there was supposed to be more." She went quiet.

Ordinarily, I can't shut myself up, but Ez's words stuck with me. I've seen that surprise in the eyes of so many men and women over the years. I wondered what it would be like when I finally met my own end. The thought alone was enough to nearly drive me insane. I survive as well as I do by drowning thoughts of my own mortality in various destructive liquids. Sitting around the fire, I wanted nothing more than to black out and forget it all, but for once, I was forced to endure.

After that night, we talked less. Well, I talked less. The closer we got to the end of our goal, the more I had to think about where we were actually going. I passed the time reading and re-reading my copied passages from the Book of the Dead, hoping to find some loophole about bringing people back. There were a few, but most involved terrible curses. The situation might have seemed hopeless, but in all my reading, there was nothing saying one couldn't just walk back out the way they had come. Sure, there were guardians to deal with, but that was a problem for another time.

We walked for seven days. Even with Ez clearing a path and receiving protection from the various deadly wildlife, it was still exhausting. On the seventh night, we set up camp as we had all the nights before, but a ghostly—well, more ghostly—silence took over the jungle. My immediate thought was La Madremonte had come back for her revenge. I grabbed my machete and pointed it out at the trees surrounding us. "It's that leafy bastard come back to finish the job."

Ez looked at me strangely. "What on earth are you talking about?"

"Uh, Nick?" Lopsang pointed to the jungle, which took on an unnatural level of movement. The trees shrank to saplings, then to sprouts, and then back to the ground they had sprung from. Leaves fell and the soil swallowed them greedily. The dirt around us trembled but remained firm where we stood.

I wondered if I had somehow been drinking from the wrong canteen. "You seeing this?" I asked.

Lopsang nodded silently.

The jungle melted away until we were left on a barren dirt field, stretching out in all directions. Stones skipped across the ground as the earth trembled and shook, rising to a low rumble. A hundred feet away, the dirt moved slowly clockwise, turning into a thick whirlpool. Stones rose from the ground, simple square shapes that revealed more complexity as they pushed their way toward the sky. Dirt fell in heavy clods as a large temple emerged.

Heavy white mist oozed out of the cracks in the earth, obscuring the scene in low fog. The structure continued to rise, revealing a full, stacked pyramid similar in presentation to Incan and Aztec architecture but combining elements from other cultures as well. Soon, the temple dwarfed the distant trees, standing tall and threatening to touch the setting sun.

My mouth fell open at the size and complexity of the building. Between the terraced levels of the pyramid, round spires crept up that looked almost Cambodian in design. Images of monsters and gods were carved deep into the walls of the temple. The reflecting sun gave the figures the illusion of movement—at least, I hoped it was an illusion. Standing sentinel beneath the temple's peak were stone statues of wild skeletal creatures. Rubies glittered in their eyes.

"I think we've got the right place," said Lopsang.

Ez and her group said nothing and walked forward.

I tried to ask about a plan, but it was clear no one was listening. Ez and her men gazed at the temple with unmatched reverence, paying attention to nothing else. I couldn't blame them. The sight could have inspired the greatest cynic to awe. "So, Ez, how do we—"

A monolithic circular stone doorway embedded in the temple's base rolled sideways. The rumble of its movement was loud enough to be heard over the settling earth. There was a mighty crash that echoed across the plain as it came to rest, leaving a dark entrance at the temple base. Without another word, Ez and her troop marched forward, drawn by some invisible force. In an ironic twist, it was as though Lopsang and I had become nothing more than ghosts to them.

The sun grew blood red and sank on the horizon, aligning with the top of the temple. At the highest point of the pyramid, a circular mirror rose, meeting the sunset and catching its light. A red beam spread out from the top of the temple, illuminating a pathway toward the now open door. Ez and her soldiers followed the light without hesitation.

"Well, they always talk about following the light..." By they, I meant countless daytime television shows about deaths in the emergency room. It was the best barometer I had. "Time to see if traveling in this horrible getup was worth it."

"You sure this will work?" asked Lopsang, shifting uncomfortably. The metal of his breastplate creaked uneasily.

"Well, if we let them get any farther ahead of us, it's not going to matter much anyway. Two conquistadors entering on their own are bound to draw suspicion." Ez's group had already made half the distance to the door. As the sun continued to set, the red path shortened. "And something tells me that if we're caught out here when the sun sets, we're going to be in trouble."

As if in answer to my warning, there was a low growl from within the thickening fog. Its white mist now rose to waist height, parting only in the red light of the path.

"Till death do us part," replied Lopsang.

"Oh, you old softie."

Together, we hustled to catch up to the group, armor clanking and crashing every step of the way. We rejoined the line right as the group approached the dark entrance to the temple. As we passed beneath the stones, I took one last look at the gruesome guardians above. One of the sculptures, a skeletal panther, crunched to life, shaking off years of dust. It looked at me with hungry eyes and bared rows of stone teeth. The growl came again from off in the distance, and I hastened through the entryway.

Behind us, the stone rolled shut, sealing the tunnel and cutting off all light. A green glow illuminated on the floor and shot forward. It split into a multitude of technicolor beams, washing onto the wall to form moving images. Scenes of life, death, and rebirth played out beside us as drawings of gods chased each other across the walls.

An image of a pregnant woman illuminated as she swallowed an emerald. Her stomach grew, filled with shimmering green light until a feathered serpent sprang from her womb, taking off into a neon sky. Next to her, the dog-like Anubis came to life. It stared at me, cocking its head to the side, but quickly fizzled into darkness.

"Gods of all cultures coming together to greet the dead," I said, dazed.

Lopsang opened his mouth to reply but said nothing. It seemed the magnificence of the temple could shock even a demi-god. An excited murmur broke out among Ez's soldiers. I supposed I would be excited too if I was heading to my eternal rest. Ez had never talked about anything else with such fervor. Her eyes were alight in the multicolored tunnel, and for the first time, a genuine smile crossed her face. I wondered if I would ever be at that level of peace.

A part of me knew it was wrong to be entering the Land of the Dead as a member of the living. It was like peeking under the wrapping of a birthday present. There was no going back after seeing what lay on the other side, and I was going to have to carry it with me to the end of my days. Dread mounted in my chest.

Trying to banish it, I focused on putting one foot in front of the other, remembering why I came. With each step, I was closer to finding James, but the truth was, we had no idea where to start. *Getting to the Land of the Dead was supposed to be the hard part...* A dark scenario crept into the back of my brain, as they often do when it isn't numbed to hell with booze. "What if he doesn't want to come back?" I asked Lopsang.

He broke momentarily from his awe. "And miss a chance to prove he's a better hunter than you?" Lopsang chuckled softly. "Have you forgotten what he's like entirely?"

"Stubborn little bastard," I responded.

"We're going to get him back."

"I know." The tunnel sloped downward, and the chill air that had been present around the dead warmed. Steam rose from cracks in the tunnel floor. Drawings faded away to blank stone. The glow that had surrounded Ez and her men for our entire journey dissipated, and their skin returned to its usual lifelike pallor, albeit still maimed and scarred.

The tunnel widened, revealing a cavernous chamber with a glowing green circular door in the center. It was well over five times my height, and a strange light swirled within. The chamber walls were covered in detailed carvings depicting souls in various states of repose rising toward the ceiling. At the top was a carving of two rulers wearing bejeweled crowns looking down at those who entered. Their faces were kind in the green light, welcoming those that entered, but I had learned never to trust a stone guardian.

I didn't have long to be suspicious. As we descended the steps, a large, dog-like creature with dark fur stepped out of the shadows and into the center of the room. It walked on two muscular legs, shaking the room with every step, and carried a long weapon in one hand.

"That's not Manchester," whispered Lopsang.

"No," I agreed. "It's Xolotl."

2

THE PSYCHOPOMP

Xolotl moved with ease across the chamber, his clawed feet clacking against the stone. He stood almost three times my height, and the weapon he held flashed in the darkness. The shaft was polished white bone, ending in a cleft patch at the bottom. The middle had been dressed with leather to make it easier to grip. A curved blade topped it like a scythe, only sharp on all sides.

Xolotl himself bore the snarling head of a dog and spoke in gruff tones. "Welcome. Please form an orderly line—we haven't got all day." He yawned as if the prospect of ferrying the dead bored him. Ez and her troop looked back and forth at one another. "Yes, I mean you. Come down the ramp to the side there and careful not to fall. Damage yourself on the way down, and you'll be dealing with it permanently."

"Not what I expected," I whispered to Lopsang as the group moved down the ramp.

"What were you expecting?" asked Xolotl, his hackles rising. The necklace of skulls he wore glowed red.

My heart leaped into my throat, making it impossible to respond.

Ez looked back at me with venom. "Do not ruin this for us."

"Don't worry, they won't," replied Xolotl. "Although I will say, a white devil and a Sherpa, both of living capacity among a procession of dead Central American warriors is quite interesting. Either way, I'll have to deal with them separately. Come closer if you will." He beckoned with a long finger, and the group walked forward.

My limbs went numb. *So much for disguise.* In hindsight, it hadn't been our best idea.

We marched forward until we were standing in a straight line, starting at Xolotl's feet. "Alright, one at a time," he growled.

Ez stepped forward. Xolotl held his free hand over her. The skulls at his neck flashed green, and flames spewed from their eyes. "My word," he breathed. "You have lived a remarkable life, and the gods will be pleased. Over one hundred kills in combat—and a few more outside it." He chuckled. "You'd give the gods of war a run for their money. No trials for you." He motioned to the portal filled with swirling green light.

Ez thanked him and stepped toward the vortex. Right before she went through, she looked to me and gave one last wink. The part of me that I wished wouldn't stir stirred again, and then she jumped through the portal. There was a soft pop followed by a hiss, then she was gone.

"Alright, next," barked Xolotl.

One of the conquistadors stepped forward, shaking beneath his armor, the plates rattling together. "Interesting. A Spanish born conqueror condemned to an afterlife with the people he sought to destroy." Xolotl chuckled. "That's not something you see every day." He held his palm out and almost immediately, the skulls at his neck went red. Xolotl closed his eyes in pain. "Cowards always wear the most armor," he murmured.

The conquistador let out a shrill scream and turned to run, but Xolotl brought his blade to bear with remarkable swiftness. It cut the man in two at the middle, and his torso landed with a horrible squish on the ground. The man was still screaming as his musket clattered to the floor. "You would have stood a better chance if you hadn't run," commented Xolotl. "Never heard of anyone completing the trials with no legs, but there's a first time for everything." He ran a finger along the wall next to him and red light spilled out, revealing another portal.

Gouts of flame shot out. With them came a moaning wind full of screams. The conquistador shook, terrified and confused as to how he was still breathing. With a swift motion, Xolotl picked up the screaming half and threw him through the portal. Then, almost as an afterthought, he picked up the legs and chucked them as well. "Want to at least give him a fair chance," he mumbled. "Next!"

As the other members of the murderous band went up for judgment, Lopsang and I exchanged nervous looks. My brain was working furiously to figure out a plan, but it wasn't going well with no booze and no time. Trying to trick a psychic deity who guarded the entrance to the underworld sounded like something out of Greek myth. *I knew skipping the lessons on the ancient order was a mistake.* At the time, a cold beer beneath a shady tree had seemed far more critical.

Eventually, the line came to us, with the rest of Ez's group being sent through the green portal. When only the three of us remained, Xolotl set down his spear and conjured a torch from thin air. He bent down to our level and held it close, examining us. "Now, what to do with you." He let out a throaty growl.

"You could let us pass," I offered. "We've made it this far after all." It was worth a try.

Xolotl laughed, and the sound reverberated through the cave. "Quite the mouth on you. I have no doubt you'd find your way up the ranks if I did let you through, but there is one issue. You are both alive as far as I can tell, and what lies beyond that door is for the dead only." He ran his hand across his head, scratching behind a pointed ear. "Why couldn't you have waited to die like everyone else?"

Keep him talking. The longer he talks, the longer you have to breathe. "We've got important business down below. He'd be angry if he found out you had stood in our way." I wasn't sure precisely who He was, but I figured it would have some connotation.

"First, he's in a hurry, now he's got an important appointment." Xolotl's bright yellow eyes came to rest on mine. "Don't look like demons to me, and we've already established you're not dead." He moved the light around, examining us further. "No, I don't think so. Who down below would possibly want to see two uninteresting humans like you?" He snorted and returned to his full height, towering over us.

"Not all of us are human," offered Lopsang, taking a step forward.

"Oh no?" asked Xolotl, growing curious. "What is it you purport to be then?" He sniffed at the air.

"The direct descendant of one of the many sun gods," answered Lopsang, deadpan. "And my friend here is a lesser trickster god."

I had to stifle a laugh. It was one thing to masquerade as a couple of conquistadors, but gods were another story entirely. Though if I was to be a god, trickery did seem like it would be my specialty.

Xolotl shifted. "Gods of the sun and I don't tend to get along," he growled.

Lopsang folded his arms. "Yes, I imagine that's true. You used to ferry the sun beyond the sunset before they stuck you down here."

Someone did their reading. I tried to remember anything about the binders Lopsang put together, but it was all lost in the airplane bender. *Next time, I'll do the homework.* Wouldn't be the first time I had broken a promise to myself.

Xolotl snarled.

"Quite disgraceful when you think about it," added Lopsang. He looked Xolotl up and down.

Maybe don't insult the psychopomp.

"So why is it you've come here then?" Xolotl's muscles tensed. "To mock my failures?" He bared his teeth.

I tried to speak, but Lopsang held up a hand to stop me. *Fine, but if we die, it's on your head, pal.*

"We've got a deal in the works with your master. There was talk of giving your position back, what with this duty rotating so much anyway."

Xolotl took a step forward, ready to strike. "You speak lies. It cannot be done." His fists clenched. "I ferry the dead now, no more."

"Does it have to be just that?" asked Lopsang, holding his hand out and conjuring a white-hot ball of flame that nearly blinded me with its brilliance. Xolotl's eyes widened with avarice as the miniature sun was reflected in them.

"It can't be true," he spoke in a whisper.

"It can, and it is." Lopsang snuffed the ball as quickly as he had conjured it.

Xolotl reached out a paw in yearning. Lopsang had him in the palm of his hand. "To do that, we need to get through." He motioned to the green portal. "Think you can help us out?"

I won't lie; I was impressed. Lopsang always astonishes me with his ability to weave a story on the spot. That's how he conned me into meeting him in the first place.

Xolotl licked his lips and grunted, considering. "I warn you. If this is some sort of trick." The skulls around his neck grew red hot again. "You will live a life of agony and regret."

I gulped, the thought of the halved man coming back to my mind.

"You may pass." Xolotl held out a hand and pointed toward the green portal.

I looked at Lopsang, who showed no sign of misgiving. Not wanting to push our luck, I hurried toward the light. "Thanks for your help." I grinned at Xolotl, and the beast's eyes narrowed.

Lopsang shot me a look that said: *Don't push it.*

I half-ran, half-jumped through the swirling mixture. A strange sensation came over me as if I were passing through hundreds of years at once. I could feel my life stretching to its end. Memories flashed before my eyes, and then there were images of things I had never seen. A lake of fire, bubbling beneath a sacrificial stone platform. A churning maelstrom with lightning and large creatures slithering beneath the surface. James playing cards in a run-down stone building. The visions only lasted a few seconds, and then they were gone.

I landed on my feet in a stone tunnel, bewildered and lost. A few seconds later, there was a popping sound. Lopsang landed next to me, looking unfazed.

"Well, that was easy," he said.

I couldn't find the words to describe what I had seen, so I lied. "Yeah, nothing to it." Something was wrong. It was as if my skin no longer belonged to me, like I was an intruder in my own body. I worked my fingers, and the muscles stretched slowly between them. It was an odd sensation, as though I was forcing them to move beyond their own ability.

Lopsang brushed himself off. "Can't believe that worked."

"I take it you're not a descendant of the sun god then?" I asked with a smirk, trying to push away the needling sensation at the back of my skull.

"Not even close." Lopsang laughed. "This," he conjured the ball again, "is a simple magic trick. The god of my parentage was something more of a lecher above anything else." He flicked the light between his fingers before extinguishing it.

"Something tells me David Copperfield isn't making those on the Vegas strip." My voice sounded odd and hollow as it echoed off the tunnel walls. I raised a hand to my skin, compelled to check that it was still there.

"You alright?" asked Lopsang.

"Yeah," I muttered, trying to shake it off. *Something isn't right here. Maybe it's that you're in the Land of the Dead, genius.* I had a point. "Let's get moving. We're nearly there." I tried to sound confident, but even I knew it was coming out flat.

"If you say so."

Together, we started down the tunnel.

3

———

CITY OF THE DAMNED

"Whars a psy-cho-pomp?" asked Albert, enunciating each part of the word as if it were equally confusing.

Nick sighed. "Were you not listening at all?"

"I was listening. Big dog thing, thought Lopsang was a god." Albert laughed as if this part was the funniest thing in the world. "Him? A god?" He made a gesture indicating Lopsang's short stature. "He's too tiny."

A look of anger crossed Lopsang's face. "Want to take it outside and see who's tiny then?" He finished his beer in a single gulp and prepared to get up from the table. Nick thought about helping, but the idea of watching someone kick Albert's ass was appealing.

Albert's eyes glazed over as if he were considering the idea, then he settled back at the table, propping himself up with his elbows. "Sorry, was rude of me." The words only half strung together in a cohesive sentence.

Lopsang called for another beer. "This one's on you," he said to Albert. Nick raised his eyebrows, both impressed and concerned by Lopsang's behavior.

"Only fair." Albert nodded to Jimmy, who filled a glass. "But still, what's a psychopomp then, eh?"

"A being that ferries souls to the Land of the Dead," Nick said, growing quickly exasperated and wondering why he had started the story in the first place. The sight of Jimmy approaching with another drink reminded him. *Anything for a free drink.*

"Right, right. And he let you pass through because Lopsang did a magic trick?"

Lopsang shifted uncomfortably, then nodded. "Pretty much."

Albert grunted. "You'd think they'd have better security is all."

"We're getting there," Nick said. "As it turns out, getting into the Land of the Dead was the easy part."

"Alright, carry on then."

Marcus let out a deep snore from beside Albert.

Nick wondered how many of his drinks he'd be able to charge to the pair of drunks. *Better be at least half.* "Right, well, we knew James was down there, but as it turns out, it's a big place…"

We emerged from a tunnel to a narrow path along the edge of an impossibly high cliff. In the distance, green-glowing lights hung, suspended in a thick mist. Above us, dark clouds swirled as though always on the verge of forming a hurricane, but no rain fell. The air was charged like it had been suspended at the moment before a lightning strike. On our right, the cliff dropped away to infinite black nothingness. On our left was a rock wall reaching to the sky until it passed through. Streaks of energy shot across the clouds where the stone pierced them. After our experiences on the mountain years ago, both Lopsang and I hugged the wall fiercely.

It appeared as though the path would go on forever, but we rounded a gradual corner, and the green lights we had seen coalesced into a sprawling city. Ahead, the trail widened and cut its way down the mountain, heading straight toward the sprawl of buildings. The town bore hundreds of civilizations' distinctive styles, much like the temple we had entered from. Toward the center, ancient temples stood impossibly tall, with thousands of torches burning on their terraces. On the outskirts, modern skyscrapers reached toward the swirling sky.

"Wow," was all I could manage. Nothing could have prepared me for it.

"I've never seen anything like it," admitted Lopsang.

"Me neither, and we've been to Shangri-La." Even the multicolored horizons of the god plane couldn't hold a candle to the staggering vista of the dead city. Looking over it, the buildings appeared to have no end. Even as we were standing at the cliff edge, I watched as a stone mausoleum fell from the swirling storm above and came to rest atop an older building. Looking closer, it was clear that some of the structures were actually made from multiple gravesites stacked atop one another.

"Must be a new arrival." Lopsang shook his head in disbelief. "How in the hell are we going to find James in a place like this?"

"Surely there's a records keeper somewhere…" The sheer size of the city was intimidating. Finding one misplaced man amid it was going to be nearly impossible. "Only logical place to start digging up some information is—"

"A bar?" Lopsang asked, anticipating my response.

I waited for my heart to leap at the idea of a drink, but it merely continued its sullen pumping. *What is happening to me?* I pushed the thought away, trying not to acknowledge it. "You must admit they're a great place to get information."

Lopsang mulled it over. "Fine, but I'm guessing whatever they're serving down here is toxic to the living."

"Isn't that the nature of a good drink?" I had suffered from mixed concoctions toxic to the living on many occasions, yet I still found myself pouring a fresh glass each night.

Lopsang shrugged. "Suit yourself."

Before we had a chance to discuss my habits any further, I started picking my way down the winding stone path that made switchbacks across the cliff. Each step was more demanding than the last, and I could feel my muscles protesting feebly. I did my best to hide my exertion, not wanting another lecture from Lopsang about the benefits of cardio, but halfway down the cliff, I had to stop. The world wobbled in an unstable wave, and I put my head between my knees, panting.

Lopsang trotted up beside me, showing no signs of exertion

whatsoever. "You do realize it's downhill, right?" he asked in a mocking tone.

"Shut it," I wheezed, putting my face in my palms as I noticed a grey patch on my right hand. Like any other human would do, I poked at it and recoiled at the cold, bloated sensation.

"Everything alright?" asked Lopsang.

I quickly hid my palm. We had come this far, and I wasn't going to turn back because of a skin irritant. "Yeah, I think I might be out of shape," I muttered. "You think after Nepal, I would have learned my lesson."

Lopsang laughed. "I told you, you should have started jogging with me."

There it was. I had always found the idea of running slowly while chatting amongst friends revolting. Grunting with exertion, I stood. "Yeah, yeah, and I always told you sitting back with a cold drink is better than any runner's high I've ever heard of."

Lopsang clapped me on the back. "Nearly there."

Lightning cracked like the Devil's knuckle in the distance, sending a menacing shockwave through my spine. We were nowhere close to 'nearly there,' but I started walking anyway. We only truly got a sense of the city's scale when we reached the bottom of the canyon. The natural formation ended abruptly, transitioning to a city street lined with tall stone buildings on either side. From ground level, their height was awe-inspiring. I found myself tense, waiting for one of them to fall. It was like strolling between giant Jenga towers, ready to crumble at the slightest movement.

While many of the buildings were traditional structures, a fair amount was built in the stacked design we had seen earlier. Burial chambers were sandwiched between rows of tombstones, mausoleums, and crypts. While they looked precarious, the buildings showed no indication of decay, with the various structures in nearly pristine condition.

I was so preoccupied looking at the towering city that I almost didn't notice how lively the streets were. Children darted in between alleyways, and corpses stood on steps chatting animatedly with one another. It seemed the dead were in various states of disrepair, with some being no more than skeletons, and others looking like they could have been alive if not for the grey tint to their skin. I tried not to think about the grey splotch on my own palm. *Need to find James and get the hell out of here.*

We walked for several city blocks in silence along a cobblestone road, taking in the sights. In my mind, the odds were that when I died, I was headed to the desolate American Land of the Dead. Or worse. Something told me it would not be nearly as vibrant as the one we were strolling through.

Other than the rot and decay, the city people seemed happy, going about their routines and, dare I say it, living. Music even floated down somewhere from above. There were no somber chords, only the twang of a carefree melody on an acoustic guitar.

I tried my best to ignore the looks we were getting from the inhabitants as we passed. To the insider, it was clear that we didn't belong. As we approached a bustling intersection, a man wearing a long black sombrero shot past in a carriage pulled by skeletal horses. Their whinny was high and unearthly, reminding me of something from a book of scary stories for children.

"Maybe I will chance it with that drink after all," said Lopsang. His eyes were wide with a mix of terror and fascination.

"That's the spirit." I found myself eyeing a man shambling across the other side of the street. *They're not zombies,* I had to remind myself. *Just because they're dead doesn't mean they want to eat your brains.* We crossed the street, and the man didn't give us a second look.

"We're in luck." Lopsang pointed up the street to a row of shops and restaurants. Hanging above a door was an old-timey sign that read: *Martin's.* Below the name was a picture of a beer mug. From inside, I heard the sound of raucous shouting that only came from disreputable drinking establishments. The sound of a bottle breaking in the back alley only cemented the image.

"That looks like the right place." As I said it, a demon burst through the door and walked down the street toward us. It staggered back and forth, propping itself up on one claw at a time in a comical hobble. *My kind of bar,* I thought. "Keep your distance, Lopsang, but don't look like you're trying to keep your distance."

We both casually moved to one side of the street, allowing the demon enough room to pass. It staggered, scanning the area with bulbous, glowing red eyes. Luckily, before it got to us, the creature stretched out a pair of grey, bat-like wings and took flight. It screeched into the night sky, knocking masonry off the building above before it drunkenly zigzagged away.

"That was close." I let out a heavy sigh. My lungs rattled—well, what my mind perceived as a rattle. The spot on my hand had left open all sorts of possibilities, and with every spare second, my brain was attributing small twinges to new symptoms. I have never had an anxious nature, and I'm still unsure how people live with it day to day. Being in the Land of the Dead brought out the worst in me.

"Still sure this bar is the best idea?" asked Lopsang.

"Trust me, if demons drink here, someone has information. They aren't often let out of Hell, and when they are, you can be sure The Devil has something to gain for it."

We approached the door to Martin's and tried to look through the two latticed windows on either side. They had been stained black, completely obscuring the interior.

Lopsang stood back from the door, wringing his hands. "I don't know about this."

"We managed to trick the guardian of the Land of the Dead. If anyone belongs in a seedy underworld bar, it's us." I pushed open the door and walked in.

4

A SEEDY UNDERWORLD BAR

Whatever image I had in my head didn't come close to preparing me for what I saw when I walked through that door. The bar was dimly lit by multicolored glass lanterns, giving each corner its own distinct hue. A blue-tinted stage in the back featured a man who was nothing but bones from the chest down, playing strings attached to his ribcage like a bass guitar. Standing beside him was a woman draped in silk to hide her features, singing a gravelly tune into a microphone. An axe protruded from her back.

I gawped at the scene. There aren't many things that can leave me dumbstruck, but The Land of the Dead was something else.

"Not from around here, are you?" asked a voice from beside me. I looked down to see a squat toad of a man sitting on a stool next to the door. He wore a freshly pressed suit that was far too large, with the collar turned up to hide a nasty gash that ran along his neck. As if sensing my unfavorable appraisal, he cracked his knuckles together.

"How'd you guess?" I asked.

"Still got that glow to you." He looked me over. "If you weren't down here, I might mistake you for one of the living." His watery eyes flicked from me to Lopsang, expectant.

"Liver cancer." I tried my best to look mournful. "Decided to end my life on my terms. Didn't want it to be messy, so took a few too many of those pain pills they gave me. Wasn't as bad as I thought it would be."

The man nodded as if that made sense. He looked back at Lopsang.

"Don't ask." Lopsang folded his arms in a gesture of intimidation. From my perspective, it wasn't working, but the man didn't question us further.

"Right, well, welcome to Martin's. Band will be on for fifteen more minutes. If you're some type of talent, see Marge in the back." He pointed to a woman with four cigarettes in her mouth, smoke pouring from her nostrils like an active volcano. "If you're going to fight, take it outside, and if you're here to drink your existential misery away, our tender is over there." He pointed to a long wood counter, packed with numerous undead people sitting shoulder to shoulder on rickety barstools.

"Right, thanks," I said, stepping past. I tried my best to ignore Marge and made a beeline for the bar. The structure ran the length of the establishment, curving around the wall at the end. On shelves behind it were various recognizable glass bottles as well as some that I had never seen before. One such container was adorned with dancing demons. Smoke hissed from beneath a cap that had clearly been taped shut. All the shelves were packed so tightly that some bottles simply hung in nets where there wasn't any more room. *They should open up one of these in Midway.* "Come on, Lopsang." I motioned toward the bar. He grunted and followed me.

As we approached, I heard a familiar voice that I couldn't quite place. "I was doing quite well for myself, actually." The man was sitting slumped over the bar in the tattered water-logged remnants of a suit. "All those years, thrown away on some stupid trip upriver." My muscles tightened. "After all that, I don't even get to go to the Land of the Dead of my ancestors because I was eaten by some——"

The rest of the bar finished the sentence for him: "Giant, shitty, river snake."

"What? Have I told you this one before?"

The bar uttered a chorus of "Yes," and several people stood up from their stools.

"But did I tell you I had a distillery?"

The bartender walked over. He was a tall man with a pencil-thin mustache and a neat red bullet hole in the center of his forehead. "Take it easy, Callum. I don't want to have to throw you out again." He passed him a glass. "This one's on the house."

"They're all on the house," Callum moaned.

"Maybe we should try another bar," I whispered to Lopsang.

"What's wrong with this one?"

I pointed to Callum and mouthed: *That's the guy I got killed.*

"What?" asked Lopsang, a little too loudly.

"Oh? New friends?" asked Callum from the bar, slowly lifting himself to a seated position and turning our way. The drunken haze faded from his eyes immediately when he saw me. "You've got to be fucking kidding me." He wiped a bloated hand over his eyes. "Nick?"

"Hi, Callum." The image of him being drowned in the river while I watched from the shore was still fresh.

"It ended up getting you too then," he said, with a hint of sadness. "I'm sorry to hear that." He raised his glass. "Care for a drink? I'd say it's better than what we were drinking in New Glasgow, but I honestly can't tell the difference."

What I wanted was to turn around and run, but that would have been pressing my luck. I sidled up to the bar, and Lopsang followed.

Callum called for a round of drinks and leaned back to look at Lopsang. "Who's your friend?" he asked.

"Remember the pilot I told you about?"

"Oh, no." Callum crossed his chest. "I was a pilot myself once. You look pretty good for being in a fiery wreck, though, all things considered."

"Died of shock on the way down," answered Lopsang.

"Lucky bastard."

The bartender came and plopped three glasses down on the bar. A familiar smell wafted from the cup. "Is this?"

"Fine whiskey," replied Callum. "Yes, and it's free. It gets old quick." He downed the glass in one gulp. "Amazing how fast you lose appreciation for the finer things when they're unlimited."

I took a swig and let the lukewarm liquid run down my throat. There was no burn. In fact, it didn't taste much like anything.

Callum must have noticed my discomfort. "Your taste buds have gone," he said matter-of-factly. "It could be rat shite and you wouldn't know the difference."

That would make sense if I were actually dead. I turned my palm face up and looked at the grey splotch. It had spread to the edges of my fingers and throbbed uncomfortably. *What the hell is happening to me?*

"Callum, right?" asked Lopsang.

"That's me," he slurred.

"Would you happen to know of anyone who keeps records for where people…" he faltered, trying to find the right word, "rest?"

The bar spun around me. Suddenly, the upbeat tempo of the band was too much. Spots sprang up, obscuring my vision. Each melancholy thump of my heart was a bass drum, shaking my ribs. A horrible notion of finality crawled over me, starting at the back of my spine and making its way to my forehead. I had the real sense that each beat of my heart could be my last.

"Sure, there are plenty of record keepers around. Wouldn't be able to reunite loved ones if there weren't." A mist came over Callum's eyes and he wiped at them. "You going to drink that?" he asked, eyeing Lopsang's glass.

Lopsang shook his head.

Callum checked to make sure the bartender wasn't watching, grabbed the glass, and drained it. "Anyways, records are easy enough to find when you know where to look."

I stopped listening. I could feel the booze sloshing around in my stomach. A horrible swelling sensation came from inside me as if I was filling up with noxious gas. *I'm dying.* I couldn't believe it. I grabbed onto the bar for stability but found my dexterity had gone. My fingers fumbled over the wood surface, and before I could cry out for help, I was toppling off my stool. The room spun around me like a carousel, and I fell to the floor.

The sound of my body hitting the wood echoed through time,

hollow and lifeless. There was no pain, only pressure. I watched in a daze as members of the bar cleared away, making room for me. Lopsang came into view, waving a hand in front of my face. "Need a little rest is all," is what I tried to say. I'm not sure if the words ever left my lips.

The bar around me shrank into a dark tunnel with one bead of light at the end. *All that work, and it's going to end for nothing.* The light shrank to a pinpoint and then went out. I was alone, floating in darkness, and then, there was simply nothing at all.

5

____

A DAMNED GOOD MYSTIC

When I awoke, I was standing on an endless grey plain. Mud squelched around my toes and a timid wind blew. I squinted into the distance and saw the glistening hump of a creature moving slowly through the gloom. A mournful cry, the saddest sound I had ever heard, echoed across the plain. It took root in my stomach and sank like a lead weight, pulling me deeper into the mud. The cold mixture slid up to my ankles.

Where the hell am I? I turned around and found the plain extended in all directions. It was a flat void of slimy mud, stretching across a never-ending, shapeless horizon.

I tried to walk forward, but each time I took a step, the mud would pull me a few inches deeper. It was surprisingly cold, quickly numbing my bare feet. After a few more fruitless attempts, I was buried to my waist. *Really? Existential quicksand?* A part of me wondered if I was in Hell, but logically it made no sense. Demons wouldn't waste time torturing, and something told me gross mud wasn't exactly their style.

The mud in front of me bubbled and churned. I tried to move away but sunk only deeper as something moved past my leg and brushed my skin. I could feel its slimy exterior, even in the dank quagmire. Before me, it looked as if the swamp water was blowing a bubble, but then a smooth head emerged. Milky-white, blind eyes stared at me, quizzically. The creature had no mouth, only taut skin where it should have been. Its eyes pulsed in the queer grey light.

Not knowing what else to do, I tried conversation. "Hi there." My voice was swallowed by the mud so quickly I was unsure if I had even spoken at all.

The creature let out a horrible, high-pitched, warbling sound that cut through my skull. I clapped my hands to my ears, trying to drown it out, but it was impossible. A blinding white light bloomed across the grey sky. The creature's warbling turned into a low, angry clicking as it waded towards me. I backed away, sinking farther into the muck, the mixture sliding up to my chest. A tentacle wrapped around my leg and yanked, pulling me deeper. The light continued to expand until it brightened the horizon like an atomic bomb. The creature thrashed, letting go of my leg and diving beneath the muck.

The brightness enveloped me, blinding me. There was no pain, or time for that matter, only the light. Then, slowly, the white swath coalesced into an ancient surgical room with various rusty implements hanging from the walls. I lifted my arm, dragging a series of tubes along with it, and nearly vomited at the horrible puckering sensation where they met my skin. Three were connected to my left arm at the joint and one ran straight into the grey spot in my palm.

I lifted my right arm and found that while free of tubes, it was not unmarked. A simple black hourglass had been tattooed on my wrist. The top glass was nearly empty, while the bottom was full of fine sand. Even as I looked at it, grains slowly rose from the bottom to the top. *Damned thing isn't even tattooed right side up.* Waking up with a new tattoo wasn't all that unfamiliar, but the lab surrounding me was.

I worked my way to a seated position, fighting all my body's natural instincts and waves of aggressive nausea. My head was about seven sizes too big, and every movement was sluggish. As I scanned the room, my eyes came to rest on two fresh-looking severed heads hanging from chains. To my horror, two tubes snaked out of the neck of each and into my arm. "What the fuck is going on here?!" I yelled, slapping at my wrist, trying to get the tubes out.

Lopsang came running into the room from a side door. "Oh, thank the heavens," he said and put a firm grip on my arm to stop me from struggling. "Trust me, Nick, you're going to want to leave those in."

From behind him, a crooked old man in a tattered lab coat staggered in, thumping a wooden cane on the floor with every other step. "See? I told you he would live." The doctor hobbled over to one of the severed heads and rapped on it with the cane. It squished, and more blood flowed through the tubes. I recoiled as the cold fluid coursed into my veins. "Almost drained. You can take those out in a minute or two." One of the doctor's eyes lolled in its socket, pointing every which way, while the other remained fixed on me.

"Who the hell is he?" Ordinarily, I'm calm waking up after a blackout, but things had gone well beyond my norm. It took immense effort not to fall into a full panic attack.

The doctor shrugged. "Not a pleasant way to treat the man who is saving your life."

I turned to look at the severed heads again. Their mouths hung open, disgusting tongues dripping toward the floor. "What is happening to me? Why do I have a tattoo?" I held up my wrist to show Lopsang.

"At least it looks cool," he mused with a smirk.

"And it's functional," added the doctor. "When the hourglass is empty, you're dead. Simple as that." He smiled as if that settled the matter. "As to my dear friends here," he motioned to the severed heads, "ironically, they're what's keeping you alive."

My head pounded, and I tried to stop the room from spinning by shutting my eyes. "Alright, two questions, and I need answers." I tried to sound authoritative, but I could hear the drunken grog in my voice. "Doctor," I paused, "are you even a doctor?"

"Of course!" The man rapped on a certificate that had been hastily nailed to the operating room wall. I would have tried to read it but keeping my eyes open for that long sounded like a marathon task. "You may call me Doctor Vasquez." The old man beamed, patting one of the heads for good measure.

"Right, Dr. Vasquez." A million questions buzzed in my brain, but I tried to quiet them and narrow my line of interrogation to two items. "Why did you tattoo the hourglass upside down?" I looked at the tattoo again. Grains of sand were still falling up, but the rate had slowed significantly.

Vasquez laughed. "It's not upside down. You were pretty close to death, my friend. We're topping you off with life right now, so to speak." He motioned to the heads.

"Right, that brings me to my second question." I opened my eyes long enough to look one of the heads in the eyes. Its tongue lolled out and hung to one side.

"Gross, Frank," chided Vasquez. "Show some respect for our company."

The head looked at Vasquez, slow and stupid, and pulled its tongue back in.

"That's better."

"Jesus Christ," I muttered.

"You had a second question," asked Vasquez.

"Right, how in the hell is this helping me stay alive?"

"It's technical," mumbled the doctor, pulling a small syringe out of his pocket. "Suffice it to say, these aren't ordinary heads."

One of them groaned.

"Yes, Cristy, you're special." The doctor let out a cackle filled with a level of madness usually reserved for black and white B-movies. "You see, they still have something to live for. It's not just their blood I'm giving you; it's that drive to keep going. Your body is shutting down and giving up. Once that happens…" He drew a line with his finger across his neck.

I nearly vomited at the thought of it all. "And this is healthy?"

"None of this is healthy, you imbecile!" He paced around the room, tapping on his syringe hopefully and edging closer to Lopsang. "I tried to convince your friend to get you out of here while you were sleeping, but he was sure that you would be adamant on staying."

"What are you planning on doing with that?" asked Lopsang, backing away from the doctor.

Vasquez put his arms behind his back, ashamed. "Any chance I could take a sample?" His eyes were hungry, and he brought the syringe out again with a delicate flourish. "Your blood must be extraordinary if you can survive down here. Something above human even." He licked his lips.

"Not a chance." Lopsang took another step away from the doctor. "Put that away and finish up here."

"Well, no need to be rude about it." He walked over to the severed head and pulled the tubes out. There was a horrible splatter as the excess liquid hit the floor, and the heads groaned. "Yes, thank you, Frank and Cristy," said Vasquez as he pushed a switch on the wall. The heads pulled up into a recessed alcove out of sight.

"Now, to answer your inevitable question, this is only going to keep you alive temporarily. I'd say you have around a day, maybe a little more if you're careful. Pay attention to the hourglass." He pointed a knobby finger at my wrist. "This infusion is not something I can do twice, and if you die again, you won't come back here, your soul will be lost for eternity."

"The grey plains," I muttered.

"Oh good, you've seen them. That should give you the necessary motivation to never return. There are horrors beyond imagining put there to torment the souls who could never find their way. Some would argue it's worse than Hell." He cackled again, rolling up the infusion tubes, ripping them unceremoniously from my arm and hanging them, still dripping, on the wall.

I flexed my arm and watched as rivulets of black blood came out of the holes. Thinking about the transfusion too long was horrifying, but despite myself, I felt better. A level of alertness had come back to my mind, but a grey fog still hung at the back. "If we're going to get out of here in a hurry, we're going to need your help."

The doctor scoffed. "I've already given my help."

"We're here to retrieve a friend," said Lopsang.

"Of course, who doesn't love a friend? You know, dying might be easier than bringing him back. I've even got a few concoctions that will make it quick. This isn't a bad neighborhood, either." His eyes swelled with excitement at the prospect.

"Or you could help us find him." Lopsang's took on a tone of menace.

"Haven't you ever heard of a phonebook?" The doctor was growing impatient.

"Doc, you're not going to like him when he gets angry." I motioned to Lopsang.

The doctor looked back and forth between us, weighing up his options. "Alright, fine, come into the next room and I'll help you find your ill-fated friend." Without another word, he bustled through a swinging door that slammed shut behind him.

"You know there's going to be a catch, right?" I said.

"There's always a catch." Lopsang sighed. "How are you feeling?"

I flexed my arm, testing it. "A little less dead than before." I thought back to my last memory: falling off the barstool. "Hey, what happened with Callum?"

Lopsang let out a long whistle.

"That good, huh?"

"Suffice it to say, he wasn't happy to learn you survived the Yacumama attack and lied to him again. Said something about revenge, making you pay, the works." Lopsang helped me off the table.

"I seem to be making a lot of friends on this side of the world."

"Well, let's see if we can get one back." Lopsang clapped me on the shoulder. "We've come this far after all."

I stepped away from the table, happy to be leaving the memory of the severed heads behind as I pushed my way through the swinging door. Beyond it was a hexagonal room filled floor to ceiling with dusty old books. The change in scenery was jarring, to say the least.

Vasquez bustled around, running his hands along the books and muttering to himself. Along the edge of the room, an iron-wrought staircase spiraled upward to a domed ceiling made of stained glass. *Clearly, Vasquez has some clout.* It depicted the four horsemen of the apocalypse riding to final judgment. The dome was propped up by four wooden skeletons that had been carved into the walls.

"Homey." Of the lies I've told, it was one of the more obvious. The carpet was a sickening shade of red, and I had to wonder how often the doctor cleaned his shoes between this room and the lab.

"One does what one can." The doctor moved up the spiral staircase toward a sign with the word 'records' neatly painted on it in cursive. "Now, what was your friend's date of death?"

"October 10th, 2010." I had never forgotten the date, and I never would.

"Right, there it is." The doctor pulled out a large book with both hands and slammed it down on a dusty table. I jumped, and my skin sagged a little too much with the upward motion. "Name?" the doctor asked.

"James Schaefer," I replied.

"Schaefer," he mumbled. "Been a while since we've had a Schaefer down here, but I suppose these mix-ups happen." The doctor flipped through the pages with alarming speed. His finger ran across line-after-line of hand-scrawled names. The process called my preconceptions about the dead and attention spans into check. Usually, they can't think about much aside from their life or eating the living, but I suppose death takes all kinds. After thoroughly checking and re-checking, the doctor slapped his bony palm onto a page. "Ah-ha! I've got it."

"And?" I asked.

"And I'd love to tell you where he is." A hungry look filled Vasquez. "But one does not simply trade something for nothing."

Lopsang stepped off the wall where he had been leaning and balled his hands to fists.

"I'm sure intimidation works in the Land of the Living, my boy, but down here you're no more powerful than I am." He reached a hand in his pocket, reproducing the syringe.

"No," answered Lopsang before the question had even been asked.

"One blood draw. Don't be such a sissy," teased the doctor, approaching slowly.

Lopsang looked at me.

"Do you have any better ideas?" I asked.

He glared and stepped forward to the table. "You really owe me after this one." Lopsang put his arm on the table face up and the doctor approached it with an uncomfortable eagerness. Before Lopsang had a chance to say anything else, the madman stuck him with the needle and hastily drew blood. Lopsang winced but said nothing.

"There, see?" The doctor capped the syringe and put it back in his pocket. "Nothing to be afraid of." He walked back over to the book. "Now, as for your friend, it looks like he's only a few stops away." The doctor went over to a small machine on his wall and punched in a series of numbers. "You're lucky I keep this around for my patients." Two tickets popped out of the machine and he handed them over. "Call it our form of parking validation."

I took the smooth, orange papers in my hand and looked them over. "What are these?"

"Head to the rail station down the road, plug them in, and you'll find your friend in no time."

"That simple?" I asked.

"That simple," replied the doctor. "Oh, and one more thing before you go." He hurried to an ornate cabinet that might have been centuries old. With a creak and a puff of dust, he pried the door open and produced a dusty bottle.

"What's that? Something to ward off the dead?" With our lack of armaments, our odds of making it much farther were feeling slim.

"Ward off the dead, here?" His look was beyond incredulous. "No, I happen to like your style and wanted to give you a parting gift. It's rum." The doctor uncorked the bottle and handed it to me.

"What'll that do?" I took the bottle, trying not to look too eager. My heart gave a half flutter.

"Keep you sane." He chuckled. "Now get going. You don't have a lot of time, and you're on a suicide mission." Vasquez pointed to another door that led to the street and hobbled away toward the surgical room, laughing. "Think of what I can do with this magical blood, Frank!" The door swung shut behind him.

"I'm sure I'm going to live to regret that," said Lopsang.

"Well, let's make sure we at least get something worthwhile in return."

6

ILL-FATED FRIENDS

The train station wasn't far and looked like the Devil's twisted interpretation of a carnival rollercoaster. The building itself was a terraced stone temple with train tracks shooting out from it in all directions. A long concourse hollowed out through the center of the structure started at the street and led to a tangled mass of wood, stone, and rail where all the tracks converged. Rail carts careened by at impossible speeds, and if I wasn't so worried about my own impending death, I might have been excited. Despite my hardened exterior, I do love a good thrill ride.

I took a long pull from the rum bottle and waited for the familiar numbness to root out the unfamiliar dead weight in my brain. "Looks like the right place."

Lopsang grabbed the bottle from my hand and took a drink as well. "After this, I think I'm done with rescuing old friends for a bit." He passed the bottle back.

"You and me both." Together, we walked down the main thoroughfare and toward the center of the temple. The sound of carts rattling on rails was deafening. Above us, hundreds of tracks spiraled off in every possible direction. With the 'fresh' blood running through my veins, I could feel the alcohol going to work. It was as if a warm blanket had settled over the darker parts of my mind, obscuring them from view. When the booze wore off, it was apt to be messy. I chose to enjoy the moment.

A purple neon sign reading 'Departures' hung at the end of the concourse. Below it was a board displaying an ever-changing series of numbers and destination names. I watched as a man and his dog shambled over to the sign and put an orange ticket into a slot below it. An arrow illuminated above them, and the man followed it to an open railway. A second later, a cart shot forward and stopped with a screech before him. Without hesitation, he stepped in and set the dog gently on his lap. It let out a playful yap, and the cart sped off again.

"It's like an amusement park, right?" I said to Lopsang.

"I've never been to an amusement park."

"First time for everything."

He gulped and grabbed for the bottle.

"Ah, ah, out of the two of us, I think I need this more." I swatted his hand away and made my way toward the sign. The dead swarmed around us, all making their way to various tracks, going about their daily business. If they hadn't been wholly ignoring our presence, it would have been the perfect setting for a horror film. A woman hopped past us, carrying her leg under one arm and a briefcase in her free hand.

The line for the ticket booth wasn't long. While we waited, I watched the concourse. The carts were moving at an incredible clip, despite being mostly solitary vehicles. Every now and then, a train of them would pass by, chained together. However, for the most part, the dead traveled alone.

"How is it that the dead have better transit than South Midway?" asked Lopsang.

"Let's wait until we've ridden them to pass judgment." When it was our turn, I approached the sign and stuck the tickets in the slot one after the other. There was a clanking, whirring noise from behind the panel, and a gravelly voice spoke from a small tin speaker: "Barrio 198442, Departing to the right. Have a nice trip."

"Thanks." I gave a small salute and walked to our right. A series of queues split out in odd directions.

"Which one do we take?" As Lopsang asked, one of the stanchions illuminated green.

"Alright, I'll admit it, the system works." In Midway, I would have stared at a map forever attempting to interpret what the hell the original city planners had been thinking. Even with that effort, I would have still been twenty minutes late to wherever I was going, assuming I was lucky.

"Perks of having all the undead city planners they could ever want." Lopsang shook his head in amazement and led the way through the queue as it spiraled up three floors. When we reached the end, there was a single empty rail track. I looked below for supports and found that there were none. The track was simply hovering in midair. I was about to comment when two carts held together by crude chains screeched to a halt in front of us. Sparks flew from the wheels and rained down on the tracks below.

"Shotgun!" I ran and hopped into the front cart. My rule about staying in the middle of a group had one clear exception: rollercoasters. Despite myself, the nervous flutter that had always drawn me to theme parks as a kid filled my ribcage like butterflies. *Maybe the Land of the Dead isn't so bad after all.*

Lopsang rolled his eyes and stepped into the second cart. I looked around for restraints or safety harnesses when the cart took off without warning down the track. I gripped the edges for dear life as we moved up a steep incline toward the top of the ancient building. Carts crisscrossed and corkscrewed around us as we headed for one of a thousand dark holes in the ceiling. The cart hurtled upward, and soon we were in complete darkness. I resisted the urge to put my hands up, not knowing the tunnel height.

A square of green light illuminated before us, and we shot out of the building toward the churning sky above. The cart accelerated to its full speed as we leveled off and hit a straightaway. The initial fear was gone in favor of elation. In the distance, I could see the cliffs we had first arrived from, and below them, the neon-lit street where the bar had been. From above, the city looked beautiful. I regretted that after that day, I would likely never see it again.

Looking at the bar brought back thoughts of Callum. His death weighed on my soul. While unlikely, I hoped that he could see his way through to understanding and enjoy the rest he had been given. *I never asked him to come with,* I reminded myself. *But you didn't try to save him either,* hissed an equally loud thought from the back of my brain. I took another drink, and the voice got a little quieter.

The cart continued to hurtle forward, passing through tall buildings and weaving around other tracks. Several times we passed through what appeared to be people's houses, but our speed was too fast to tell for sure. The city thinned away, and soon we were traveling alongside smaller mausoleums and more traditional crypts. Here, the dead shambled and crawled like the horror movies of old. On our left was a hilltop where several skeletons fought with crude weaponry, bashing each other to bits, only to put themselves back together and try again.

I turned to Lopsang. "We're a long way from Kansas."

His eyes were wide as he stared at the grim surroundings. "No one is ever going to believe this."

"No, but it would make one hell of a story."

Mausoleums gave way to rolling hills littered with gravestones where the buildings no longer reached above a single story. Plains stretched out over the land to a series of temples and castles far off in the distance. Each had its own distinct style, representing the culture it had come from. Lightning flashed behind an Aztec pyramid, casting shadows of skeletal royalty on the clouds above.

"What are those?" asked Lopsang.

I had only skimmed the Book of the Dead, but the castle and the crowns made the deduction easy. "If I had to guess, that's the king and queen."

"The dead need a monarchy?"

"Everyone needs to bow to something, be it science, royalty, gods, or all of the above." I wondered what the king and queen of an undead realm looked like and hoped that we would never have to meet them. On cue, green flame twisted and swirled to the sky from behind the temple, punching a hole in the clouds before extinguishing.

"And that?" asked Lopsang.

"Some things I think we're better off not knowing."

Before we had a chance to discuss it any further, sparks flew from the carts' wheels as we slowed down. The track lowered to ground level, and we stopped next to a squat building that was constructed entirely of gravestones stacked atop one another. A few crude windows made of shattered glass panes covered holes in the siding, giving some semblance of home.

I stepped out of the cart and took it all in. *So, this is where James has been spending the past year.* It wasn't what I expected, but then again, nothing about my journey to find him had been. Lopsang stepped out and came to my side. The carts took off from behind us, off to carry the next group to their destination.

"Think he's in there?" I asked. My heart found its lost vigor and pumped heavily in my chest.

"Only one way to find out."

At the front of the house was a simple wooden door with an ornate metal knocker. The dwelling was utterly at odds with itself stylistically, and I wondered where they had found all the materials. It was this wonder that allowed me to stay rooted to the spot and avoid the eventual task of knocking on the door.

"Nick?" Lopsang put a hand on my shoulder. "We don't have all the time in the world."

I looked down at the hourglass tattoo on my right arm. Sure enough, sand was falling to the bottom half of the glass. Time was short. "Alright. He can't possibly still be mad about it, can he?"

Lopsang said nothing but pushed on my back until I was walking forward.

When I reached the door, I raised a hand hesitantly and then rapped three times. The door opened on its own accord, revealing a dank stone chamber decorated in the same style as a college dorm room. Two men were sitting around a table playing cards. James was not among them.

I only had a second to process this when he emerged from behind the door, looking exactly like he had the last time I saw him. "Nick?" he asked. "Is that really you?"

7
______

REUNIONS

I was shocked speechless. Our entire journey had been centered on finding James, but I never imagined it would be as easy as him opening a door to let us in. He wore his parka, ripped where the yeti had slashed his stomach open. The skin beneath was dark, blotchy, and sewn together by a series of black stitches that barely held. From the neck up, it almost looked like the same old James, albeit a little paler.

"Nick?" asked James again. A tremor had crept into his voice.

"Yup," was all I could manage. To see him alive again was almost too much. We had finally done it. After all the time slogging through the god-forsaken jungle, we were here.

James's eyes were glazed over and unreadable. *This is the moment,* I thought, wondering whether he would embrace us or turn away. I winced in preparation, knowing that either way, there was a good chance he was going to punch me. James moved forward with alarming speed, and there was a sickening squish as he wrapped his arms around me in a hug. "Took you long enough," he said.

I clapped him on the back. "I've missed you, kid." Despite the alcohol in my system, it was a rare moment of emotional clarity.

"Surprisingly, me too." James pulled away and turned to Lopsang. "He roped you into coming down here?"

"Wouldn't have missed it for the world." Lopsang hugged him as well.

I took a long drink from the bottle of rum, trying to chase away the intense barrage of emotions hammering my conscience.

"I see that hasn't changed." James raised an eyebrow.

"There's the sarcastic shit I remember." Despite being far from our goal, the weight of my journey to bring him back had lifted. We had him, now all we had to do was get him out.

James laughed, and there was a horrible ripping sound as the stitches holding his stomach together split open, spilling his intestines onto the floor. He looked down at them with annoyance. "Shit, Diego, I told you those weren't going to hold." He knelt and casually scooped up his innards.

Alcohol crept up my throat, fighting to get out, but I successfully fought my gag reflex.

"Oh, relax," said James. "You get used to it after a while." He finished putting everything back in place and held the wound with a hand. "Give me a minute to fix this up," he said, embarrassed. "Have a seat." He motioned to the table where two men sat playing cards. "These are my cousins, I think." James walked out of the room.

I looked to Lopsang, who shrugged and moved to the table. The two men seated there were dressed in modern clothing and sported near-identical gunshot wounds in their chests. "Thanks for having us," I said, awkwardly.

One of the men looked at me, grunted, and returned his attention to the cards.

Tough crowd. "James, when you've got yourself stitched up, be ready to move," I called. The sand was falling quickly to the bottom of the hourglass on my wrist. "What the hell? I think this thing is broken." I showed it to Lopsang, but his attention was fixed on the room James had entered. "Lopsang, either his potion didn't work or——"

"Uh, Nick." Lopsang pointed toward the door.

I looked up and saw James standing in the doorway, flanked by three men. On his right was Callum, and on his left, two of the people I wanted to see the least in the world. Despite being blown to smithereens, Paul Mansen stood back at his full height, badly burned but seemingly intact. Next to him, his brother Rick glared at me, still dressed in the khaki suit he had worn in his final television special. It had also been the same night I watched a madman dressed as sasquatch gut him.

I grimaced. "What a wonderful reunion this is." I did a quick mental check on the exits. Our assailants had obviously come in through a back door, but I didn't like my odds of barreling straight through them. The door we had come through was close enough to make a run for, even if it left our backs exposed momentarily.

"Nice to see you again," said Paul. "That was a dirty little trick with the silver filling. Hurt like a bitch." He rubbed at his jaw.

"Yeah, well, transforming into a werewolf wasn't exactly fair either, was it?"

Paul scoffed.

"Been waiting a long time for this," growled his brother.

I had to laugh. I've never been good at knowing when to shut up. "The two of you," I motioned to Callum and Paul, "I feel some sympathy for. But you," I pointed a finger at Rick, "were an idiot that was in well over his head. If you'll recall, I told you to turn back."

"Nick, maybe not the right time?" asked James, his voice shortening as Callum put a blade to his neck. The gesture was semi-futile given James's already reposed nature, but I supposed having another mortal wound could be inconvenient.

Rick started forward, a knife in his hand.

Paul put a hand out to stop his brother. "We can't hurt them. They've got an appointment with an old friend that I wouldn't want them to miss."

James's eyes went wide. "Which old friend is that?"

"Exactly the one you don't want to see." I could picture Manchester's smug face. Death at the hands of the Mansen idiots almost seemed better.

"Christ," groaned James. "He's down here too?" He struggled, but Callum tightened his grip. "Can't say I'm surprised."

"Better stand up and get walking before someone gets hurt." Callum was seething. Any kinship we had shared in life was gone, replaced by the need to do me fatal harm.

I moved my hands toward my head, checking my wrist. Sure enough, the sand was falling even faster than before. *Come on, give me a break.* I turned toward the door, palms firmly on the back of my head. "If Manchester wants to talk, we'll talk," I said over my shoulder.

"Screw that," replied James. "Diego, help us out here."

I had completely forgotten the other men seated at the table with us. One of them who sported a thick mustache and long, greasy hair looked up. "You're too loud, cousin, keep it down. Tell your friends to take it outside." He returned his attention to the cards and pushed a few chips toward the center of the table.

"Really, man?" James let out an exasperated sigh. "What happened to cousins having each other's back?"

The man who I now assumed was Diego looked up again. "We only told you that so you would stop freaking out."

"So much crying and whining about the yeti," chimed in the other, making a gesture of mock despair.

"Pricks." James spat on the floor. Diego waved a hand at him, and I tried to make a move for the door amidst the confusion.

"Easy now." Paul stepped up behind me. "Let's take this nice and slow." He put a hand on my back and pushed me toward the door we came in through.

"I can't believe this," said James, his voice again cut short by Callum's knife. "Easy with that thing. I'm barely holding myself together as it is."

We were marched out to the front of the house where six rail carts sat chained together on an older looking track that hadn't been there a moment ago. "You three will ride in front," ordered Callum.

"Should be a change of pace for you," seethed Rick. "He likes to cower in the middle of a lineup."

"Yes, Brother," answered Paul. "You've told us."

Paul pushed me into the first car of the train with James and Lopsang behind me. The other three men loaded in, and the carts sped off. The ride was much rougher than before. The tracks stayed lower to the ground, and the carts jostled over bumps and chips in the railway. Rather than moving toward the city, the tracks veered off in the direction of the plains we had passed.

We were only out in the open for a minute before the tracks headed straight for a barrow and sloped down into the earth. *How in the hell are we going to get ourselves out of this one?* Instinctively, I looked at my arm and watched as some grains of sand fell upward, filling the top half of the glass. There weren't many of them, but it was a start. *Apparently, we're doing something right.*

Lopsang leaned close to me and whispered: "James says, 'hold on.'"

There it is. Before I could argue, there was a mighty snap, followed by the screech of metal on metal. Somehow, our carts picked up even more speed, and we rocketed ahead.

I looked back to see James grinning like a madman. "Manual override!" he yelled, laughing hysterically. "What could possibly go wrong?!"

8

_____

AN ILL-ADVISED MINE CART CHASE

We were flying like a bat straight out of hell to the center of the earth. A yellow light illuminated the front of the cart as we passed into a darkened tunnel, casting a bright cone of light on the tracks ahead of us. I held on for dear life as the cart twisted and turned through caverns and catacombs. Looking behind us, I could catch no sight of the Mansen brothers and Callum. "How long before they figure out that manual override trick?" I yelled at James.

"Not long enough," he said. "Don't worry, the track splits up here, we should be able to lose them." He spoke with a confidence that I usually reserved for when I was blind drunk.

"How do you know that?" I yelled.

"Gut feeling," replied James, putting a hand to his stitches. "I get a lot of those lately." He laughed like a madman and gripped the lever controlling our speed.

"Need I remind you that not all of us are dead already?"

"Don't be such a baby."

A smile crept over Lopsang's lips as he gripped the sides of the cart with white knuckles.

"What's got you so happy?"

"This is the most fun I've had in a long time." He laughed and returned his eyes to the track ahead.

I resigned myself to the same, knowing there wasn't much I could do. The tunnel opened, and the tracks crossed onto a stone bridge over a cavern filled with stalactites and stalagmites, as though we were passing through the maw of some ancient subterranean monster. Below, slimy creatures picked their way through the spikes. They hopped between pools of inky black liquid, producing slow bubbles when they went under. The scene was far too close to the grey plains for my liking.

Ahead of us, the track split into three, with one going straight forward, one up and to the right, and the other farther down. "I'll be damned, kid, you were right." He was turning out to be more like me every day.

"Lucky guess," he said with unbridled confidence. "I'm liking our odds up rather than down," he called. "Any objections?"

"Flawless logic as usual." I looked behind us to check for the Mansen crew right as a voice called out from the other side of the cavern.

"You can't escape us!"

Spoken like a true villain. Sure enough, the Mansen twins and Callum had been gaining on us and caught up. "How in the hell did they manage that?"

"Looks like they've done this before." James gritted his teeth. "Hold on!" He yanked a lever to the right, and the cart took a sharp turn at the fork. The left wheels lifted off the rails, but as we straightened out, they slammed back down onto the tracks. My stomach pitched and rolled, but I managed to hold its contents in. Something told me undead vomit was worse than I could have imagined.

I looked behind us to see if our pursuers had made the turn. Their carts split off, each taking one of the three directions. "Clever bastards." Rick Mansen had taken our track and was quickly gaining. "Any chance you can make this thing go faster?"

James shot me an angry look. "With no idea of what's coming around the next bend? Sure." James pushed a lever, and the cart jumped forward with blinding speed. "I thought you were the one who didn't want to die." The track bent into a sharp incline, and my stomach turned as my guts were pressed toward the floor.

"You're not getting away from me, Nick!" Rick's eyes were wide with anger as he held onto the front of his cart with an uncomfortable hunger.

"Even in death, you've still got the corniest script. Easy to see why you never won an Emmy." I thought back to his disappointed face at the only award show he had ever been invited to. It was one of the sweetest television moments I had ever witnessed.

Rick swore, and his cart picked up speed.

The hill abruptly ended, giving way to a flat section of tunnel. Our cart left the rails, and I was left floating. I did my best to hunker to the bottom, hoping my back wouldn't smack into the tunnel ceiling. The cart continued to rise, but the crunch of the rocks above never came. We smashed back onto the tracks, and I landed with a heavy thump on the cart's metal rim, knocking the wind out of me. I turned, wheezing, right as Rick crested the hill. With the lighter weight of a single cart, he shot off like a rocket straight into the tunnel ceiling. There was a horrible crunch, and then a burst of green flame as the cart exploded.

"Jesus, what the hell are these carts filled with?" I looked down at the floor below me, nervous at all the jostling we had been doing.

James shrugged. "There's a reason they go fast."

Lopsang put his hands in the air and let out a joyful whoop.

"This isn't an amusement park, Lopsang!"

"But you said earlier—"

"Fuck what I said!"

Lopsang laughed at me and James joined in. After a moment, I couldn't help but laugh as well. We continued to careen down the long tunnel, reducing our speed, knowing the track behind us had been blocked. The tunnel took another sharp turn and widened to reveal an orange-lit cavern. Heat blasted me from all sides, and my pores screamed out in agony.

I looked over the edge to see volcanic vents spewing lava. The whole floor of the cavern bubbled and boiled like a witch's cauldron. Even worse, the track converged ahead with two other rails. "What are the odds those are the same tracks?" I asked, already knowing the answer.

I looked behind us as we careened over the pool of lava. Paul was speeding along on the track to our left, and Callum slowed on our right. "Must go faster, James." The carts were gaining on us, and neither of their passengers looked happy. We needed to get to the other side of the cavern before they had the chance to get on either side of us.

"Look, Nick, all he wants to do is talk!" shouted Paul, speeding up.

"Right, and you deserved ten seasons for a show where you stole artifacts from local tribes, Paulie." His car shot past us, and I could see a grimace of anger on his face. Paul waited until he had crossed the point of convergence and slowed his cart down.

"Any ideas?" I asked.

James looked over the edge of the cart at the lava below. "Well, jumping is out."

"Great deduction, Sherlock, but we're in very real trouble here!"

Lopsang looked ahead, then behind. "Punch it?"

"What good is that going to do?"

Lopsang did some quick mental calculations. "You jump into Paul's cart, kick him out, we hop forward, put the brakes on in the last car, and stop Callum on the bridge."

"Are you kidding me?!"

"Any better ideas?" asked James. "Because he's starting to slow down."

I looked forward and saw that Mansen was edging closer with every second, as was Callum. "Ah, hell." I checked my wrist. The sand grains weren't falling at all. "Damnit, the tattoo agrees." I took a deep breath. "Punch it, James." I moved to all fours in my cart, preparing to leap at Mansen when we collided.

James pushed the lever to the floor, and our carts accelerated. I watched as Mansen's expression turned from vengeance to surprise. Time slowed down as our cart plowed into his. I sprung out, pushing off hard with my back legs as the sound of our collision filled the chamber. There was a sickening moment where I thought I had overshot. I braced for what was sure to be a horrible death under the wheels of Paul's cart. Ez's words: 'Death is always a surprise,' rang in my head.

But it wasn't quite my time.

I slammed into the front edge of the metal cart and was blinded by pain in my chest. *No time for broken ribs,* I told myself. Flipping around, I made a pitiful gesture of balling my fists up to fight. Mansen and I were uncomfortably close and both a little too stunned to come to blows. We locked eyes, and instinct took over. I kicked upward, catching him in the jaw with the heel of my boot, snapping his head up. "Really sorry to do this to you twice in the same week." For what it's worth, I really was.

Mansen turned his gaze to me, unfazed, and knocked me to the floor. I tried to struggle, but he quickly pinned me. Behind him, I could see James and Lopsang moving forward through the carts. Mansen put a forearm to my neck, pushing me hard toward the floor. "You're lucky he wants you alive, Ventner." He smashed my head into the metal.

Stars burst in my vision and pain shot through my head to the base of my spine. *Well, at least that's working again.* My thoughts were dull and sluggish as if they were being filtered through a veil. Mansen released the pressure on my neck. I was expecting a witty quip, but instead, his fist struck the side of my head. After the first impact, I didn't feel much of anything at all. There was dull, throbbing pain and the occasional run of adrenaline up my spine, but nothing more.

When I was on the verge of blacking out, he stopped. "Don't worry, Ventner, I'll bring you to him alive. But I wanted to have a little fun first." Mansen laughed maniacally.

"You never learned," I coughed up black blood, "to mind your surroundings."

A look of confusion crossed Mansen's face, but before he could turn around, Lopsang grabbed him and picked him up. There was a horrifying moment where Mansen held on to my collar and I was lifted off the floor. Lopsang took his free hand and brought it down on Mansen's forearm. The shock loosened his grip, and I fell to the floor. Lopsang hefted Mansen out of the cart and flung him out over the abyss. His body spun like a ragdoll. I heard him cursing the whole way down, right up until he landed in a volcanic vent. His voice died off in a fiery gurgle.

"Nice shot." I spit blood over the edge. "From range too."

"You owe me one."

I looked over his shoulder and could see Callum stuck in the middle of the bridge behind our locked cart. "Can't believe that worked."

"Let's find a place to stop this thing." One minecart chase had been enough to last me a lifetime.

James pushed the lever, and we flew into the darkness.

9

———

JUDGE AND JURY

When the mine cart finally came to a stop, we found ourselves in an abandoned rail station. Defunct ticket machines gathered dust in a corner, and fluorescent lights flickered to life above. I stepped out of the cart. Glass crunched with each footfall. "Now, this feels more like Midway," I commented. At my feet were the remnants of a poster reading: *Have you seen the King and Queen lately?* It depicted the temple we had seen earlier. A comical lightning bolt had been drawn above the battlements, illuminating two skeletal figures.

I pointed out the poster to Lopsang. "Look familiar?"

He paid no attention and paced around the platform, looking for exits. "I don't like this."

Truth be told, neither did I. There were only three exits. Two were rail tunnels, including where we had come in, and the third was a dark corridor with a green exit sign. *I guess they can't afford to keep the lights on everywhere.* I contemplated how they kept the lights on at all, but it made my head spin more than it already was, so I ignored it. On top of that, the air had grown oppressively hot. Even in my state of half-death, I was sweating.

James bent low to the ground, poking through the refuse. "This place hasn't been used in a long time," he said.

"Glad to see those tracking skills haven't gone to waste."

"Oh, screw off." James gave me the finger and continued to look around. When he had finished his cursory search, he stood up and faced me. "You planning on telling me what the hell is going on?"

I hadn't been expecting the direct line of questioning. "Well, we appear to be in an abandoned rail station," I started.

James cut me off. "I mean, your old friends who were so keen on turning us into worm food, asshole."

I chewed at the inside of my lip. One of the Mansen's might have been a coincidence, but both *and* Callum? Manchester clearly had a plan, and it involved far too many reunions for my liking. "Remember that job in Clearwater?"

"I remember driving your ass out of there in a hurry and getting shot at."

I smiled at the memory. 'Car chase' had been on my adventuring bucket list. It had been the first and the last time. "Well, Rick is the one who got killed by that psychopath I was hunting on the mountain."

"The one who pretended to be Bigfoot?"

"That's the one."

James whistled. "Deep cut for Manchester. Sounds like he's been doing his homework. What about the other brother? Out for revenge?"

Lopsang scoffed.

I glared at him. "Not exactly…"

James continued to stare me down, unwavering.

"I may have killed him about a week back in gladiatorial combat…"

"Been busy," noted James.

"In my defense, he was a werewolf at the time."

"And the other guy?"

"Might have gotten him killed too," I replied, distracted by a gust of wind from the tunnel we had come from. With it came the hot stink of brimstone.

"Jesus Christ, Nick. How many people did you murder to get here?!"

"Wasn't murder." I leaned down to listen to the tracks. They emitted a dull hum.

"Semantics!" yelled James.

"Shut up," I hissed. "We're about to have more company." The tracks hummed with the sound of approaching carts. "We need to get out of here right now."

"Dammit. I didn't even get to ask about Manchester."

"Well, if we don't get out of here quick, you can ask him yourself."

James balled his fists up. "Fine, dark and creepy tunnel it is."

We took off at a run. For a few paces, the light of the rail station illuminated the tunnel, but soon after, we plunged into complete blackness.

"Keep your hand on the wall," called James. "You don't want to know what kind of things lurk in the dark down here."

I had quite the imagination. With every stumble, I pictured something cold, dead, and sporting thousands of teeth ripping me to ribbons. My shoes clicked along the tile floor, their sound bouncing off the walls and echoing back. We turned a corner, and I lost all sense of space. If it weren't for my hand running along the smooth stone wall, I might have been lost forever.

"You in there, Nick?" called a woman from behind us.

My blood froze, but instinct took over. "No," I panted. "Wrong tunnel." More straightforward solutions had gotten us out of more dire circumstances.

"Pick up the pace. He's up ahead." A cacophony of footsteps joined our own echo in the tunnel, making it impossible to tell how many pursuers there were. For all I knew, it could have been an army.

I plumbed the depths of my energy and ran faster. With each step, the tunnel grew hotter. My nostrils burned with every labored breath, but I pushed forward. "That's never a good sign."

"What choice do we have?" spluttered James, trying not to inhale too deeply.

"None. Run faster," replied Lopsang.

"Thanks for the pep talk, coach!" I heard his footsteps passing me in the tunnel. A light bloomed ahead of us, dim and dark red. *Please don't be another lava pit.* Red light underground was rarely a good thing. As it grew stronger, and the tunnel hotter, I knew I was right. The tunnel ended abruptly, revealing a large cavern.

The light source came from a bubbling pit of lava that extended as far as the eye could see. A narrow stone bridge extended some distance over the pool, ending in a wider platform decorated with carved stone plinths. Each bore a set of rusty chains, connected to a ring about halfway up. Along the chamber's sides, staircases led to hollowed-out alcoves with a good view of the platform below.

The three of us skidded to a halt as we approached the cliff edge. "Well, this is so much worse than I thought," I muttered.

"Yeah, I think we might be in trouble," said James. Behind us, three hooded figures emerged from the tunnel, brandishing swords. I turned to run toward the staircase, anything to get us away from what I now assumed was a sacrificial platform. More figures in hoods came rushing down the stairs toward us. I stopped and reluctantly backed toward the platform.

"Tell me you've got a plan, Nick," whispered Lopsang.

"I'm working on it." I looked at my wrist. Sand grains were falling at a quick clip. Apparently, whatever plan I was working out wasn't quite good enough.

The three figures from the tunnel advanced but only enough to block our escape. Recesses in the cavern walls opened, and more hooded figures entered the room. Before we knew it, we were surrounded. None of them spoke a word, but each pointed a weapon at us, cutting off the notion of escape.

"Been waiting a long time for this, Nick," said one of the hooded figures, tightening their grip on a sword.

"You're not the first one who's said that to me today," I commented, trying to place the voice.

"More friends of yours?" asked James.

"Let's hope not."

"Well, well, well, look who finally decided to show up," a cold voice called from the crowd.

I would have recognized him anywhere. "Evening, Harvey. So nice to see you again."

Manchester stepped through the group, sporting his wide-brimmed black hat. In the dim light of the lava, his scarred face looked somehow worse than before. "There are a lot of people who have been waiting for this moment, Nick. Seems that you've got quite a lot of friends down here." He laughed and the crowd joined in.

"Oh good, I love reunions."

Manchester's lip curled in a sneer. "Something tells me you aren't going to enjoy this one. Why don't you introduce yourselves?"

One by one, the figures surrounding us removed the dark hoods obscuring their faces. Whatever I had been expecting, the reality was worse. As each member of the crowd unmasked themselves, a deep sense of shame grew within me. I've made many mistakes in my life, but before that moment, I had never truly been accountable for them.

"Good to see you again, Nick," said a woman bearing claw marks that ran across the better portion of her face and chest. I immediately recognized her as one of my first apprentices. Our encounter with a water demon in Singapore had been quick and bloody, and while I managed to kill the creature, she didn't make it.

The front row was almost entirely apprentices, but there were many others. Somehow, Manchester had even recruited his own team from the mountain a year prior. The faces of the mercenaries we had fought with against the yeti were almost unrecognizable. I thought back to the mauling the yeti had given them. The attack hadn't been my fault, but there was no getting around the fact that I had escaped relatively unharmed.

More surprising were the stony faces of Rick and Paul Mansen. It appeared that no matter how hard I tried, I couldn't get rid of them. Rick's skin looked like a used charcoal briquette, but he was still upright. Paul stood bent and crooked with jagged bits of burnt bone poking out from his charred skin. Considering he had been blown up and run over, he looked well. "You two are looking healthy." I gave a small salute. "Sorry about the lava pit, Paulie."

Paul glared at me. "Keep talking. It's not going to save you this time." His voice was hoarse and gravelly; nothing like it had been in life.

"His time is coming, Paul." Manchester rubbed his own burnt skin, producing flakes of ash. "Recognize anyone else?" he asked me.

Both James and Lopsang looked at me sideways. I could feel their silent judgment.

"I have to say, as far as surprise parties go," I looked around the room, "not my ideal guest list." The various states of gruesome deformity represented by my past colleagues and professional enemies were sobering.

"It took some time to track them down, I'll admit." Manchester twiddled his fingers in excitement. "But time flies when you're having fun."

"I'm touched. And here I thought you were some run of the mill psychopath." To be fair, it was more effort than anyone had gone through in my entire life, and in some sick twisted way, I felt validated. "You really know how to make a guy feel special."

Manchester's eyes were daggers. It was clear we didn't have long before things were going to get uncomfortably violent.

James broke his silence. "So why bring *us* down here too?"

Manchester looked surprised, pausing to think before answering the question. "Because he would have gotten in the way." He made a flittering gesture to Lopsang. "His blind loyalty has already gotten Nick out of more than a few binds that should have left him six feet under."

"Better than working for someone like you," Lopsang pointed out.

"Ah, yes, there it is." Manchester smiled dramatically. "Well, I think I've had about enough of our little chat, and there are some who are anxious to get on with the next part." His eyes glittered with malice.

"Let's see, torture racks," I gestured to the platform behind me, "no punchbowl, and a whole lot of swords…we're not going to sit around and catch up, are we?"

Manchester chuckled. "We'll see if your sense of humor stays intact after a little time before the fire." There was a murmur of anticipation from the crowd.

"I always put on my best face for you, Harvey." Then, knowing I was already in as deep as I could go, I dug another foot down. "Wish I could say the same for you."

Manchester's cheek twitched in irritation. "String them up. Leave the apprentice with me."

10

———

EXECUTIONER

Before I had time to complain about the cliché, we were strung up on a dais at the end of a stone walkway over a lake of bubbling lava. Lopsang and I were side-by-side, but Manchester kept James among the other hooded figures. I hoped to hell he wasn't swapping stories with my other apprentices. Over the years, I had lost quite a few of them. I wasn't exactly blameless. There was a particularly burned man that I suspected might have been the 'virgin' I had traded to a group of natives for a treasure map. The plan had always been to rescue him before things got out of hand, but as it turns out, the chief had been more than a little volcano-happy and tossed him in before I had a chance to intervene.

"Any chance you can poof your way out of these ropes?" I asked Lopsang.

He grunted in annoyance. "Do you think I would have let us get tied up if my powers were working?"

"It's happened before," I offered, remembering the cult that had nearly executed us in the mountains.

"Not this time." Lopsang struggled with his ropes. "I may not be dying like you, but it appears this land stripped me of something else."

"Perfect." I thought through all the scenarios in my head and couldn't see one with a positive outcome. Manchester had us strung up, right where he wanted us. The worst part was his cocky swagger towards all his best-laid plans coming to fruition. I wished to hell I had been a little smarter and planned a trick of my own.

"How many of these people are you responsible for killing?" asked Lopsang, his tone quiet and firm.

My head was still spinning from seeing them all. Until that point, I lived my life on the simple principle of emotional and moral avoidance for my misdeeds. Being confronted by the undead representations of my past had never been part of the plan. "Look, Lopsang, I wasn't always the upstanding moral citizen who stands before you today."

He scoffed. "So, all of them."

"This is a dangerous line of work. They knew what they were signing up for." Most of them had known. Some wanted to see the world and knew the Army wasn't the right lens to view it through. Might have honestly been safer.

"One of these days you're going to have to reckon with what you've done."

"Oh, don't worry, I think that time is coming." Manchester had broken off from the group and was approaching with James, his arms swinging casually at his sides.

"Why is James—" started Lopsang.

"Unbound?" asked Manchester, his tone condescending as ever. "I would think it was obvious by now." James didn't make eye contact, but I could read the anger on his face a mile away.

"Ah hell, you talked to them, didn't you?" I wasn't sure what the apprentices would have to say about me, but I knew it wasn't going to be good.

"Worried they might not be willing to give you a reference?" Manchester knew he had won. A wide grin was plastered on his ruined face as his cold eyes cut into mine.

"You're a real sick son of a bitch, you know that?"

Manchester gave a little curtsey, taking it as a compliment.

"You really think you're in a position to judge?" James's voice was low and conflicted. He raised his eyes to look at me. "Do you see how many lives have been lost because of your carelessness?"

He might as well have stabbed me. A cold, wrenching pain took root in my stomach. Manchester I could handle—he was an asshole—but coming from James, it hurt. I looked to the hooded figures standing at the edge of the lake of fire. Hopelessness overtook me like a tsunami. One of the two allies I had in the world was now standing on the wrong side of the dividing line, and I didn't have a way to bring him back.

"It's the same reason I ended up down here, Nick!" yelled James.

Manchester watched the conflict play out with delight in his eyes. "It appears one can only lie for so long before it all catches up with him." Somehow, beneath the charred, burnt, and broken skin, his eyes still sparkled.

I looked at James. After all that we had been through going to save him, he was the reason we weren't going to get back. No, that wasn't right; I was going to be the reason we weren't going to return. For once, I wished I was back in the damned jungle, and that any moment I'd wake up in a cold sweat, huddled under a tarp. The scene was too vivid for a dream. "What do you want me to say?" I asked. "I came back for you, didn't I?"

"What about them, Nick? There have to be at least twenty people on the other side of that bridge you didn't come back for."

"Not all of those were my—"

"It doesn't matter! It's not the number." James paced back and forth. "Christ, you don't get it."

Despite the lake of hot lava below and impending death a few feet away, I would have taken a stiff drink over someone cutting my bonds. All the guilt and rage that I kept deep down was creeping up in my throat, choking me. "Of course, I do." The words came out leaden and foreign as if someone else had spoken them. *Oh god, too long without a drink, and the truth is coming out.* "You never forget those things, James." My head sunk low to my chest. It seemed that without my numbing companion, there was no more running from it. Memories rolled through in waves.

I saw Rick Mansen coughing and choking on his own blood in

the frozen plains at the top of Clearwater Mountain. He was an idiot, but no one deserved to go like that. I saw Lucas, my first apprentice, staggering toward me, his back full of blow darts because I had asked him to scout ahead. I remembered the numerous heartless phone calls I had made to significant others and parents, letting them know that their loved one's 'study abroad' program had taken a deadly turn.

After every phone call, I would drain a bottle by myself in the apartment until I stopped remembering everything except how to piss and sleep. Then, the next day, I would wake up to a message from another eager, young upstart who had discovered the mysteries beyond common sense and wanted to join me on my adventures. It was the same reason I hadn't wanted James to follow me into the mountains in the first place.

"My, my, are those tears?" Manchester's voice carried a horrible mocking ring to it. "I wasn't sure you were capable of feeling."

James's resolve broke, but not for long. "Can't be real." He spat at my feet. "It's a ploy to get out of the ropes."

On most days, he would have been right. "James, I'm sorry," was all I could say. "Do what you're going to do." Surrounded by my demons, I didn't care anymore. One way or another, I wanted them out of my head. Whether that was through drink or death wasn't a pressing concern.

"I didn't think you would break so easily." The bravado went out of Manchester's speech. "I must admit, I'm a little disappointed."

All my witty lines and pithy quips were miles away. I could do nothing but stare and try to hold back the shame burning behind my eyes.

"Well, I can't say this isn't what I wanted." Manchester strolled over, taking a good, long look at me. "I had thought lowering you slowly over the edge and watching you burn to death would be fun. Even bought a cage for it." There was a creaking sound as a metal structure was raised from beneath us on a winch. "I do know how much you love those old adventure movies."

Numbness prickled through me. My face held slack, unable to process anything.

"But, given the turn this has taken," Manchester looked at the cage, longingly, "I think I've got a more poetic end in mind." He opened his coat and retrieved a long knife. The blade sparkled in the dim light reflected in his eyes. "Oh, how I want to take this and flay that guilty frown right off your face." There was a hunger in the statement that bordered on cannibalistic appetite. "But no, I think we should give the opportunity to the person who would hurt you the most." He flipped the blade so that the handle was towards James. "What do you think? Up for the job?"

James looked from me to the knife, his limbs numb with apprehension and disbelief. *He's considering it.* Even in my wildest nightmares, I had never pictured my life ending by James's hand. There were plenty of others who would slit my throat for less, but he was the one person I trusted no matter what.

"Don't do it, James. You'll never outrun this," said Lopsang. "I won't let you."

It was good to know I hadn't lost all my friends.

James snatched the knife from Manchester's hand and pointed it at me.

"And to think I was happy to see you," I said.

Manchester laughed and put a hand on James's back. "Make it slow. I want to enjoy this."

James's eyes looked directly into mine as he approached. Manchester shadowed him every step of the way. I could see the desire to kill behind those eyes. He had made up his mind, and there wasn't anything anyone could do to change it. It seemed that after all my years of running, the end was finally approaching. In a way, it was fitting.

"I forgive you." There was nothing else for me to say. If I had been in James's position, I might have done the same thing.

James raised the knife, ready to strike, and then whispered: "Likewise."

I had a second to watch confusion flicker across Manchester's face before James spun around in one fluid motion and stabbed him in the side of the head. "Oh Christ, not again," he said, staggering and reaching to pull the blade out. "You really are a little shit."

Before he had a chance, James yanked the knife back with a sickening squelch and kicked Manchester in the chest, sending him toppling over the edge and screaming toward the pit of lava below.

It all happened so quickly that I didn't have time to process. James cut the ropes binding my hands. "You killed him," I managed, stunned.

"Oh, I wouldn't be so sure about that. He's come back once, let's not risk it by waiting around."

"But you were going to kill me." None of it made sense.

"Don't be an idiot, Nick. He pushed me through a magical portal at gunpoint, remember?"

"Vaguely." I fell to my knees as the rope broke. Everything in my body was heavy and sluggish. I looked at the hourglass on my wrist and found the grains were still falling much faster than I would have liked.

James moved and worked at the ropes binding Lopsang. There was a confused murmur spreading from the hooded figures on the other side of the pit. Lopsang landed on his feet and clapped a hand to James's back. "Well done," he said. "You even had me going for a second."

James approached me and lifted me to my feet. "Make no mistake, Nick, I thought about it. But you came back for me, which means you do, somewhere deep down, possess the capacity for change. Don't make me regret this." He put a firm hand on my shoulder, nearly knocking me over, and smiled.

I found my footing as the hooded figures approached. "What about them?" I asked, still dazed.

"Well, you've already killed them once."

"Some of them twice," I corrected.

"Think we can do it again?"

11

———

APPRENTICE ROYALE

What happened next can only be described as a literal and existential blood bath. The path between us and the hooded figures was thin, meaning they could only come at us two at a time. James was the only one with a weapon, and the horde charging at us brandished swords, spears, and a couple of sharp implements I wasn't familiar with.

The first two to reach us were some of my earliest apprentices. Harold had been the virgin I threw into the volcano, and Paula, well, she had learned the hard way not to kiss a crocodile man. They made a macabre pair as they advanced. James brandished the knife, trying to keep them at bay as both advanced wielding rusty swords. I had never been great with edged weapons, but I have a simple rule: Don't bring fists to a sword fight. My odds of survival would get infinitely better if I could get my hand on a weapon of any kind.

"Hello, boss," slurred Paula, her jaw in complete ruins, dripping black ooze onto the ground below.

"You're looking quite well, Paula." I backed away. "Aside from this whole thing." I made a sweeping gesture toward my own jaw.

Her face contorted into what might have been a scowl.

200

"And you, Harold. Sorry about the who—"

"Daniel. My name is and always has been Daniel!" He charged at me just as the volcano below us rumbled, spitting gobs of lava into the air. Daniel flinched, and it was the split-second distraction I needed. Thankfully, he had never been great at self-defense. I hadn't had much time to train him after all.

While he was busy cowering at the lava, I grabbed his wrist, my fingers slipping over the mix of charred flesh and slimy muscle beneath. He yelped and dropped the sword. I caught it with my free hand. "Really sorry to do this to you again, Ha—" I paused. *James said you had the capacity for change.* "Daniel." I tossed him over the edge and tried my best to ignore the string of curses he uttered as he fell gurgling to his death for a second time.

Paula was turning to face me when James swept her legs out from under her. I put a foot on the blade of her sword as she slipped off the edge of the platform. Lopsang scrambled to pick the weapon up, and the three of us turned to face the rest of the horde. It seemed that many had stayed back, waiting to see how the others would fair. With how quickly we had dispatched them, most dropped their weapons and ran.

While those that remained looked nervous, there was one who was steadfast. Callum's legs did not shake, and his gaze did not waver. Like those we had taken on the boat with us on our fateful river trip, he held a metal spear. There was hatred in his eyes, plain and simple. "Come on then, Nick!" he yelled. "You and I have a score to settle!" He flipped the spear in one hand, advancing slowly.

I had never been a fan of one-on-one combat. It was always touted as a matter of respect, which never really fit in when lives were on the line.

"What's the plan, Nick?" asked James.

I looked to see who had stayed aside from Callum. Rick Mansen had turned to flee, but his brother remained, irritated and badly burned. Beside him were a mercenary named Styg who had been killed by the yeti, a few of Manchester's ill-fated crew, and two apprentices that I had a shockingly poor memory of. "Well, looks like Callum has his heart set on me. Think you can take care of the rest?"

"I count six others," said Lopsang.

"Great, five for me, one for you," joked James.

"Cocky little bastard, aren't you?" It was good to see James having some of his humor back.

"Only when I'm cleaning up your mistakes."

Together, the three of us advanced. Callum stepped off to one side of the cave and waved away the others. They begrudgingly obliged. It never ceases to amaze me when people follow the rules in combat. "Fair is fair," I muttered. We stepped off the bridge, and I turned to face him. "It doesn't have to go like this," I offered. "We could try to sneak you out too." We were already pressing our luck trying to get one dead man back into the Land of the Living. I didn't see the harm in one more.

"I thought of you as a friend." Callum's eyes brimmed with angry tears. "You watched me die, Nick!"

Weariness overtook me in a wave. From behind, I heard clashing swords. Lopsang and James had wasted no time in getting started. "I'm sorry, Callum." I meant it. "There was nothing I could have done."

"You knew that snake was going to be there. The only reason it attacked us in the first place was because of that cursed book of yours." Callum jabbed forward with his spear, testing my defenses. I parried it effortlessly and sidestepped. Every part of me wanted to let him go peacefully, but he was not making it easy.

"You've been deceived. Manchester was the one who set the Yacumama on us."

Callum laughed mirthlessly. "Funny, he said you might try to spin a story like that." He jabbed again, this time lower. The tip of the spear caught the leg of my pants before I was able to get out of the way, tearing the fabric. There was a loud rumble, and the earth shook beneath our feet. A gob of molten lava shot up from the pit below and landed ten feet away, cooling quickly from red to black.

"Something tells me we don't have long to talk, one way or another. It doesn't have to go this way."

"Better we finish this quick then." Callum readied himself for another attack.

"Look, I've already tossed two people in a lava pit today, and there's no reason for a third."

Callum advanced rapidly with a series of jabs aimed at my chest. I parried them, sidestepped, and swung my sword towards his arm. It caught him on the wrist, cutting deeply and sending a spurt of black blood into the air. He looked at his hand and snarled. "I had a family, Nick. I was going to see them again!" He rushed forward, brushing my sword aside with his spear and checking me with his shoulder.

We fell to the ground, and I dropped my weapon. I tried to speak, but the weight of him on my chest was too much. He raised the spear for a killing blow, but the cavern shook violently in the same instant. The sound of cracking stone filled the chamber as stalactites dislodged above. The ground shook with impacts as the rock bombs fell, exploding around us, and rocky debris shot out in all directions.

There was a heavy thump as rubble struck Callum's back and he fell off me. Seizing the opportunity, I rolled away, grabbed my weapon, and ran for cover. My sudden movement caught Styg's eye. She spotted me and broke into a run. A stone column fell, crushing her instantly and spraying the surrounding ground with blood.

I froze, stunned and horrified. We were running out of time.

"Oh no, you're not running away," came Callum's voice from behind me.

I spun around, holding my sword out defensively.

Callum had taken on an entirely new look. Blood streaked down half of his face from where the rock debris had struck his head. He looked insane, like something out of a horror movie. "We've got unfinished business." He let out a maniacal laugh to top off the image.

Meanwhile, a set of dismembered hooded figures crawled toward the tunnel. I turned to Lopsang and James, who both shrugged. "We held up our end of the bargain."

I scoffed. "He's a lot spritelier than he looks."

Callum took to a stumbling run, leaving a swath of blood behind him.

I looked into his eyes and saw that rage had consumed him, but I still didn't want to kill him again. I wasn't exactly sure what would happen. Paul and Rick had gotten lucky coming back a second time, but the memory of the grey plains still haunted me. If there was a chance he would end up there, I wanted to avoid it.

I pointed my sword at Callum. "Please, don't make me do this."

Callum renewed his grip on his spear and leaned into the charge. Behind him, a gout of lava erupted, sending a small wave over the rock platform. The red light silhouetted him as he approached. "You're all going to pay!" he shouted.

"Alright, I warned you." With what little speed I still possessed, I met Callum as he charged. He tried to stab me again with the same move as before. I parried it and swung toward his head. There was a horrible, tearing sensation as my blade caught in the rotting fibers of his neck and then came free. Blood spattered the tunnel wall, and Callum looked surprised as his head toppled to the floor.

His body continued to move, swinging wildly with the spear. I sidestepped it. "Oh, you son of a bitch," he growled. "Real cute." His body lunged with the spear, striking one of the tunnel walls and toppling over.

"Good enough?" I asked James and Lopsang.

They shrugged in agreement.

"Alright, let's get the hell out of here." I started to walk away and then looked at Callum's head lopsided from the floor. "Good luck finding a seamstress," I added and ran down the tunnel.

12

THE GREAT ESCAPE

The cavern rumbled behind us. Scorching air singed my nostrils with each struggling breath. Still, I held my hand to the tunnel wall until we emerged back into the rail station we had entered from. Our carts were sitting in the loading station, with three more from our pursuers abandoned behind them. Without hesitation, the three of us jumped in the carts, and James pushed the accelerator to full.

We shot out of the station as a river of lava poured from the mouth of the tunnel. I winced at the thought of Callum being burned alive, but I had given him every opportunity to choose a different path. The cart rattled and jostled as we headed up the tracks. I slumped down with both relief and extreme weariness; nothing sounded better than a cold drink and a warm bed. Eerie green light bloomed above us as we exited the darkened tunnels and rocketed into the 'fresh' air.

We were almost there; I could feel it. Elation should have been sweeping over me, but something was wrong. We were out of the tunnels, but the light in the sky was growing darker by the second. I propped myself up on the edge of the cart, trying to get a look at

205

the scenery, but it was distant and fuzzy. "What the—" The words sloughed out of me, dying before I could finish them.

"Nick?" called Lopsang's voice from somewhere distant. The world took on a muted, underwater presence, everything passing by at a snail's pace. "Are you alright?"

I lifted my arm, and dread slid over me like a cold blanket. The top half of the hourglass was nearly empty. It appeared the twenty-four hours had been an estimate that didn't anticipate life-threatening combat and extreme physical exertion. I turned the tattoo towards Lopsang. His face went pale.

"James, get us back on the main tracks as fast as you can. We need to get him out of here."

I remember snippets of images as we passed back through the city. Buildings were nothing more than colorful blurs interspersed with darkness. When the light grew dimmest, I could hear the hollow echo of the grey plains and feel the slimy mud caking around my feet. I don't know how it happened, but the next thing I knew, I was on my feet and we were walking back up the hill towards the entrance we had come through.

"We were carrying you; that's how it happened," said Lopsang, interrupting.

Nick took a sip of what Jimmy had assured him would be the last drink of the night. "Really?" he slurred. "I definitely remember being on my own two feet."

Lopsang laughed and shook his head. "You would remember it that way because it makes you look better. I've listened to you take liberties with our stories on more than one occasion."

Albert goggled at me through boozy eyes from across the table. It was unclear if he was processing the argument intently or if he had simply passed out while sitting up again. "He's ri—" he started to say, but his words wilted into incoherent mumbling as his head slumped down to his chest.

"Wake up, Albert." Marcus belched, the stench rank enough to raise a dead man.

"Whar?" muttered Albert.

Hillbilly smelling salts, thought Nick.

"They're almost to the end of the story, and Nick's bullshitting again. Gotta keep him honest."

Albert nodded, wiped at his eyes with beer-soaked hands, and propped himself up on the table.

Satisfied, Marcus returned to Nick and Lopsang. "So, you were carrying Nick?"

"If anything, they were supporting me slightly."

Lopsang raised an eyebrow. "Story has changed from walking on your own two feet."

"Fine, whatever makes you happy." Nick waved a hand.

Lopsang finished his beer and set the glass down with a few bills underneath it. "If you don't mind, I'm going to step outside for this last part." There was a firmness in his voice that made for no argument.

"Yeah, alright, see you out there," replied Nick, trying to keep himself steady. "It'll only be a moment, and then we can split the cab."

Lopsang nodded and clapped him on the shoulder. "Have a nice evening." He waved to Albert, Marcus, and Jimmy in turn.

"Be safe out there. Watch out for snipes," grumbled Albert.

"I will." Lopsang walked out through the double doors, leaving a cold whistle of wind in his wake. It seemed appropriate.

"So, they were carrying me back to the Land of the Living."

"Like a wee babe," added Albert.

"I'm never telling you a story again…"

———

I DON'T REMEMBER MUCH about the journey back, but lucidity washed over me in waves as we came closer to the exit. Regretfully, I looked down at my hand and saw that the grey bubbling mass had spread up my wrist. The world bumped and turned as Lopsang carried me. After an eternity, I could see the cave entrance that marked our way back to the Land of the Living.

"We made it," I slurred. "Look, James, that's where the portal is!" I hopped down from Lopsang's shoulders, nearly tumbling off the mountainside.

"Easy, Nick, we're not through this just yet." Lopsang watched the cave warily.

"Well then, let's get moving." The world had regained some clarity, and I almost felt alive. My heart skipped a beat and thudded heavily in my chest, reminding me otherwise. "I don't think I've got much time left." Dragging one foot after the other, I hobbled my way toward the cave entrance. Inside, the portal shimmered, casting glowing green light on the stone walls.

Despite the urgency, Lopsang slowed down and eyed the portal suspiciously.

"What is it?" James squinted, looking for whatever Lopsang was seeing.

"I think we might be in trouble." Dismay crept into Lopsang's voice.

As we drew closer to the portal, a massive figure moved in the shadows. It's hulking, muscular form shook the surrounding environment with each step. The portal light reflected off yellow eyes, and the creature let out a bone-shaking growl. Its fur bristled as it drew nearer, and the sharp edge of a weapon glinted in the darkness.

"What the hell is that?" James backed away.

"Oh, just another god we've pissed off." I patted my sides, hoping to hell that I had kept one of the weapons from our brawl. All I found were the ragged, tattered edges of my shirt, fluttering in the otherworldly breeze. Chills racked my spine, nearly causing me to fall over. Adrenaline pumped through my veins, keeping my vision steady. Still, it was clear I didn't have much time left.

I turned to Lopsang. "Don't suppose you brought any of those swords?"

Lopsang shook his head. "I was too busy carrying you."

Xolotl marched forward, letting the portal's green light spill over him. The skulls around his neck glowed red hot as he growled again. Small stones fell from the cavern ceiling and shattered.

"You really don't work well with deities, do you?" James balled up his fists, preparing to fight.

I couldn't help but laugh at the gesture. "What are you going to do, go ten rounds with a god? Go on ahead, I'll sit here and watch. Better we get it done before we bother trying to bring you back from the dead."

James went to retort, but Lopsang held out a hand and whispered. "He may not know we lied yet."

"I don't think this is going to work—"

"We have returned from meeting with your king!" boomed Lopsang, his voice taking on a deep baritone.

"Is that so?" asked Xolotl, spinning his bladed staff idly. "I suppose I should be thanking you then. Going to the King of the Dead on my behalf?" A wide smile spread across his face, but there was no friendliness in it.

He knows, I thought.

"You know, the funny thing about that. I've just had a visit from a colleague of sorts." Xolotl's breath was heavy and filled the room. "He said that you're a bunch of con men trying to cheat death."

I regretted our premature celebration.

Lopsang held out his hand and produced the ball of light. "Have you forgotten?"

"Your silly little parlor trick?" he asked. "No, and I'm still angry about it if I'm being honest." He stamped a foot on the ground and the room shook. "I'm not one for tricks."

Lopsang was silent.

"Lucky for you, I've got someone interested in having a meeting with you after all. Why don't you follow me?" He extended a hand towards the portal.

I took a woozy look back at the Land of the Dead, wondering if we could make a run for it.

"Come on, Ventner, you don't have much time left." Xolotl let out a harsh chuckle. "Lucky for you, your friend wanted to meet on the other side. Said he needed some quality time."

I looked at Lopsang and James. Neither said anything. "Well, it beats dying here." Reluctantly, I marched forward.

Xolotl eyed me carefully as I approached the portal. "You try and run for it on the other side, and I'll see that neither of them makes it back."

"I think I've done enough running for one day." I stepped through the portal, and a cold snap of electricity shot through my body. In an instant, I fell forward into the Land of the Living, gasping for breath. My heart guttered back to life like an old sedan and pumped blood desperately to my recently decayed limbs. Tingling life spread from my core to the edges of my body. The sensation was beautiful, like I was being drawn to life by some divine artist.

Two loud thuds came from behind me as James and Lopsang skidded through the portal. James fell to his knees and looked down at his torn parka with wide eyes. Cautiously, he pulled the zipper down and looked at the torn shirt beneath. A scar ran across his stomach, but that was all. Against all odds, he was alive.

A smile spread across my face. We had done it. The kid was alive.

Lopsang came through next, landing on his feet and turning immediately toward the way out. He looked down at me, no doubt noticing the wetness around my eyes. "No time for celebration, Nick. Remember?" He put a hand around James's back and hoisted him to a stand.

I pushed myself up, my sense of danger mounting within me once more. "Right, let's get moving before big, dumb, and ugly gets—"

A low, ragged remnant of a laugh cut me off.

Oh, come on.

Manchester emerged from behind a pillar, nothing more than a charcoal pile held together by some demonic intervention. Despite his condition, he still maintained the same, condescending, confident stride. "You know, I think dying gets easier every time I do it." He laughed again, and the horrible sound of it filled the room. "Don't worry, you'll get the hang of it soon enough."

13

MAN BITES DOG

It didn't take long for me to realize how well and truly fucked we were. The three of us backed away from the advancing dead man. Even as we did, Xolotl came through the portal, landing on the stone with a crash. I looked toward the exit. It wasn't far, but even with my newfound vitality, I wasn't going to outrun a god.

"Nick," whispered James.

"Before you ask, no, I don't have a plan."

"What else is new?" He pointed a finger toward the stone circle that contained the portal we had come through. The light had gone out, but in its absence, I could see a pile of weapons and armor next to it.

The memory of the man who had been cut in two by Xolotl came back to me. "Only the righteous get to keep their weapons when they move on." It made perfect sense.

"What are you babbling about?" asked Manchester. "I was hoping for a bit of begging and pleading, but this religious drivel is nothing short of—"

I didn't let him finish. Before he could say anything more, I was scrambling toward the pile of weapons. Xolotl had barely moved past them; I hoped that I could sneak by with the element of surprise. Whatever idiocy had planted that idea in my brain was quickly exposed to the cold, harsh light of reality. Xolotl grimaced and swiped at me with a thick paw.

Dropping to both knees, I tried to slide beneath his attack. The action might have looked cool in theory, but in reality, all I got were bruised knees and bloody shins. Seconds before Xolotl's arm came down, there was a blinding flash of light, followed by colorful smoke erupting out of nowhere. I waited for the pain of claws raking across my flesh, but it never came.

The thick smoke took a few seconds to clear. A shadow moved through it, running right for me. I rolled over, ready to fight just as James skidded to a halt. "Lopsang's doing his thing," he said, breathlessly. James dropped to his knees and began searching for a weapon that wasn't bent, broken, or otherwise unusable.

"God, I love it when he does his thing." I followed James's lead and rummaged through the pile, looking for anything usable. The first item that caught my eye was a World War II-era rifle with a bayonet at the end. I turned in time to see Manchester running towards us. He held a bloody dagger in one hand, and while I couldn't be sure, it looked an awful lot like the one James had plunged into his head an hour earlier. "No time to be picky, James, choose something. I don't know if we're going to be able to bring you back again."

"Don't rush me," he hissed. The clank of metal against metal was audible as he dove deeper into the pile.

I racked the rifle, pointed it straight at Manchester, and pulled the trigger. The shot rang out through the temple, louder than I anticipated, and struck Manchester in the shoulder. Bits of ash and charred flesh flew off from where it had hit, but he continued forward unfazed. I was stunned that the weapon had fired at all.

With each step Manchester took, ashes fell to the ground, revealing the blackened skeleton beneath. Ordinarily, he would have wasted away to nothing, but the ashes rose back to his body, reforming only to be torn apart again. *Now, if that isn't some black magic bullshit...* I pulled the trigger again, but nothing happened. *Bolt action, idiot,* was all I could think before he was on me.

Manchester charged, brandishing his blade. I tried to stab him with the bayonet, but he side-stepped me and struck. White-hot pain lit up my right leg as the knife sunk in, making it all the way to the bone. Manchester tried to maintain his balance, but with his weapon stuck, he stumbled. I tried to pull the knife from my leg, but the pain was too much. My fingers shook, and waves of nausea crashed over me.

Manchester regained his balance but stopped short as another gunshot rang out. Black ash and bone exploded outward as his right arm completely disintegrated. He howled in frustration and ran toward James, who was tossing aside the antique musket he had fired.

The kid wasted all his time to pick that hunk of junk?

Before James could pick up another weapon, Manchester hit him with more force than any mortal could have possessed. The kid flew backward into the pile of weapons with a mighty crash. It was damn near a miracle that none of the rusty blades pierced him along the way.

I tried to stand, but my leg buckled. Blood leaked steadily from the wound as Manchester returned his attention to me. In the background, I watched as Lopsang danced circles around Xolotl, deftly dodging the creature's angry swipes and blinding him with light. *At least one of us is winning the fight.* I knew Manchester would be no match for Lopsang, but that was only if we could survive long enough.

As if answering my thoughts, Manchester swung a fist and connected with my jaw, sending me spinning to the floor. The pain gave way to a dull throbbing sensation as adrenaline finally kicked in. *If we get out of this, I'm really going to need to see a doctor.* A fog came over my vision. I had almost risen to my knees when a melted boot crashed into my ribs, knocking the wind from me.

"You know, they say being in the Land of the Dead dulls your senses." Manchester landed another kick. "So, in a way, I'm glad you escaped our little reunion down there."

I tried to wheeze a response, but Mansen's kicks continued, furious and unabated. As the punishment continued, I lost all sense of everything. The world was a continuous throb of dull pain, punctuated by the harsh tones of Manchester's cocksure monologue.

"You know, in life, I merely thought of you as a nuisance. A hunter that couldn't be bothered with the finer things and would never truly reach his potential." Manchester flipped me onto my back so that I was looking directly at his scarred face. "Now I see you for what you truly are." He reached down and tore the knife from my leg, sending fresh agony from the wound.

"What's that?" I asked, spitting up gobs of blood with every word. "Better than you?"

Manchester snorted. "No, a worthless drunk who's gotten incredibly lucky. I've killed plenty of my comrades, but at least it was for a purpose. You, on the other hand, have no end game other than filling those glass bottles you're so content to throw your life into."

It was hard to argue with him. He was right. Even at that moment, I was dreaming of a scenario where I waltzed out of the temple and into a tropical bar. "You've got me there."

"What, no humor left?" he asked, towering over me. There was a crash, and the thunder of falling stone as either Lopsang or Xolotl was thrown into one of the temple's walls. "I always pictured you trying desperately to have the last laugh."

"Oh, you can be sure I will." It is written out in my will that I will be buried with both middle fingers outstretched toward the sky. One final 'screw off' to the god that won't accept me. Out of the corner of my eye, I watched James slowly rise to a stand. "But this isn't that end."

"I'm quite sure it is." Manchester advanced on me with the blade.

"After all that, you underestimated the kid again. Learn from your mistakes, you pathetic old fool."

There was a soft thunk, and a spear stuck out of Manchester's left eye socket. Bits of burnt skull and gristle rained down on me. "James, you better get ready to hit him again, that's not going to finish the job."

Manchester stood awkwardly with the spear still poking from his eye. He jerked forward, pulled the weapon out of his head, and turned to face James. "Do you have any idea how much that stings?" he asked and charged, knocking the spear aside and tackling James to the ground.

I scrambled to my feet, grabbing the knife Manchester had dropped, and plunging it into his spine. If nothing else, it was going to hurt like hell. Manchester grunted and put his bony hands around James's throat. He squeezed tight. I removed the knife and brought it down again to no avail.

James choked and spluttered, grabbing for Manchester's hands but unable to move him.

"I may not have much left in me, Nick," breathed Manchester. "But I'll be damned if I'm going to give you a happy ending." He pressed harder, and James's eyes bulged.

"Not again, you son of a bitch!" I yelled.

"Sorry, old frie—"

Green lightning shot around the room, illuminating the entire temple in bright, static light. A bolt arched out and struck Manchester, sending him spinning backward into a temple wall. Thunder followed swiftly on its heels, shaking me to my core and knocking me onto my back. I didn't take time to look and see the source and instead crawled to James.

To my surprise, he was breathing. Black smoke rose from the tips of his singed hair as he coughed and spluttered, rising quickly to his feet. "What in the holy hell was that?" he asked.

I looked down at my own hands, curious and hopeful. Had I somehow inherited godlike powers from my time among the dead?

"So, these are the ones that have been causing so much trouble," rumbled a deep voice from the center of the cavern.

I looked up to see a tall skeletal king standing in the middle of the room with a scepter. The tip crackled with green light.

"Oh, shit…"

14

KING OF THE DEAD

The king easily stood fifteen feet tall, cutting an imposing figure even in the vaulted room. When he moved, his bones creaked, filling the temple with their discordant notes. He wore a black cloak, embossed with an image of another skeleton in a crown, presumably the queen. His teeth were filed points, and there was a burning orange fire behind his eyes that waxed and waned with his mood.

"I assume you know who I am?" he asked, his voice low and rough but filling the room.

I stood, wincing in pain at the wound in my leg. My vision blurred. I nearly fell over. In the corner, I could see both Lopsang and Xolotl recovering from their bout. Both looked equally worse for wear, and I was reminded to never mess with Lopsang.

"Oh, my," said the king. "You're losing a lot of blood, and that won't make for decent conversation on this side of the portal." He waved bony fingers adorned with gold rings and jewels through the air. Wisps of white mist appeared and floated down to my leg. There was a cool numbing sensation as the wound knit itself back together.

"Wow," was all I could manage. I tested my leg with a slight hop and found it to be as good as new.

"Wonderful." The king made a yawning gesture, more out of show than anything else. "Now, I'll ask you again. Do you know who I am?"

I looked up to the bejeweled crown atop his head. "I'm going to guess the King of the Dead."

"Miclantecuhtli also works. It's the name the Aztecs gave me. Over time, I've actually come to like it."

"Right, Miclant—" I stumbled on the word. "Mickey work?"

Fire flashed bright behind the King's eyes and then died to embers. "It's a little unorthodox, but I'm not sure what else I would expect from you."

"So, you know me?" I tried to feel fear rather than flattery, but I'm a simple creature at heart. The fact that the King of the Dead knew me was enough for a momentary swell of pride.

"I know everyone who passes through that gate." He pointed to the portal as it illuminated with green fire and then snuffed out. "Especially when it's someone trying to cheat us."

From the back corner of the room, I heard Manchester groaning as he got to his feet. I turned toward him reflexively and got into a fighting posture.

"That won't be necessary," said Mickey. "He's not going to try and start any more fights, are you, Harvey?"

I couldn't help but smile.

Manchester muttered something that sounded halfway between a curse and an acknowledgment.

"My, my, you've really done a number on him." Mickey looked from me to James, himself rising to his feet.

"He's an old friend," I replied.

"Indeed, and we've seen how you treat old friends." His fingers made a bony clacking noise as he drummed them upon his skull, thinking the situation over. "You know, for once, my queen and I are of a different opinion on what to do with you."

"Is one of the options mercy?" I asked.

"In a way." The king knelt to look at me. "She would have had you killed, strung up, tortured, and then killed again." His jaw shifted to the right, giving the impression of humor. "Ordinarily, I would quite enjoy something like that but given all you went through to get down here, I had a more mutually beneficial proposal in mind. Less short-term satisfaction, of course, but the sweetest delights do take time."

The words 'mutually beneficial' were never good coming from a supernatural enemy. Bargains struck with deities often come at the price of a soul. While dirtied, I was attached to mine.

"Let me kill them for you, my liege," slurred Manchester, his speech obscured by the gaping hole in his face where he had been stabbed repeatedly.

The fire grew hotter behind Mickey's eyes. "You've wasted enough of my time on this little vendetta of yours, Harvey. I let them into the realm on your explicit promise that they would never leave. Three souls for the price of one, you said." The king intertwined his fingers and stared at Manchester. "Tell me, Harvey, do you remember that conversation?"

"Yes," said Manchester, slowly approaching me. I took a step in the opposite direction.

"Good," purred Mickey. "Then you'll remember the consequences outlined for if you failed."

Manchester bolted towards me, sprinting with a speed I didn't know he possessed.

"Pity," said Mickey, raising a hand lazily. Manchester was stopped and lifted into the air, mid-run. The sight of him floating was uncomfortably familiar, and I wondered if he was about to be burned to death for the third time. "You really shouldn't have tried that," Mickey said. "Xolotl!"

Obediently, Xolotl stepped to the wall and ran a finger across it. The red portal he had sent the unworthy warrior through opened again.

"You will pass through The Nine Trials."

"No!" screamed Manchester. "Give me this, let me finish him off!"

"I'm afraid you haven't earned it. Finish The Nine Trials and we'll talk."

Manchester's good eye widened and looked right at me. "Mark my words, Nick, I will find you again."

"Of that, I have no doubt." I gave Manchester a friendly wave. "But those trials aren't going to make it easy."

"I will—"

Mickey snapped his bony fingers with a loud crack and Manchester flew screaming through the portal. Xolotl held out a hand and closed it.

Given my ever-growing hatred for the man, I thought I would feel relief. Instead, I got the same hollow feeling as the first time I had watched him die. I stared at the spot where Manchester had been a few seconds earlier, unable to believe he was truly gone. To be honest, I still don't.

If he had found his way through the Land of the Dead once, I doubted even Dante's rungs of hell could stop him, let alone The Nine Trials. In the absence of Manchester's commanding presence, the room went silent. Seeing the man literally go to hell had been high on my bucket list, but there was no time to savor the moment.

"He'll complete the trials," said Mickey, breaking the silence. "I can see the force of will within him. But you'll be dead by then anyway."

"That a threat?" I asked.

"No, I don't make threats. Don't worry, today's your lucky day. I admire your spirit, and taking it away so easily wouldn't be much of a sport." The fire shone brightly in his eyes as he looked directly into mine. I could feel the gaze going deep into my soul, rooting out my fears, my schemes, everything. There was no fighting the King of the Dead, I knew that. Whatever he was going to offer, we had to accept or face a gruesome end.

"You will live, Nick Ventner."

I let out an all-too-audible sigh of relief.

"Don't celebrate yet."

Xolotl chuckled from the corner.

"Down boy," called Mickey.

I almost laughed, still transfixed by the king's gaze.

"No one can cheat me without paying a price."

"There's always a catch."

"Yes, there is. When you die, you will face The Nine Trials as well, and when you are finished, your soul will come directly to me."

I didn't like the idea, but it seemed better than dying on the spot. All the same, a little negotiation never hurt anyone. "So, my soul comes to you, then what? Do you have a term sheet? Maybe a few bullet points about the quality of life in your care? Do the dead need health insurance?"

Mickey laughed. "You're not exactly in a position to bargain."

"Even so, I'd like to know the terms."

"You'll retain bodily autonomy down here, but there may be times when I need your help. When that time comes, I'll call on you, and you'll answer."

"Great. Simple favors, I assume?" I had watched Godfather one too many times to know how those ended up working out.

"Precisely. It took quite a lot of bargaining with the rulers of your Land of the Dead, but in the end, we were able to come to an agreement."

"All that for me?" I couldn't lie; it wasn't hurting my self-esteem. "Sounds like a good enough deal." It sounded like a shit deal, but a few more years in the Land of the Living would help me find a way to weasel out of it. "What about them?" I asked, motioning to Lopsang and James, who remained uncharacteristically silent.

"Yes, that is a matter I have thought a lot on. This one," he motioned to Lopsang, "has proved himself a capable warrior. It's in our code to honor him. He may leave without penalty."

Lucky bastard.

"You, on the other hand." The king turned to face James, who had been keeping quiet and still, perhaps hoping he wouldn't be seen. "You're an escapee, and letting you go would set a bad example."

I could see tears brimming in the edges of James's eyes. His hands moved reflexively to his stomach, where his mortal wound had been.

"Don't worry, you can keep your newly healed form, but you

must understand, death has to be absolute. There's a balance to strike."

"No," I said firmly.

Mickey turned on me faster than I could blink. "This is not a negotiation." Fire flashed from his eyes, licking toward my face. I began to sweat. "I've given you one of my best deals, and you're poised to reject it for your friend here? Perhaps you'd like to start The Nine Trials a little early?" Rage filled his voice.

"We're not leaving here without him. Lopsang, get ready for a fight." White-hot anger filled my brain at the thought of leaving the Land of the Dead without James, even if the other option was a fight we stood no chance of winning. We had gone through too much. If this was how it all ended, at least it would be for something worthwhile.

Mickey stood to his full height and laughed. He picked up his staff, and lightning crackled at the end of it. "A bold but poor choice."

"Well, I've fought more than a few undead pricks today, might as well add another to the pile." I scrambled toward the pile of weapons.

"Such a waste," he muttered. "But I can't say this hasn't been fun." Electricity buzzed through the air, and I winced in anticipation of whatever horrible juju came out the end of Mickey's staff.

"Wait!" shouted Lopsang, stepping forward for the first time.

The lightning calmed temporarily. "Ah, do you have more sense than your friend?" he asked.

Lopsang looked at me and James, in turn, pain clear across his face. "Enough people have died today."

"Dying is good business for me." Mickey smiled. "I don't see the problem."

"What do you want in exchange for James?" Lopsang's voice was low, as though he already knew the answer.

Mickey rapped his bony fingers on his skull. "Well, that was quite a light show you put on earlier. I could have a lot of fun passing on a divine endowment like that."

Lopsang's face fell.

"Maybe I'll give it to our good friend, Xolotl. He has missed his time in the sun."

Xolotl growled.

Lopsang remained silent, rooted to the spot. A tear ran down his cheek.

"I don't have all day. Kingdom to run and all that."

Lopsang wrung his hands together and then thrust them out. "Fine. Take it. I don't need it anyway." The last words came out choked.

"Well, I'll be damned, it appears you are correct Mr. Ventner; this was a negotiation after all." He held out his hand, and light shot out of Lopsang's fingers in streams. Mickey grabbed it and twirled it between his fingers, swirling and shifting between his knuckles with dazzling brilliance. "Are you sure this is what you want?" He let the power flow back into Lopsang momentarily. "You are above these mortals and one of the finest warriors we have ever seen."

"He did hit me with a few cheap shots," grumbled Xolotl.

Mickey held up a finger to silence him, and Xolotl cowered to a corner.

Lopsang was pensive but turned his eyes to the king resolutely. "I'm not leaving here without them. My powers for his life."

Mickey threw back his head in a gale of ghostly laughter. "Well, this is a boon I could have never hoped to receive. Deal." He put a hand on Lopsang's head. The light blazed once more and danced around Mickey's fingers before disappearing. "Very well, you are free to go."

Mickey removed his hand, and Lopsang fell to his hands and knees, panting.

I ran to his side. "You alright?"

"He feels what it's like to be mortal for the first time," commented Mickey. "Most would think of it as a curse."

At that moment, I hated the king for what he had done.

"Why would you go and do a stupid thing like that?" asked James.

"Well, this has all the makings of a touching reunion, but I think it's time I be going. Xolotl, be a dear and see that our guests find their way out." Mickey snapped his fingers. There was a flash of green lightning, a deep rumble of thunder, and he was gone.

"We need to go," said Lopsang, his voice weak.

I helped him to his feet, and under the watchful eye of Xolotl, we exited the temple. We passed by the neon pictures of the gods dancing along the long upward slope in silence. I wasn't sure what there was to say.

After a short walk, we emerged from the temple into the sweltering heat. Moisture hung in the air, clinging to my skin. The buzz of the insects was almost instantaneous. "Out of the frying pan and into the fire," I muttered.

James stepped into a beam of sunlight shining through the trees, closed his eyes, and fell to his knees, weeping.

I sat next to him. "I told you I'd come for you."

"You're just lucky I hadn't figured out how to haunt your ass."

"Well, we're not out of it yet," said Lopsang. "Don't suppose Mickey," he spoke the name with disgust, "gave you any food or water to survive the journey home?"

"Sure didn't." I hadn't thought about it. The mistake seemed asinine in hindsight. "I guess it's a good thing we have our tracker back. Welcome to the jungle, kid. It's hell."

James wiped his already sweating brow. "How long did you say it took you to get here?"

"Trust me, I don't think you want an answer to that question. Now, come on, get to work, kid. Just because you got resurrected doesn't mean this is a free ride."

James smiled at me, and before I could do anything about it, he wrapped me in a firm embrace. "Thanks for coming back."

I patted his back awkwardly. Displays of affection have never been my thing—a problem that's ended more than a few relationships. "Anytime, kid." A weight settled heavily on my heart when I considered the cost. I needed a drink and needed it quick. "Alright, that's enough of that." I shrugged James off.

James laughed. "Good to be back together again. Let's go home."

EPILOGUE

The bar had gone entirely silent. Part of Nick regretted telling the story, as he always did. With the silence came a thick tension that couldn't have been cut with the sharpest knife. Nick attempted to anyway. "So, that's really it, I suppose. Unless you've got a few more hours to hear about our trek out. No more monsters, so to speak, but James did get his ass bitten by a piranha."

A single tear rolled down Albert's cheek. "Poor bastard." He wiped the tear away. "All that for a lousy drunk like you." He chuckled. "You are some kind of con."

"King of the Dead sounds like a real ass," replied Marcus.

Jimmy emerged from behind the bar. "I think he spent four hours feeding us a line of bullshit."

Albert and Marcus looked at each other and grunted.

Nick was lost in his own memory of the event. A melancholy brewed within him. "I think I'll take off as well. Thanks for the beers, fellas."

"Hey! Those drinks were not on the house!" shouted Jimmy, but Nick ignored him and walked out of the bar.

There was an uncharacteristic chill in the air for Midway. Rain fell in sheets. He looked down at the hourglass on his wrist to see if he should worry. No grains fell. *Still have some time left, then.* He looked out into the parking lot illuminated by a single lamp, trying to see where Lopsang had gone. He was about to walk into the downpour to find him when a voice called out from the darkness.

"Hey, stranger."

Nick wheeled toward the side of the bar, where a woman stepped out of the shadows. It was his date. His heart simultaneously performed somersaults and freefalls. James and Lopsang stepped out next to her, and Nick's confusion deepened.

"What the hell?" he asked, the words pouring from his mouth in a way that only a drunk could manage.

"Recognize her?" asked James. "Because she claims to be an old friend of ours."

Nick looked at the woman long and hard. "Of course, I do! She was my date." He paused, calculating the next sentence in real-time. "Weren't you going to get a taxi?" There was a horrible gurgling in his stomach, and he suspected that he was on the cusp of what was going to be an unpleasant afterparty in a nearby gutter.

"You didn't recognize me either," said the woman to James.

He shrugged. "I was just the driver. We didn't talk much."

"The driver?" Nick asked, staggering to the side. "The driver when?" His eyes widened as he looked deep into hers. It was as if someone had lifted a veil. Facial features could be changed, but eyes stayed the same. The familiarity from earlier struck again. "Shirley?" he asked.

It had been years since their misadventure in Clearwater, and he hadn't seen her since he put her in contact with The Order. "Shirley Codwell?" She had certainly come a long way from the disgruntled tabloid reporter he had first met almost three years ago.

"See?" she said, looking to James. "I told you he'd get it eventually."

"What happened to your face?" he blundered, still unclear as to what exactly was happening.

"Well, as it turns out, The Sixth Side is better at finding people than you thought." She rubbed a hand over her neck, tensing. "But we were able to come to an agreement. They spared my life and in exchange, I started working for them. After a few necessary procedures," she motioned to her face, "I was the perfect candidate."

Rage boiled inside Nick. "You're working for the Sixth Side?!"

"Sixth side of what?" asked James.

"The Pentagon, James, the sixth side of the Pentagon."

"Pentagons have—"

"I know how many sides they have! It's a stupid fucking name for a government organization that preys on the weak and covers up all the—" Nick stopped mid-sentence and vomited into the parking lot. *Witch's brew. Never again with the witch's brew.*

"Government agent?" asked James.

"Not quite," she answered. "Think he'll come around?"

"When he's sober. If the pay is good enough. Probably."

"Good." Shirley pressed a jet-black card into James's hand. "There's enough on that for airfare and expenses for the three of you. If you can bring him around to the idea, meet me in New Orleans in three days."

"All this for a rogue necromancer?" asked Lopsang.

"Your words, not mine." Shirley disappeared into the night.

Lopsang and James bent down to pick up Nick.

"Oh, piss off, we aren't working for the government," he slurred, the drunkenness coming back in a massive wave. "Unless they have cheeseburgers," he added. "I think I could use a few cheeseburgers right about now."

"Guess we're going to the Big Easy then," said James.

"You know there's no way we can control him in that city, right?" Lopsang hoisted Nick onto his shoulders.

"No open container laws," slurred Nick. "Nah, I'm sure we'll be fine…"

AFTERWORD

Nick, James, and Lopsang will return in Maelstrom

ABOUT THE AUTHOR

Ashton Macaulay is a fiction writer living in Seattle, WA. His works include Whiteout, the tale of drunken monster hunter Nick Ventner, Man of the Mountain, an intriguing audio drama surrounding a man trying to maintain the Bigfoot legend, and various short stories published through Aberrant Literature.

Nick Ventner is a drunk with a blatant disregard for others. He's also damned good at hunting creatures that aren't supposed to exist. From amateur necromancers in the bayou to Sasquatch impersonators in the Pacific Northwest, Nick's seen it all. Even if some of the details might be a little fuzzy.

In *Whiteout*, Nick faces his greatest challenge to date. Accompanied by his trusty mountain guide, Lopsang, and his testy apprentice, James, Nick journeys into the Himalayas to settle a matter of pride and payouts, as he searches for the lost riches of Shangri-La rumored to lie within the mountain's peak.

However, the sudden arrival of Nick's greatest adversary, Manchester, complicates matters, and pits the two in a race towards the top, and both soon find that they have not just one another to contend with, but also a mythical and elusive yeti that has been terrorizing the mountain.

Featuring death-defying obstacles, hair-raising encounters with creatures
from beyond, and a heavy dose of sarcasm along the way, Whiteout is sure
to satisfy anyone looking for a fast-paced adventure novel brimming with
action, suspense, and imagination. Not to mention the occasional whiskey
on the rocks.

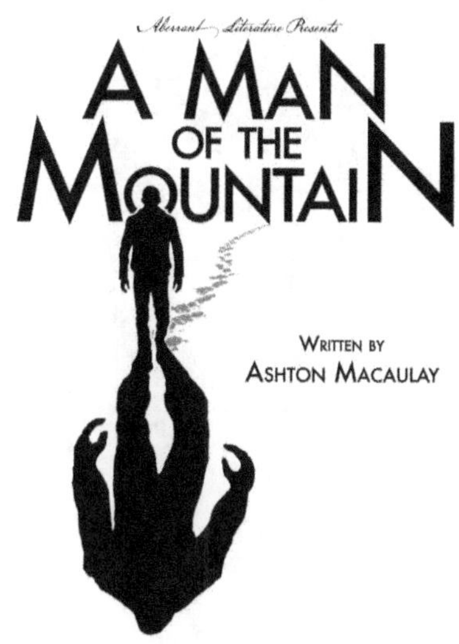

Jonas is a recluse. He lives in the mountains alone, appreciative of the peace and solitude the wilderness has to offer. It also enables him to keep his unusual line of work a secret.

At the behest of mysterious employers, Jonas has been instructed to wear a fur-covered suit and terrorize hikers at a local mountain range, all in an effort to maintain the mythical legend of Bigfoot. While typically uneventful, there are times when a hiker gets too close and the situation becomes...messy. Jonas may not be bloodthirsty, but he always does what's necessary to uphold a certain level of discretion.

After several high-profile 'accidents' are written off by authorities as bear attacks, tabloid reporter Shirley Codwell notices a pattern and sets out to unravel the truth. Convinced that the killings are the work of a legendary beast, she calls upon the monster hunting community for assistance. The

events that transpire are like nothing she could have expected...and will
send Jonas running for his life.

Set in the Whiteout universe, A Man of the Mountain is a thrilling dark-
comic adventure that will keep you turning the pages right through to it's
incredible, shocking conclusion.

With *Aberrant Tales*, you truly never know what type of story you will encounter next. So prepare to fully immerse yourself in this collection of twelve fascinating tales filled with suspense, intrigue, and imagination. You'll find it to be one hell of a ride.